ROCK BOTTOM

◇
◇
◇

Also by Sarah Andrews

In Cold Pursuit
Dead Dry
Earth Colors
Killer Dust
Fault Line
An Eye for Gold
Bone Hunter
Only Flesh and Bones
Mother Nature
A Fall in Denver
Tensleep

ROCK BOTTOM

◆
◆
◆

Sarah Andrews

MINOTAUR BOOKS ✷ NEW YORK

ROCK BOTTOM. Copyright © 2012 by Sarah Andrews Brown. All rights reserved. Printed in the United States of America. For information, address St. Martin's Press, 175 Fifth Avenue, New York, N.Y. 10010.

www.minotaurbooks.com
www.stmartins.com

Library of Congress Cataloging-in-Publication Data

Andrews, Sarah.
    Rock bottom / Sarah Andrews.—1st ed.
        p. cm.
    ISBN 978-0-312-67659-9 (hardcover)
    ISBN 978-1-4299-7765-4 (e-book)
        1. Hansen, Em (Fictitious character)—Fiction.   2. Women geologists—Fiction.
I. Title.
    PS3551.N4526R63 2012
    813'.54—dc23

                                                                        2012013576

First Edition: August 2012

10   9   8   7   6   5   4   3   2   1

With love to Damon and Duncan, who rowed Lava Falls on their ways to other great exploits. With thanks to four great geology teachers: William A. Fischer, who took his last ride through those waters, John H. Lewis, who taught me to love geology, Frank Ethridge, who taught me how to use it, and Edwin Dinwiddie McKee, who taught me how to tell its story.

Acknowledgments

A great number of people assisted me in preparing this story, providing facts and background information, making suggestions, and, finally, fact-checking and making sure I spelled place names correctly. Primary among them were Allyson Mathis, U.S. National Park Service science and education outreach coordinator for Grand Canyon National Park, and Edwin D. McKee, who was chief naturalist there from 1929 to 1940. Eddie was my mentor much later at the U.S. Geological Survey in Denver, and his legacy of scientific research still inspires everyone who visits the park or, like Allyson, has the great pleasure of living and working there.

This book might not have been written had the real Don Rasmussen, paleontologist extraordinaire, not asked me to name a character after his beloved wife, Jerry. I had promised that I would, and that kept the story alive in my head through a long season when life got in the way of writing.

I thank Sherry Rhoades Kane for accompanying me to the Grand Canyon during a splendid research/road trip!

I deeply appreciate the faith shown by my editor, Kelley Ragland, who gave me a contract to write this after a significant lapse of time in a turbulent publishing market.

I'd like to thank the real Jerry Rasmussen for catching a slew of those niggling large and small errors that crept insidiously into this manuscript.

I thank the intrepid and august members of the April Fools Rafting and Drinking Society who accompanied me, my husband, Damon, and our son, Duncan, downriver on a private trip during April 2007, providing the best background research money can't buy. Among those intrepid rowers and paddlers, I wish to acknowledge Jerry "the Gummer" Weber, Damon's mentor in geology, for having the sense of humor to let me apply his name to a character in this book, and for "sneaking" me through a rapid or two without getting me wet.

Most of all, I thank all of us, the citizens of these United States, who have set aside the wilderness of the Grand Canyon under the protection of the National Park Service, so that all who visit may be inspired, each in his or her own way, by its majesty.

ROCK BOTTOM

◇
◇
◇

U.S. National Park Service, Grand Canyon National Park
Transcript of communication received by satellite phone by dispatcher
Cleome James
April 16, 0945 hrs.

"—Gotta talk fast 'cause these satellites cross over the aperture of this canyon like hot lead. We're missing one of our party."

"Say your name, sir."

"Fritz Calder."

"Your location, please."

"The Ledges. River mile 151.5."

"You're with a river party?"

"Yes. A man is missing."

"Are you reporting a drowning, sir?"

"I sure hope not."

"State the circumstances."

"Woke up this morning and he was gone. I don't know what happened. We've done an exhaustive search of the immediate area. His boat is here, his life vest, all his gear. The only thing gone is him. If he left on purpose, he sure didn't tell anyone, and he sure didn't hike out, unless he's a fly and can go straight up these cliffs. Request a ranger—"

End of transmission. Connection lost.

APRIL 1: LEES FERRY

I'D HAD A MORBID FEAR OF MOVING WATER EVER SINCE I WAS A KID AND my brother drowned in the irrigation ditch on the ranch I grew up on back home in Wyoming. It sucked him under. I watched him go, and could do nothing to save him. And that was just a man-made ditch, almost narrow enough that I could have jumped across it. Now I stood on the bank of the Colorado River at the upper end of the Grand Canyon, wishing like hell that I was almost anywhere else.

"Isn't this great!" A strong pair of arms wrapped around me from behind: Fritz, my beloved, my husband of six months.

I plastered a grin across my face and turned toward him to burrow into his hug, trying to press from my brain the image of the roiling water that swept between our heap of equipment and the naked red ground of the Moenkopi Formation that rose above the far bank. We'd unloaded everything out of the hired van: four sixteen-foot rafts, three kayaks, a heap of tents, camp stoves, waterproof duffels, and an impossible mound of food and beer, twenty-one days' rations for sixteen people. And I was one of those sixteen. Or it would have been sixteen, except that three days earlier, we'd lost our leader, which was another little problem I had with this expedition. What in hell's name was I doing rigging up to help Fritz row one of those rafts down a gigantic river? I was ready to puke with anxiety, and the water that flowed by the launch beach here at Lees Ferry was hardly a riffle; what was I going to do when we reached the giant rapids that awaited us downstream? Sockdolager, Hance, Horn, Crystal, and the horrendous Lava Falls; Fritz had been going on about them for months, exulting over what an adrenaline rush they were. The rapids on the Colorado River through the Grand Canyon were so large that they had their own rating system, and as water levels fluctuated, some of them got worse with higher discharge and others got worse with less. Oh, woe was me.

I know that I should have told Fritz about my little phobia, but I hadn't had the heart. His friend Tiny had sprung this raft trip on us as his present at our wedding, all happy because it had taken years of entering the lottery to get a private trip permit, and he had been so sure of things that he had put Fritz down on the application as alternate trip leader. By the time Fritz was done slapping Tiny high fives and doing his happy dance and finally turned to me to share his excitement, I'd had time to kid myself that I could maybe do this thing. At worst, I figured that I could look pleased now and sort it out with him later; I mean, how could I disappoint him on our wedding day? But it only got harder to tell him. Tiny had worked damned hard to get a private permit, and Fritz was incandescently excited to take along his son from his first marriage, thirteen-year-old Brendan, who could only come if I was there as substitute mom (you should have seen the stare his ex-wife fixed on me, after she was done glaring at Fritz), and . . . well, it all just snowballed.

Brendan shuffled past us carrying a heap of life preservers, struggling to carry more than his short arms and small frame really allowed. "Where should I put these?" he asked.

"Over by the dry bags is fine," said Fritz. He had bent his own frame down from its eagle's-nest height and was kissing my neck now, really nuzzling in. Into my ear he whispered, "It's too bad Tiny couldn't be here."

"Yeah, he worked so hard to put this trip together." Tiny had slid his

Harley across Interstate 80 west of Salt Lake City. Tiny was in the hospital in traction. Right now that sounded like a smart place to be.

I felt something metallic jab into my back. "What's that?" I asked Fritz, shoving my hand between us to find out what was poking me.

"Sorry," he said, pulling my rock hammer out of his belt loop. He gave it a heft. "I'm glad you brought this along. It's got a thousand uses."

"No geologist would consider leaving home without one," I said. I reached for it, but he snapped it away.

"I'm not done with it yet," he said. "I was using it to make a couple of adjustments on our rigging. The outfitting company that rented us that raft had it set up for someone with short legs."

"Everybody's legs are shorter than yours, Fritz."

"Oh, hey, here's the ranger!" Fritz loped over to greet a petite woman in uniform who had just climbed out of a National Park Service truck. He bounded up to her like a Saint Bernard puppy, all loose-jointed and full of delight, announcing, "Hey, hi! Tiny couldn't be here, so now I'm trip leader."

She looked up at him, shifted her gaze uncomfortably toward the rock hammer, stiffened her spine, and said, "You're the alternate?"

"Yes, Fritz Calder." He poked the spike end of the head of the rock hammer at the list on her clipboard. "Right there."

"That's just fine, sir. Now please round up your party so I can check your requirements." The ranger lined us up and began going down her list of persons who were going on this expedition with us, checking IDs. "Okay," she said, "so your original leader couldn't make it, so you have fifteen instead of sixteen, but I only count fourteen of you. Where's your fifteenth?"

Fritz said, "Not here yet."

She looked at him over the frames of her sunglasses. "Expecting him anytime soon?" she asked drily.

Fritz colored slightly, hard to see under his tan, a sort of blotchiness. He had not in fact met the fifteenth member of our party. There were several people on the list he hadn't known before we arrived, but all the others had shown up when we did, the night before, and we had all had dinner together at the café up above the cliffs and had camped out on the riverbank and gotten to know each other a bit. This fifteenth guy figured he was special somehow, like he didn't need to show his face until launch day. Tiny had put him on the list at the last moment, just before he went and stacked up his motorcycle, without discussing his decision with Fritz. We knew almost nothing about him. The story was that they had met in a bar. Tiny had justified his decision by stating that the guy had a lot of experience on the river. "It'll be a really good thing to have him along," he said. "I'm not getting any younger, and, well, I just think we should avail ourselves of real talent and knowledge. He built his own dory," he concluded, as if being able to handle a hammer and saw made him our dream date in the middle of Class 10 rapids.

The mystery man's name was George Oberley, but he'd told Tiny that he went by "Wink." I wanted to kick Mr. Oberley's ass from the moment I heard that nickname, but having a saucy moniker was the least of what worried me about him. Here was every other thing Tiny had been able to recite on the subject of Wink Oberley:

He was a geologist. ("One of your brethren," Fritz had said brightly.)

He was working on his Ph.D. in geology at Princeton.

He had been a professional boatman and was soooo experienced that this would be his forty-third trip down the river.

He used to be in the army, an Airborne Ranger.

My basic distrust of anyone who'd let himself be called Wink aside, when I heard this summation of our supposed Colorado River expert, little klaxons and sirens had gone off in my head. That group of factoids sounded more like something on a SAT test than a résumé, one of those questions where you're supposed to figure out which item doesn't fit with the others. There was just no way that an Ivy League geologist Ph.D. candidate river rat had ever been an Army Airborne Ranger. Geologists make crappy soldiers on account of we question all authority, including our own. We do not play well enough with the other boys and girls to make it into an elite, tightly knit cadre like the Airborne Rangers. Shout orders at a geologist under fire and you get someone who wants to sit down and open a beer and have a conversation about the plan, parse it down to a gnat's eyelash, maybe offer up a few alternative concepts, and then do none of the above. Putting one of us into a parachute and telling him to jump out of a plane over a jungle full of people who are shooting at dangly things in the sky would not be a viable proposition, because while "geologist" is, for bizarre reasons, considered by insurance actuaries to be one of the most dangerous professions, we like to choose our dangers rather than having them chosen for us. We are each a one-person herd of cats. And the fact that Mr. George "Wink" Oberley and his wonderful homemade dory had yet to appear tended to support my case.

In fact, before we left home, Fritz and I had had words over my concerns. This was stupid, but there you go. Fritz had been elite military, a jet pilot, an experience that can bring out the chauvinist in a man, so he had felt compelled to defend this Army Airborne Ranger he had not yet met, even though on another day and in another situation the competition between the navy and the army might have come to the fore. Fritz had ended our debate by stating quite firmly that my paranoia and prejudice had no place on a river trip where we were going to have to get along together and rely on each other for three weeks at the bottom of this canyon. I'd let it go because Fritz was my darling sweetheart, but this was one of the times in our acquaintance that I found him to be a bit credulous. They say opposites attract, and he stays on the right side of me most of the time by not pointing out too many of the places where I run a bit thin, so here I was.

The ranger lady looked at her watch and then back at her list. "This fifteenth name is handwritten. I can't make it out."

"George Oberley," said Fritz.

The ranger stiffened. "George *Oberley?*" she echoed. "You don't mean *Wink?*"

Fritz nodded.

Her face began to twist into an unpleasant smile which so contorted her cheeks that her sunglasses slid askew. "Holy Mother of God, Wink Oberley! I thought he was . . ." She caught herself and pressed her lips flat, trying to look official again.

At that very moment a beat-up pickup truck pulling a trailer with a big wooden Grand Canyon dory on it rumbled down the road that led from the cliff tops into the parking lot, kicking up a cloud of dust as it left the pavement and turned onto the launch ramp. It pulled to a stop. The shotgun-side door opened and a guy stepped out and racked his shoulders back in a stiff little stretch. He was forty or so, a bit under average height, thickset. He wore a sagging Princeton T-shirt, frayed cutoff army camouflage fatigue pants, a cheap pair of flip-flops, and an expensive pair of wraparound shades that were too narrow for his face. Below the edge of that reflective plastic I could see a three- or four-day growth of beard, and he'd pushed his faded ball cap down hard enough that his shaggy hair stuck out straight. As he idly surveyed the scene, he used his left hand to reach around and have a good scratch at his right armpit, then pulled up his T-shirt and had a go at his belly.

The driver of the pickup called to him through the open door. "So let's get this thing unloaded, shit-wad," he shouted. "I gotta be back in Page by dinnertime or Eleanor will put my balls on the menu!"

"Keep it zipped," said Mr. Armpit Scratcher, who was now strolling down the beach toward the ranger. "Well if it ain't Maryann Eliasson," he said.

"Long time no see," replied the ranger, in a tone that suggested that perhaps the long time hadn't been quite long enough.

"Oh, give an old friend a hug," he insisted, mashing one on her before she could jump sideways and escape.

The driver of the pickup gunned the motor, racked the gears into reverse, and began to back the trailer down toward the river.

Ranger Eliasson had a fight on her hands trying to wrestle free of Wink's bear hug, which seemed focused on making pelvic contact. "You son of a bitch, get your mitts offa me," she said, and as the struggle continued, she lowered her voice and growled, "I haven't forgotten what you did to Cleome!"

"Cleome? Oh, now, we're all one big family on this river!"

"Family? Sure, but you and me, we're not kissing cousins, so back off!"

My attention was split between this display and some honest gawking at the dory, which looked to be about sixteen feet long and between four and five feet at its widest. Everything about it was curved, its flat sheets of plywood bent so that the bow rose to a high point and the small transom at the stern almost equally upturned. It looked like it had been through the wars, its paint bruised and faded and the plywood patched in multiple places, attesting to long and hard use. A pair of eyes were painted in the bow, one to either side, and toward its stern we were all treated to its name: *Wave Slut*.

Fritz moved in and broke up the tussle between river ranger and river trash by forcefully offering the man a hand to shake. Fritz is tall and muscular and knows how to be imposing when he has to be. "You must be George Oberley," he said, like it was an order.

"Wink." The masher abruptly let go of the woman and lifted his sunglasses, squeezed one eye shut like that was real cute, then snapped that plastic visor back in place.

"Wink," said Fritz, his jaws tightening. "Nice of you to put in an appearance. So, you need some help launching that dory?"

Wink's face went slack. "For what? Hank can handle it."

Hank now had the trailer up past its axle in the water. He got out of the truck and waded around the dory undoing straps, and as the boat began to float up off the cradle, he paid out the bow line, letting the river take it down the beach a ways. It rode high in the water, its up-curved flanks almost begging the water to challenge it. When it looked like it was about to slam into the row of rafts, Hank gave the line a tug and pulled it neatly into place in the rank, then selected a rock to use as a crude anchor. He then immediately turned his back on the boat, stalked back over to his truck, reached into the bed, hauled out a large gear bag, which he dumped unceremoniously on the ramp. He next unlashed a pair of oars and dropped them next to the duffel so hard they bounced like pickup sticks, then he jumped back into the pickup, gunned the engine, and drove away.

Wink gave him a merry wave. "You can pick it up the end of the month at Diamond Creek!"

The driver of the truck extended one scrawny arm out the window and flipped him off.

To anyone who might be listening, Wink said, "It's a great boat. I've taken it down this river a hundred times. My friend here's had it stored for me in Page while I've been at Princeton working on my Ph.D." He emphasized the words "Princeton" and "Ph.D.," just in case people were listening.

I wasn't quite sure how you can take a boat down a river a hundred times if you've only been down the river forty-two times, but mathematics seldom matches hyperbole.

As if nothing odd had just occurred, the ranger hitched herself up all officious again and began ticking down her list of requirements, checking our life vests, the fire pan, the military surplus rocket boxes we would use to carry out our poop. She cast a gimlet eye on my rock hammer and asked Fritz, "You have a permit to collect rocks?"

Fritz said, "No, and we know not to collect anything but memories. I use this for driving in tent stakes."

"Each boat has a spare life vest?"

Brendan lifted up our spare.

Wink stepped toward Brendan, snatched the vest out of his hands, and turned it over. "I see you're renting your equipment. What a bunch of crap," he said, then stuffed it back into Brendan's hands and gave him a not entirely playful swat across the top of his head.

Brendan clutched the life vest to his belly and shot a worried look at his father, who had his hands balled into fists and planted on his hips. And so began our trip down the Grand Canyon with the marvelous Wink Oberley.

Landed by helicopter above Lower Ledges Campsite and deployed Zodiac raft. While helicopter searched for missing man, I continued to Lower Ledges, river right mile 151.5, found party of 14 making sandwiches. All in a somber mood. Missing man had not been found.

Trip leader Fritz Calder stated that he woke at 5:15 A.M. and all seemed normal in camp. Four rafts, one dory, and three kayaks were as left the night before, tied up riding the current at the bottom ledge of rock. Kayaker Olaf Jones slept in the middle raft, was unaware of the disappearance until informed by Calder. Kayaker Lloyd Oshiro slept on a ledge near the rafts and likewise noticed nothing amiss until morning. All others slept in tents or under the sky on camp mats up near the cliff base. Missing man last seen drinking alcoholic beverages at the campfire by oarsmen Mungo Park and Dell Oxley when they turned in at about 10:30 P.M.

Calder stated that he started the stove for coffee and made a routine check of campsite. He noticed nothing amiss except that the campfire appeared to have been left to burn itself out rather than being properly extinguished. Assumed missing man was in tent belonging to Glenda Fittle.

Glenda Fittle said no, she slept alone, had gone to her tent at 9:00 P.M., fell asleep immediately, did not notice she was alone until she woke in the morning.

All awake by 7:30. Search begun @ 7:45 A.M. At 8:30 A.M. Calder commenced attempts to reach Park Dispatch via sat phone to advise of possible drowning. Consensus is that missing man might have fallen into river, passing out while urinating.

Fittle asserted that missing man had been "vibed out" of the trip, so I inspected the site for signs of a person having left the campsite by any means other than going into the river, but found no footprints, etc. Cliffs would be difficult if not impossible to scale and it's a long way to nowhere up beyond the rim. Nearest side canyon this side of river is 150 Mile Canyon, a mile and a half upriver. Access would require at minimum very careful ledge walking, but in darkness? And again 150 Mile leads into the middle of nowhere. Nearest dowriver side canyon is Havasu, about 4 miles river left. Checked water temperature. Hypothermia would render anyone unconscious in half that distance.

Inspected the missing man's equipment, which seemed intact. It included:

Paco Pad and sleeping bag
PFD + spare
hat
1 pr. flip-flops
small dry bag, containing:
    3 T-shirts
    1 pr. cargo shorts
    fleece jacket
    1 pr. athletic shoes

    small ziplock bag with toiletries
    paperback book (*Atlas Shrugged* by Ayn Rand)

On questioning party members, it was surmised that the missing man had been barefoot in camp during the evening. He was not observed to have had any footwear or clothing or gear beyond an additional plaid shirt and cutoff camouflage pants worn last night in camp.

I am inclined to agree that he fell into the river by mishap, and it follows from there that he is drowned. I advised the party that bodies without PFD usually sink and do not reemerge for 2–14 days, if ever.

At 4:45 P.M. contacted NPS group working downstream to watch for a body and advised Calder's party to remain at Ledges Camp a second night until a preliminary report is filed at HQ.

APRIL 1: FINAL PREPARATIONS

THE WATERS OF THE COLORADO RIVER RISE AT THE CONTINENTAL Divide along the Rocky Mountains in northern Colorado above 10,000 feet elevation, joining sheet wash into rivulets and rivulets into a creek. As myriad tributaries add their strength the river grows, tumbling west-southwestward down and down to Grand Junction, a town so named because the upper stretch of the Colorado was, for a period of time, called the Grand River by Euro-Americans. Earlier human inhabitants of this continent had other names for it; the upper reaches of the drainage is *Seedskeedee* to the Crow Indians, and as its course flows through other tribal lands, it becomes *Tó Nts'ósíkooh* to the Navajo and *'Aha Kwahwat* to the Mojave. At Grand Junction the river is joined by the Gunnison River, growing into a mighty force, then turns northwestward for a few dozen miles, crosses into Utah, and bends to the southwest. Below Moab, the Colorado joins hands with the Green River (which heads in Wyoming) and flows into what was once Glen Canyon and is now Lake Powell. The Spanish named the lower stretch Colorado, their word for red, because they found it choked with mud and sand that washes off the oxidized desert slickrock that reaches to its banks.

I've seen photographs of the lovely twisting side canyons that fed into Glen Canyon, a vast fairyland of red rock smoothed into a symphony of compound curves by the load of abrasive silt, sand, rocks, and up-rooted trees that were tumbled into the river by the purging rush of flash floods. Now all these sediments and flotsam—thirteen to twenty-seven tons per day depending on runoff—are captured by the lake, a great settling basin created by the construction of the Glen Canyon Dam, which was built in the dam-building heyday of the 1950s and '60s to regulate the flow of the river and provide power generation and rec-reational opportunities for powerboaters and water-skiers. Both lake and water regulation were by-products of the United States' poorly cal-culated water debt to other basin states, which brought the problem to the Bureau of Reclamation, a federal agency that existed to build dams and thus did so. The bureau reckoned it a "cash-register dam" that would help pay for other reclamation projects and extend the life of Hoover Dam downstream.

Lees Ferry, where I now stood tightening cam straps that held our gear to our raft, is fifteen miles downriver from Glen Canyon Dam. I wore neoprene booties on my feet as I waded through the shallows around the raft, because while the river's springtime temperatures used to rise quickly from winter's thirty-two degrees Fahrenheit on the way to summer's eighty, it now shot under the dam near the bottom of Lake Powell at forty-seven degrees, a temperature that delivered up rapid hypothermia for anyone who went swimming without a wet suit.

I glanced up the beach to where Fritz stood with a beer in his hand, directing the final loading of the rafts. Fritz and Tiny liked to call themselves the April Fools Rafting and Drinking Society, a name they acquired when they first started rafting farther up the Colorado River near Moab. The guy who led those trips preferred spring over summer in the canyons because it's not so beastly hot and not as overrun with touri, his faux Latin name for tourists. I don't know the man's real name, because they always just called him "the Gummer," a tribute to his ad-vanced age. The Gummer had taught them how to scout and row rapids without getting killed, so they thought they were hot shit and always told themselves they'd do the Grand together. Tiny tried for years to get them in on a private trip, and when that didn't work they finally coughed up the money for a commercial trip. Tiny went commercially again the next year and the next, but by then Fritz was busy starting his aviation businesses—air charter and designing a new plane—and such expenditures of time and money weren't an option. Tiny became so charged up by those commercial trips that he started applying again for a private permit, and it just happened to come together for him about the time Fritz announced that we were getting married, so like I said, he waited until our big day to make his really big announcement.

I did enjoy the preparations for the river trip, and the idea of being around all that slick rock did please me. And I was glad Brendan could come, because he was of an age now when he needed to be out doing manly things with his dad rather than sitting home watching his mom paint her toenails and bitch about her second husband (okay, so she's a dish and a rough act to follow and I have a little thing about that, but I've got to believe that Fritz chose me precisely because the epithet "princess" could never be applied to me). I was also glad that Fritz and Tiny had seen their way clear to let me invite along fellow geologist Molly Chang from the University of Utah. She was my main professor when I took my M.S. there. She said she'd come if this geologist with whom she's doing a project could also come, a guy from Denver named Don Rasmussen. Don said he wouldn't come without his wife, Jerry.

So now I was getting to know Jerry a bit, visiting with her while we all finished rigging our rafts and most everyone else was busy running up and down the beach carrying gear.

"So you and Fritz are newlyweds?" Jerry asked. "How lovely. This is a fine way to honeymoon."

"Mm-hm."

She dug into one of the big coolers that was strapped in behind the oarlocks on her raft and pulled out a couple of Sapporo beers. "We should have a toast. Here." She handed me one.

I popped the tab on the top of the thing and we clunked them together. "To marriage," I said.

"To marriage." She took a nice long pull on her beer. "And to finding a good man, which makes it all worth it," she added. She took another draw, and smacked her lips with satisfaction. "Don and I honeymooned while working for the Forest Service in a lookout tower up in Montana named Porphyry."

"Porphyry. Like the rock?"

"Yes. It was built on a high peak that has an Eocene ignimbrite porphyry right at the surface."

"So are you a geologist, too?" I inquired.

Another voice cut into the conversation: Wink Oberley, who sat stretched out across the aft seat of the *Wave Slut* with his feet up on the near gunwale. "Hey, those beers look pretty good there."

Jerry had her back to the dory and did not look around at him. To me she said, "I manage an office for an oil company."

Wink spoke again, louder. "You got a beer for *this* man?" When another ten seconds went by and she still had not replied, he swung one of his oars on its pivot and tapped the big round rubber flotation tube that ran all the way around her raft. He hit it just hard enough that the whole raft jiggled, bouncing her a bit. "Hey, lady! I'm sooo thirsty here!"

Jerry was bent over from the hips, pulling hard on a cam strap. "I heard you," she said evenly. "And as you can see, I'm sooo busy here."

"In that case, I can wait a bit," he said, like he was doing her some kind of a favor. He yawned and stretched and gazed at her bottom. "It's such a fine day, and the view just can't be beat."

Without straightening up, Jerry said, "Oh, well, then, Dink, if you have all that free time, there's plenty to do around here. There are provisions to be loaded into the fourth raft, and it would be just great if you'd fill those water jugs there. And when that's done, you could ask Em here what sort of vegetables you could be prepping for dinner; you know, like some of those carrots Brendan loaded into your hold for you.

I'm sure the deck of your dory would make a fine place to put a cutting board."

"Wink," he said, correcting her. He crunched his face into the old one-eye again, even though Jerry still kept her back to him and continued with her work. It occurred to me that she knew damned well that she had his name wrong. It occurred to me also that Jerry was one smart cookie. It occurred to me most of all that I was going to enjoy getting to know her.

Wink stared at her back and her beer for a while longer, then got up and found his way out of his boat and down along the launch ramp, stopping to rummage through a box of stores for something to eat. He reminded me of a film I once saw of a rogue bear loose in a campsite where humans had unwittingly left food lying around. Grotesquely fascinated, I turned to adjust the oar on that side of our raft so I could watch him out of the corner of my eye. He found an orange, hefted it up and down a couple of times like a baseball, then gouged into it with his right forefinger to break through the peel, which he removed rather messily, setting off a spray of juice that splattered the front of his T-shirt. I gave him points for not dropping the peel onto the ground, but his progression along the ramp as he ripped juicy sections from the orange and stuffed them into his mouth suggested that the extent to which he was civilized was fragmental. He stopped at the bulletin board by the covered picnic area for a moment, read something that was posted there, gave the page a tap with his index finger and smiled, then continued down the ramp to a stretch where another group was beginning to inflate their rafts. He struck up a conversation, and in about a minute flat, he had a beer in his hand and began knocking it back like it was water, gassing away at that crew while they worked their pumps.

Our rafts were sixteen-footers, each built like a giant squared-off inner tube with two inner cross tubes and a rubber floor. The tubes were about two feet in diameter, and the forward end was lifted in a prow to address the waves. The rafts were self-bailing, which meant that if they shipped water in the rapids it would drain away down through portals between the tubes and the flooring. There were D-rings welded at strategic points along the tubes so we could lash equipment to the rafts using one-inch-wide cam straps. It was not comforting to know that the reason all objects had to be lashed down was that these big wide monsters could easily flip in the rapids.

Still working on the lashings in her hold, Jerry said, "So I run the office for a small oil company, and I'm current president of the Denver Chapter of the Desk and Derrick Club, which is an association of people who do what I do." She looked up at me and smiled pleasantly. "And I have little patience for those who can't figure out how to keep themselves busy." Her tone was light, matter-of-fact.

"No pucky."

"No pucky whatsoever."

"He's on the no-beer list."

"Who?"

"Mr. *Wave Slut* here. It was one of my tasks to do the calculations on how much beer to bring, so Fritz gave me the list of who's drinking and who isn't. Tiny rigged it that way because the nondrinkers generally don't want to subsidize the drinkers' beer."

Now it was me that Jerry seemed not to hear. I supposed that she didn't want to get any further into a three-cornered conversation or, worse yet, a whining fest about our resident mooch, so I let the point go, but the fact was that I thought it was damned rude for Mr. Oberley to sign up for no beer and then expect to get some. Had Jerry been willing to engage in this gossip, I might have told her also that I had overheard Fritz and Tiny discussing this issue, because the beer was the least of it. Wink, it seemed, did not wish to be charged for his portion of the permit, satellite phone rental, the shuttle that would move our vehicles down to Diamond Creek, or for any of the other bits of equipment and logistics that go into a river trip. Fritz had found himself in the middle of negotiations between Tiny and Wink, who seemed to think his expertise was of such value that he should perhaps not even pay for his share of the food. He claimed poverty. He was a graduate student with a family to feed, he told them, and while he was on the topic, he felt that we should all pitch in to buy him a plane ticket to get him out here from New Jersey. Fritz had pointed out to Tiny that it was a permit stipulation that costs be shared equally among participants, and said he sure didn't want to have to explain to the others why they were having to pay an extra couple hundred dollars apiece to treat this unknown like a prince. There was plenty of river experience among the other participants, most of whom owned their own rafts and had been here before, so Tiny had begun to crumble a bit, admitting that he wasn't sure why someone who had "humped his leg" to get onto the trip was now trying to get it for free.

I moved back to the side of our raft that was nearest Jerry's and adjusted the cam straps on the Paco Pad that Fritz had placed across the main seat as a cushion. A Paco Pad is the gold standard of waterproof foam mats used for camping on river trips, and the air so carefully trapped inside this one was starting to heat up in the sun, making the whole thing swell to the point where I was concerned that a seam might rupture. I opened the valves and let out some air, then dipped some water out of the river and spilled it across the expanse of rubber to cool it off. As I bent to do this, I noticed that Wink had now wandered over to where Brendan was working to carefully pack loaves of bread into waterproof storage boxes.

"Who are you?" Wink asked him.

"I'm Brendan, Fritz's son." He offered a hand to shake.

"Oh, so you're with Fritz?" Wink ignored Brendan's hand and instead planted his feet and stared down at the kid, watching him work. His jovial expression skewed halfway into a sneer.

My emotional radar went nuts. An unpleasant tone had crept into the man's voice, something that made me feel crawly. I wanted to tell Wink to get to work and leave Brendan alone, but that would make for a bad beginning to our three-week enforced acquaintance. I told myself that the fact was that his boat didn't need to be rigged, a point in favor of a wooden dory as compared to a rubber raft. Rafts were big and buoyant and carried a lot of gear, but they arrived flat as a pancake and thus had to be inflated, and rigging them with all the rocket boxes and coolers and dry bags and what-have-you was a lengthy process that, in part, was going to have to be repeated daily, while the dory had floated off that trailer as pretty as you please and all Wink had to do was load in his dry bag and Paco Pad and accept that delivery of vegetables.

It occurred to me to make sure that those veggies were properly stowed. I waited until Wink wandered up the ramp to use the bathroom and then hurried over to the dory, lifted the after hatch, and took a peek. "Holy Moses, this thing is awash!" I told Jerry. "Is this thing going to make it down the river?"

"I noticed that he was running a pump earlier," she said. "The wood looks pretty dry. Maybe it will swell up and seal after it's been in the water a while."

"But won't things get wet?"

"Well . . . maybe we won't have to wash those carrots so much."

"His granola bars are afloat."

"They aren't his granola bars."

I closed the lid and turned to look at her. "Then whose . . . ?"

"He sweet-talked Don into giving him one, saying he couldn't afford to go up to lunch at the café with the rest of us. I noticed when Don turned his back he took a few more. Like maybe half the box."

I smiled. Nothing got past Jerry Rasmussen, not a single blessed thing. I moved to the forward hatch and gave it a tug. It was latched, and I couldn't figure out how to get it open. Was it locked? This guy was beginning to be more than a little bit of a puzzle to me.

I strolled over to the bulletin board and looked at the item Wink had tapped. It was a listing of the river parties set to launch that month. I supposed that he had looked it over to see if any of his old friends or colleagues might be on the river the same time he was, but I wondered if sharing the river with old chums would be a good thing for him, or bad.

I found our trip on the list (private, twenty-one days from this launch ramp to the take-out at Diamond Creek). There were several others, mostly commercial trips, and it appeared that the park was running a botanical survey. I also noticed a still-moist smudge of orange pulp next to one of the commercial trips, which indicated where Wink had tapped the page. He had identified a group called God's Voice; why?

Molly Chang strolled past me on her way back from an errand to her car. She leaned close and read the page. "God's Voice. Isn't that one of those fundamentalist Christian groups? You know, the one with the big television program."

"I can't say as I watch that kind of programming."

Molly shook her head. "Don't you remember them? Their preacher worked himself up into a real fervor one Sunday and dropped dead right in front of about a million or so of his TV faithful."

"I missed that one."

"You gotta read the tabloids, Em. You're falling behind on your gossip." She gave me a pat on the shoulder and continued back to the raft she was helping to rig.

I headed back toward the rafts myself, trying to sort out this new bit of data about Wink Oberley. Certainly the canyon inspired plenty of awe but it didn't make sense that someone as profane as Wink would take an interest in a church group, unless he had tapped the page out of contempt; but no, he had been smiling, apparently happy to see whatever it was that had caught his eye.

Something about Wink Oberley was very wrong, and I wanted to know what it was. Forewarned was forearmed. I had just an hour or so before we launched to find out what I could about him. Even here at Lees Ferry I could raise no cell phone signal, and once we were afloat, my only communications with the outside world would depend on very expensive calls over the satellite telephone we had rented in case of emergencies.

Part of the idea of a raft trip was to leave behind the modern world of high-speed Internet and flush toilets and box stores and TV and its violence and prescription drug ads and most other things that we let define us, but right that instant, I wanted access to information.

The pay phones next to the bathrooms at the top of the ramp weren't working. I straightened up from my work and stretched my back, trying to remember how far up the road I'd have to go to find another one. The best person to call would be Faye Carter, my closest friend and Fritz's business partner. I had first met her while working with the FBI agent who became her husband. My life always did have a way of getting snarled in such ways, but Faye was a smart cookie and knew me well enough that she wouldn't take my concern for unfounded paranoia.

I told Fritz that I was going to move our vehicle to the long-term parking lot and headed up the road. It turned out to be a five-mile drive to the nearest working telephone, but I was lucky and caught Faye at the office.

"What's up?" she inquired. "Forget your water wings?"

"Ha ha, I need a favor," I told her. "Could you flip onto the Internet and see if there's anything in the Princeton University Geology Department about a George Oberley? He's supposedly a Ph.D. candidate there. Sometimes graduate departments have stuff about who's working with whom."

I listened to Faye tap keys. "Nope. I'm not finding anything in their search window . . . Let me try this . . . No, I went back to Google and typed George Oberley and Princeton and got nothing. Got something else you want me to check?"

"Put the name into 411.com for New Jersey."

"So how are Fritz and Brendan . . . Okay, on that 411, I've got an address in Rocky Hill. That's right next to Princeton. I had family back there. In fact, they're still there, and I think one of them is in administration at the university; you want me to do some digging?"

"That would take a while. We launch in an hour."

"Business is slow. It would give me something to do. Fritz said he was going to call me on the fifth or sixth with a resupply list, so I could shovel my dirt then."

"Maybe this is going further than I should."

"Is this Em Hansen I'm talking to?"

"You know I promised Fritz that I'd stay away from contentious stuff; you know, investigations where people might get mad and someone—like me—might get hurt."

"Oh, so that means you're not supposed to look after him when he gets a ringer on his prize river trip? Come on, this is enlightened self-interest, and it will be like old times: you, me, maybe a miscreant . . ."

A good friend is someone who supports you in doing what instinct is screaming for you to do. "Sure," I said. "I'll talk to you on the fifth."

◆

When at last every last piece of gear was secured and we'd handed our car keys off to the crew that was going to shuttle the cars to locations at the South Rim (for those who couldn't make the full three-week run, and would therefore hike out at the halfway point at Phantom Ranch) and at Diamond Creek (for the rest of us, and for those who would hike in and row only the lower half), Fritz called us all together for a final powwow and safety briefing, after which he said, "Okay then, we launch!"

A chorus of cheers went up. Pop tops popped. Fourteen souls pushed the rafts and kayaks into the water and pulled away from the beach with great gusto. Our fifteenth waded his beat-up plywood marvel off the beach, climbed in, and pointed its high nose downriver, but he seemed distracted by the route that led down from the rim. I wondered what was he looking for.

Fritz led the procession until the kayakers sped past him in search of riffles to play in. Aboard our raft, Brendan settled himself in the bow and I climbed up on top of the load behind Fritz, lifted my eyes to the rim rock—the gorgeous sweep of vermilion Wingate Sandstone—and silently chanted the mantras I had worked out with the psychotherapist I had covertly consulted about my phobia ("I float like a cork, I float like a cork. . . . The water is chocolate Jell-O, the water is chocolate Jell-O").

It really was a lovely day: The sky was cobalt blue, we had a light breeze and seventy-five degrees, my life vest (PFD, or personal flotation device, Fritz was teaching me to say) was pleasantly snug, and the rhythm of the oars was darned close to soporific. Fritz began to sing a little ditty about his happiness. Swallows flitted through the air.

Over eons, the river had cut down through thousands of feet of layered sedimentary rock but at Lees Ferry, the river level stood at 3,107 feet above sea level. I leaned back and studied the strata that lined the river: naked red and brown rocks that had been carved into fantastic shapes stair-stepping back, the hard sandstones and limestones forming cliffs, and the soft shales forming slopes. I could see great red cliffs of Wingate Sandstone, stepping away toward the sky. In the solidity of stone I was at peace.

Four miles downriver, we slid under the high span of the bridge that carries Highway 89A from the east side of the river to the west. A huge bird circled overhead, one of the canyon's resident California condors out looking for something dead to eat. ("I float like a cork and I don't taste like chocolate Jell-O or anything else you might like to eat," I told it in my head, regarding its nine-foot wingspan with respect.) The chocolate brown Moenkopi Formation opened downward, and beneath it emerged the white cliff-former of the Coconino Sandstone.

I studied the river guide, a waterproof flip-book that illustrated the canyon and the river and all of its tributary canyons and important features such as sandy beaches big enough for overnight camping, symbolized by triangles. The river was represented by a sinuous blue band between cliffs, which were picked out with contour lines showing elevation above the banks. Each mile downriver was indicated by a number framed in a hexagon. Riffles were marked by single lines crossing from bank to bank, and rapids were a series of lines that looked like ladders reaching downriver. Each rapid was named, and that name was followed by numbers in parentheses that gauged the magnitudes of the rapids, some of which grew or lessened in difficulty with increase or decrease in river flow. Dashed lines showed where side canyons presented dry tributaries that might wake up and deliver flash floods. I concentrated on the little triangles that meant I got to walk on land.

The river ran south for the first sixty miles through a section of the Grand Canyon known as Marble Canyon, cutting down through the Hermit Shale, the four rock formations of the Supai Group, the Surprise Canyon Formation, and, by river mile 23, the massive Redwall Limestone. Fritz had shown me photos from his prior trip. The Redwall was hundreds of feet thick and rose nearly vertical from the water's edge. The towering red cliffs, the deep blue sky, and their reflections on the swirling water formed a tableau so mesmerizing that photographers could not keep their cameras at bay. Fritz promised that the subject of his snapshots would bring me tranquillity and serenity, punctuated by moments of raw thrill as we shot over rapids. "You'll love all that stone," he'd said. "How can you not?"

Indeed. I leaned back, closed my eyes, felt the sun on my face, and descended into the landscape of the river.

U.S. National Park Service, Grand Canyon National Park
Transcript of communication received by satellite phone by dispatcher
Cleome James
April 18, 0820 hrs.

"I need to speak to a ranger, and quick!"

"State your name, please."

"Sherry Rhoades. I'm with a river party and we've found a body."

"A body, ma'am? Is that a human body, or an animal?"

"A human body, goddammit! Do you think I'd get this excited about a dead jackrabbit?"

"Hold the line, please, ma'am."

"Get me someone who can—"

"You've found human remains?"

"Yes, we've got a goddamn dead body in our goddamn campsite!"

"Where are you located?"

"Whitmore Wash. River mile 188 right. I—"

"Is this person known to you?"

"No. Never saw him before."

"A male? Describe him, please."

"Yeah, I'd say it's male, all right, but—"

"Height? Weight? Age? Skin color?"

"Height? What do you mean, height? He sure as hell ain't standing up! I'm trying to tell you that the man is dead!"

"Is this an average-height, muscular, white male?"

"Ah . . . okay, I see what you're saying. Yeah, you could say so. That would describe him. Sure."

"Brown hair? Brown eyes?"

"His hair is brown, but the eyes . . . Um, listen: He doesn't look so good. And we didn't check for ID. I didn't touch him. Kathryn! Hey, anybody! Anything in his pockets?"

"We've had a man go missing from farther upriver, so that's probably him. Please cover the body with a tarp or something and—shit, lost the connection. I hate these damned sat phones! Howie, hand me that radio. Has Seth Farnsworth checked in yet this morning? Damn it. Is this recording device still running?"

End of recording.

APRIL 1: SHAKEDOWN CRUISE

OUR FIRST NIGHT ON THE RIVER WE CAMPED AT THE MOUTH OF BADGER Canyon, just below Badger Creek Rapid, the first stretch of whitewater large enough to kick up what Fritz called "a soporific veil of white noise." Badger was rated a 5 out of 10 at high water and an 8 at low because large rocks stuck out then. Lucky for me the river was running high that day. "We caught some luck; someone up at the dam turned the river on," Fritz told me. He thought it was a good thing that we not take on heavy challenges on our first day going down our first rapid, and I heartily agreed. The river guide indicated that we made a fifteen-foot drop over the course of the rapid, but you could have fooled me; I had my eyes closed. I hardly got splashed. I hoped that maybe this wasn't going to be all that tough after all.

We had come eight miles from Lees Ferry rowing on otherwise flat water, though there were plenty of places where the water sort of spread out into flat boils, indicating who knew what was going on below. At Badger Canyon, we pulled over to river right, brought the rafts up to the bank, and tied them to the stoutest trees we could find, paying out twenty feet or more of line. As he paid out our bow line and tied his best Eagle Scout knots, Fritz explained that tethering rafts was a tricky business: Because the river waters rose and fell with the requirements of the

Glen Canyon Dam's need to generate electricity for all the traffic lights, air conditioners, light-emitting diodes, and automated pool sweeps in this region of the Southwest, we had to be careful not to tie our boats too close to the high-water line, lest we find ourselves having to drag them across a naked sandbank in the morning. Similarly, if we paid out too much and the water rose, we might find the boats a rope's length downriver banging against whatever rocks or tree stumps lurked in that direction.

Our first night in camp went fairly smoothly, considering that it was a shakedown exercise for unloading the rafts and setting up camp. A key element in laying out our camp was to choose a sanguine spot for our portable toilet. National Park Service rules required that we carry out all solid wastes, especially those that came out of the aft ends of humans. It was okay to pee in the river, but not on land, and our feces had to leave with us. A system had therefore been devised for the efficient packaging of poop using vessels large enough to double as a commode yet small enough to be easily transported back to the designated raft each morning when we broke camp. Our system depended on repurposed army surplus rocket boxes. The rocket boxes were the height of a standard porcelain toilet, and they handily came with two big, friendly handles for ease of lugging them about. Their lids were tightly sealed, but once in position in a suitably private alcove among the brush that lined the riverbanks, the lid was popped and a toilet seat was clipped to the top. Stick a roll of toilet paper on a nearby twig and voilà, eco-friendly frontier toilet. "The groover," as Fritz called it, was positioned downwind from the campsite yet not so far that it be difficult to find or reach should midnight peregrinations be required. Daytime pee stops were another matter. Fritz explained that at lunch stops, "The ladies shall head upstream and the gentlemen shall head downstream.

Skirts up and pants down," Jerry added cheerfully.

All hands helped bring elements of the kitchen up to the clearing we had chosen. A simple yet functional setup was devised using two light-weight folding aluminum tables, a pair of propane camp stoves, a fire pan, various utensils, and a sizable filter pump for creating potable water. A galvanized tub filled with river water served as a beer cooler. Food, plates, and flatware were brought up from the various stowage boxes and coolers on the rafts, and each of us was in charge of transporting his or her own folding camp chair, tent, and sleep gear.

I helped Fritz and Brendan pitch the tent we would share for probably longer than would be quite comfortable for all of us, and, when Fritz had trouble driving in the tent stakes, I fetched my mineral hammer from my gear box on the raft and gave each a good whack.

Molly Chang and Mungo were in charge of dinner that first night, and I could hear Mungo cussing as he dug through one of the giant coolers and rocket boxes that were lashed to the various rafts in search of fresh chicken and vegetables to make a big stir-fry, it being requisite to eat up whatever would spoil first. One of the other huge coolers had been taped shut to keep it cold as long as possible; it had been packed solid with frozen vacuum-packed meats and set in a walk-in freezer for a couple of days before we left Utah to get it as cold as possible and try to keep it that way for as long as possible. It had been something of a challenge to pack enough eats for sixteen people for twenty-one days, while keeping the menus simple enough that dinner could be tossed together within an hour in a high wind or downpour as necessary yet still sufficiently interesting that morale didn't collapse by the end of the second week. It was a good thing no one needed me to manage that project; I would have packed those coolers solid with junk food.

Bedding was another major challenge. There were two schools of thought here: tents and no tents. Those who wanted privacy—or such privacy as could be afforded when that many people are crammed together on a small beach—liked tents. Olaf Jones, who was at ease up to his gizzard in churning rapids, slept in a tent because he was totally paranoid while on land. Just say "Spider!" or, worse yet, "Scorpion!" and the man was gone. Even "Ants!" made him jump sideways. He didn't like insects crawling on him while he slept, but he told me that the real reason he brought a tent was to keep himself separated from mice. "They all carry diseases like hantavirus. Little buggers crawl on you in the night if you sleep outside," Olaf growled. "On an earlier river trip, one of those little sons of bitches bit me right on the nose, and I had to rim out and find a frikkin' doc. And watch out for the skunks. They carry rabies. You gotta take care you don't get rabies. Horrible way to go."

I said, "But you don't mind the idea of drowning, or hitting your head on a rock."

"Water is clean," he said, sweeping a hand across an imaginary surface. "Gives you a good bath." Suddenly he grinned, showing me a gap where a tooth was missing. "You get water in places where you didn't even know you had places!"

Olaf was a safety kayaker, one of our crew of three. I was glad they were with us. It would be their job to zip about in the churning spume while the rafts shot through the whitewater so they could catch anyone who fell out of a raft, or catch everyone if the raft flipped. Kayaks were infinitely more maneuverable than rafts, which pretty much went only one way: downriver. A kayaker could hover and play in the water, go upriver if the gradient wasn't too steep, and, Fritz had explained to me, he could "eddy out" along the side of a rapid and be right there to shoot out into the current to catch a "floater." If I "went for a swim," he assured me, one of the kayakers would be there "right quick" to give me an assist. In the unlikely event that this should happen, I should grab the safety strap at one end of the kayak and let him tow me back to my raft. I decided that I would hold on to the safety straps on our raft very tightly. A "swimmer" I was not. But this didn't seem to worry Olaf.

I looked out across the "clean" river. It looked like it was carrying one heck of a lot of sediment to me, but maybe that was just the geologist in me, and I was being a bit too literal about things.

Molly's stir-fry and Mungo's dessert of fresh fruits with yogurt really hit the spot. Everything tasted better out of doors, and, per the dictates of our copy of the National Park Service's *Noncommercial River Trip Regulations*, our bible for avoiding Trouble with the Man, we built a "warming and aesthetic fire" in our "metal fire pan measuring 300 square inches . . . The lip of the pan must be 3 inches high on all sides . . . [and] must be elevated using manufactured legs (not rocks, empty cans, etc.)." The upstream source of sediment had been cut off when the Glen Canyon Dam was built, so the river was now eroding the beaches faster than they were being built up, and likewise the cleansing high flood stages of the river were gone, so it was incumbent upon us to keep what beaches remained in as good shape as possible. They were a finite and dwindling resource. I could see how fragile the canyon was, and I appreciated the care taken by those who had gone before us to keep these campsites clean.

We sat around the fire telling stories about ourselves and earlier river trips, and those who weren't yet acquainted began to get to know each other. Brendan was the only kid along, or should I say a kid on the cusp of young manhood. He was thirteen and his voice was cracking, though he hadn't started his growth spurt yet. Olaf Jones, who at twenty-two was the next youngest person on the trip, had already developed a series of nicknames for Brendan, all focusing on his short stature: He called him "Low Pockets" and "Stump," or just "Hey, Runt."

I looked around the fire, studying the groups that manned each boat. Fritz, Brendan, and I formed raft number one. Raft two was manned by Don and Jerry Rasmussen, the geologist/oil company office manager couple from Denver. They were experienced rafters, a couple of empty-nesters of advancing middle age who were gathering no moss. The plan had been for Tiny to share rowing their raft, but because he was not here, the safety kayakers had kindly offered to spell Don and Jerry at the oars, especially on long days when we might find ourselves rowing into the wind.

The kayakers—Olaf Jones, Lloyd Oshiro, and Gary McClanahan— were a mixed bag of sinewy adrenaline junkies with ragged haircuts. We knew them from here and there. Olaf was one of those guys who lived for adventure and had no permanent address. Lloyd was a Ph.D. candidate currently studying with Molly, and Gary rode Harleys with Tiny when he wasn't working on a highway crew somewhere.

Raft three was Dell Oxley and Nancy Skinner, two friends of Tiny's whom neither Fritz nor I had met before we all arrived at the put-in. Dell had a professorial air to him—I think he taught in a college somewhere—and Nancy was a bookkeeper for the navy who had taken early retirement. She had brought her knitting to the fireside and looked like life suited her just fine. Also on that raft was Danielle Burtis, a pal of Dell's from somewhere in Florida who did something Floridian for a living.

Raft four held Mungo Park, Molly Chang, and Julianne Wertz. Mungo was a big, hairy guy who was a physicist in real life, and Julianne was a young, unemployed schoolteacher who had always, always, always wanted to do something like this but could only afford to come on the first "half" of the expedition. She and Danielle would hike out the Bright Angel Trail from Phantom Ranch, and two others would take their places. The upper half of the river was actually more like the upper two-fifths; Phantom Ranch lay eighty-eight miles downriver from Lees Ferry, and our pull-out was at Diamond Creek, which was at mile 226. We planned to reach mile 88 on our tenth night and would camp at a site called Cremation.

The canyon was full of quirky names, as Wink Oberley explained. "Batchit Cave is my personal favorite," he said. "There's an old story that Eddie McKee, who was park naturalist here back in the 1930s, took his lovely wife, Barbara, there during some of his fieldwork, and she said, 'Why, there are nothing but unmarried men here; how nice that they'd name this place after what bachelors do,' but she had it wrong! It got that name because it was full of bat guano! Get it? Bat-shit!" He laughed like a machine gun, savoring his own joke.

Julianne said, "Oh, Wink, you're so funny!"

Wink scanned our faces for additional appreciation.

"What day do you think we'll get to Nankoweap?" Don asked Fritz. "That's such a spectacular site. We'll overnight there, yes?"

Fritz said, "Yes, in fact Tiny and I planned for two nights at Nankoweap. It's such a big beach that it has several good campsites, so we won't be putting anyone out by staying over. I'm personally looking forward to hiking up to the granaries with Brendan here." He reached over and ruffled his son's hair, and got a good-natured swat in reply. The kid never looked up from his pre-algebra homework, which he was doing by the light of his headlamp. In order to bring him along it had been necessary to pull Brendan out of school for a month. His eighth-grade teachers had cheerfully assigned independent study projects, delighted by the idea of how much the kid would learn on a trip like this. The math teacher had been the only hard-ass in the bunch.

Wink cut back in. "It will be fun to run the rapids there several times if we want. I'm sure our kayakers here would let some of us big-boaters take a shot." Ignoring surprised looks from Olaf and Lloyd, he reached a hand out to Julianne and stroked her forearm. "It's just a three on a scale of ten. Good practice for you."

Julianne beamed. "Would you show me how, Wink? I've never been in a kayak."

He leaned closer to her and said, "There are a number of things I'd like to show you, honey."

Julianne raised her shoulders to her ears and tittered in glee, then threw back her head and stared at the sky. "Oh, aren't the stars marvelous! The desert air! Oh! That one's moving!"

"That's a satellite," said Jerry.

"Oh."

"Chariots of the astronaut gods," said Mungo.

"I tried out for the astronaut corps," Wink informed us. "Interesting set of challenges, and I would have been available if they'd mounted an expedition to Mars. Think of that, the first geologist on Mars!"

Fatigue suddenly weighed on me. "I'm going to find our tent and crawl inside it," I announced. "See the rest of you in the A.M."

Fritz said, "I'll be along in a bit." He looked over at Brendan, who was still focused tightly on his homework. I felt bad that I'd missed that cue. Solidarity was important to thirteen-year-olds who were stuck doing pre-algebra in one of the most beautiful places on earth, especially those who were a long way from their mothers, whether they entirely got along with them or not. I was supposed to be standing in for her, and here I was thinking of no one but myself.

Nancy Skinner stuffed her knitting into its carry bag and arched her back into a catlike stretch. "I'm right after you," she said. "Nothing like fresh air and exercise to wear a woman out."

Wink stood up and made quite a display of stretching this way and that. "Well, I'm off to sleep on my dory," he said. "The rest of you can shlep your gear up and down the beach if you like, but it's a lot easier to sleep on my boat, and with the gentle movement of the water, I sleep like a baby."

Julianne said, "Oh, Wink, I'm so impressed with your simple ethic!"

Mungo coughed like something had caught in his throat. People began to scatter.

Before heading up to our tent I "used" the river. Wading into a private spot in the shallows, I dropped my shorts and crouched into the position. It was times like this that I envied men their plumbing, but pretty much the rest of the time I was fine with mine.

As I walked up the path afterward toward our tent afterward, a spark flew up from the fire pan, and I followed it upward until it winked out of existence over my head, lost in the dazzling lights of the night sky. *From the ridiculous to the sublime, the Grand Canyon has it all,* I mused.

Unfortunately, *it all* would prove to include trouble that would have us sleeping apart before we reached Diamond Creek.

I arrived at Whitmore Wash by helicopter. Noncommercial group led by Sherry Rhoades was packed and ready to leave site. Rhoades and party member Kathryn Davy showed me to the place along the riverbank upstream from the campsite where the body was found. Davy stated that she had been bird-watching and moved through the tamarisk to see what a group of turkey vultures were "finding so interesting."

The body was a white male, average height, husky build, dark hair. The birds had already been at his face, so immediate ID was not possible. It could be the one missing from the Calder party upriver. Calculating flow, the timing is about right. As to speculation that the victim drowned, something does not look right. Something about this corpse is not consistent with other remains I have examined.

I released the Rhoades party to continue downriver and requested that Chief Ranger Gerald Weber notify the coroner and investigate the scene before corpse removal.

APRIL 2: GEOLOGY LESSONS

THE MIDDLE OF OUR FIRST FULL DAY ON THE RIVER, IN A SECTION OF THE canyon known as the Roaring Twenties, Julianne Wertz managed to flip Molly and Mungo's raft in a "not very big" (Fritz's words, not mine) rapid called Indian Dick. Mungo commented that "Dick" probably wasn't the name of the Indian after whom this tumble of water was named, but rather a description of his sense of humor.

Julianne was chagrined, though the incident wasn't entirely her fault. Wink had assured her that she had the "stuff" to row a rapid. I felt sorriest for Molly, who got pretty cold swimming the raft to shore.

Wink was helpful in getting the raft right side up. He knew what he was doing—where to place it relative to the current, how to rig the lines, who should push and who should pull—and we had things back in order in jig time. Julianne awarded him a big, lingering hug. Mungo cussed continually beneath his breath during these proceedings, and I heard him mutter the words "nookie motive" more than once. He didn't have much trouble persuading Julianne to ride the next few miles downriver in the dory with the marvelous Mr. Oberley at the oars.

It was about in this stretch of river that the Redwall Limestone first appeared. I pointed it out to Brendan, hoping that he would take an interest in the geology of the canyon and put it into one of his independent study reports, but so far he seemed more interested in rowing the raft. "It sure is red," he said, trying to be polite.

I told him, "The stone is actually gray, but it's stained the same brickred as the strata above it; see? Iron oxide is easily mobilized and washed down over the face of the Redwall. And it does form a wall: Instead of the stair-step setbacks of the Supai Group strata above, this limestone forms a vertical cliff."

Looking bored, Brendan leaned over and dragged a hand in the water to watch the ripples.

I tried another tack. "The Grand Canyon's really neat because the river has cut through all three major kinds of rock: sedimentary, metamorphic, and igneous. These rocks here are all sedimentary, but we'll get to the metamorphic and igneous rocks later on in the trip. Sedimentary rocks are kind of easy to read because they tend to form these nice broad layers. That's because, well . . . they're formed from sediments that fill in a . . . a basin, and . . ." I was quickly getting balled up in the jargon of geology, and Brendan wasn't even bothering to look up. "What would you like to learn about these rocks?" I asked.

Brendan rolled onto his back and stared up at the cliffs. "How'd they get there?" he asked.

"That's exactly the question geologists ask!" I replied. "And we've found a lot of answers. The rocks tell the story." I gestured up the wall of the canyon, sweeping from river level to the sky. "One of the basic rules of geology is the Law of Superposition, which says that the layer on the bottom was laid down first, and over time each layer above was stacked on top, sequentially.

"Well, duh," said Brendan.

I glanced at Fritz. He was concentrating on his rowing, diplomatically staying out of our conversation.

I said, "Well, every once in a while you get faked out by a thrust fault, but generally that law holds true. The cool thing is that you can compare these ancient rocks to sediments you'd find in a tidal flat, say, or a riverbed, or a sand dune, and you can match them up. The Redwall Limestone, for instance, was deposited at the bottom of the ocean. As creatures that lived in the ocean died, their shells dropped to the bottom, building up a layer."

"I don't see any shells," said Brendan.

"Neither do I, looking from the middle of the river here," I agreed. "But remember the park ranger Don and Wink were talking about? Eddie McKee? Well, he studied those rocks for over fifty years, and he found plenty of fossils in them. He found corals, crinoids, foraminifera, brachiopods, trilobites, cephalopods—"

"What are all of those?" asked Fritz, hinting that I should speak plain English around his son.

"Well, corals you know about," I said. "Crinoids are more commonly called sea lilies. The rest are various sea creatures both small and large that had shells made of calcium carbonate—a chemical that's also known as lime, hence the name 'limestone.' Most of those shells are so tiny that they make up a sort of mush, but we'll see lots of fossils on this trip. Nautiloids, trace fossils, there were also fish, and—"

"We're a long way from the ocean, Em," Brendan said dubiously.

"Yeah, but the Redwall here, it was deposited in an ocean, and the rocks are now thousands of feet above sea level! What do you suppose happened?"

"You tell me," he said, but when his father shot him a look, he added, "Please."

My head spun a bit as I tried to feature explaining the theory of plate tectonics to him with only words and hand gestures. I considered trying to impress him with the fact that marine shell fossils could also be found near the top of Everest, five miles above sea level. I could explain that the Indian subcontinent had come roaring up from down near Antarctica and slammed into Asia, heaving the strata up that high, but that opened a whole can of worms about plates of the earth's crust moving around like sludge on the surface of a spherical pot of boiling oatmeal.

"Let's just stay with how the rocks were formed for now," I said. "So, look at these gnarly layers just above the top of the Redwall Limestone. Those rocks are actually a stack of formations called the Supai Group, named after the town of Supai on the Havasupai Indian Reservation. McKee studied all of those layers and matched them to modern sediments he had looked at. When you get deep-sea creatures made of limestone, that's one thing, but here he had fewer fossils to go by, so he had to look at the sizes of grains in the rock and how they were arranged. He found shallow marine, lagoon, and river sediments, and a few sand dunes. All of those rocks were formed in environments right near the ocean. So now you've got the Redwall, which was deposited at the bottom of the ocean, and the Supai, which was deposited in the band between shallow marine and the shoreline."

Brendan rolled onto his back and stared up at the cliffs. He had previously sounded trenchant, but now that he'd let down his guard a bit, he seemed a bit more interested.

I said, "Next you get the Hermit Formation, that dark red slope up there at the base of that buffy-colored cliff. The Hermit was deposited by rivers flowing off a mountain range, so as we follow the sequence we're moving from the open ocean onto the land and then going inland. Above that, the buffy-colored cliff is the Coconino Sandstone. It's all sand dunes. This tells us that at this location, during the period of time when the sediments in these rocks were being deposited, the land was rising relative to the oceans. It went from a full ocean environment to a high, dry land environment."

"How do you know they're sand dunes?" Brendan asked.

"McKee wanted to know that, too, so he went to White Sands National Monument in New Mexico and cut open a modern sand dune to see how it looked inside. He got the military to do it using one of their D9 Caterpillar tractors."

"Cool!"

"Yes, it was. And what did he find inside? The sand that blew downwind from the crest of the dune had left thin layers as it slid down the slip face, called 'cross-beds.' Other kinds of sedimentary structures have cross-beds, too, but the kind that builds up on the leeward sides of sand dunes is steeper than those you get underwater where a river moves sand along its bed or dumps it out to sea along the front of a delta. The cross-beds in sand dunes are especially big and they curve at the bottom because as the wind blows over the crest of the dune it whips into a vortex and reworks the sand at the toe. If you climbed up that cliff and looked at the Coconino Sandstone, you'd find cross-beds that look exactly like the ones McKee studied at White Sands."

Brendan was squinting at me, a look that said, *Prove it to me.*

I said, "He also found the footprints of lizards up there in the Coconino, the kind that walked only on land, so that was another clue, but the footprints always went up the dune slip faces in the rock and never down."

Fritz smiled. "So somewhere out there when the Coconino was being formed there were a whole lot of lizards perched on top of sand dunes trying to get down, eh?"

I laughed. "McKee wanted to figure out that riddle, too, so he went out and found a chuckwalla lizard and had it march up and down a modern sand dune, and you know what? The chuckwalla made nice orderly tracks going uphill, but when it turned around and went down, it set off avalanches in the dune slip face that obliterated its tracks."

Brendan said, "So its uphill tracks were still there, but its downhill tracks were erased."

"Exactly. But McKee had another problem with his modern lizard: The chuckwalla liked it fine on that nice hot sand and didn't want to move, so you know what he did? He put the lizard on the dune, then stood there creating shade on it until it cooled off and decided to move into the sun."

Brendan laughed. I was getting somewhere.

"And how old are these rocks?" Fritz asked.

I said, "The Redwall is Mississippian time, about three hundred forty million years old, and the younger strata, through the Coconino, were deposited from the early Pennsylvanian Period to the early Permian Period, a span from approximately three hundred fifteen to two hundred seventy-five million years ago."

"Three hundred forty million years," said Fritz softly. "That's hard to imagine."

Brendan suddenly frowned. His tone took on the ring of a preacher as he said something that sounded like a quotation, "And the waters returned from off the earth continually: and after the end of the hundred and fifty days the waters were abated."

I stared at the lad, wondering what I had just heard.

Brendan's gaze flickered toward me and away, and in the instant of connection he stiffened ever so slightly pulling his shoulders up around his ears as if for protection. I felt him withdraw, as if he were no longer on the raft with me and his father in this beautiful place in nature.

I looked from son to father and back again, wondering if I had said something wrong.

Notes of Gerald Weber, Chief Ranger
RE: Human remains found at Whitmore Wash
April 18

Flew to helo pad opposite Whitmore Canyon to examine body of white male discovered there earlier this morning. River Ranger Seth Farnsworth met flight and transported to beach just above Whitmore Rapid to avoid contaminating scene with rotor wash.

Corpse was located in shallows adjacent to beach just above Whitmore Rapid. Photographed scene in detail.

Body lay on its back. Body showed no postmortem bloat and little decay, but face and belly etc. had been attacked by vultures. Gross examination of corpse yielded scrapes and bruises but not cause of death.

Searched pockets. All were empty. Collected fingerprints to send FBI for ID. Placed body bag next to it and rolled it into bag.

Preliminary matching of missing persons suggests that this is the man reported missing from Ledges Campsite, but agree with Ranger

Farnsworth that corpse did not lodge in eddies upriver as expected and therefore its presence here is suspect. Therefore called helicopter to beach, loaded body for transport to Mohave County coroner to determine cause of death.

APRIL 3: VASEY'S PARADISE AND OTHER SURPRISES

WE STOPPED FOR LUNCH ON OUR THIRD DAY AT A CAMPSITE CALLED South Canyon, near Stanton's Cave, again on river right. Most campsites in that part of the canyon are on the right, or west side of the river, because the left bank is part of the Navajo Reservation. Arizona is a patchwork of public lands of varying descriptions. We could land briefly during the day as needed on reservation lands, but not hike out to the rim above and not make camp. I say respect is a good thing; I wouldn't want anyone pitching a tent on my front yard without at least asking.

Stanton's Cave was named after a railroad surveyor who for some reason took his survey party down the river in 1889 and 1890. I wonder what that was like. They didn't have rubber rafts, and as far as wood goes, I'll bet Wink's beat-up dory would look like a floating palace next to what they used.

While Brendan stood at water's edge kicking sand into the river, I took my lunch to the place where his father sat watching him while he ate his sandwich. "What gives?" I whispered. "I haven't had a moment alone with you, without Brendan in earshot. What's going on with him?"

"I'm not sure what you mean."

"Yeah, you do. You nudged me into talking to him about geology yesterday, and when you got me to say something about the age of the rocks he curled up like a hedgehog and started spouting Bible verses."

Fritz stared at the ground, his sandwich forgotten. "He has a good memory for such things."

"Help me here, Fritz! I don't want to upset the kid! Has someone put the munch on him about biblical reckonings of time or something?"

"Well, his mother . . ." He stuffed his quickly mummifying sandwich into his mouth and chewed, hard.

Suddenly the whole scenario hit me like a brick: Early in our relationship, when Fritz had told me that the former Mrs. Calder had been a bit on the religious side, I had cheerfully assumed that meant she was Catholic or something. But Catholics didn't spout verses from the Book of Genesis. They might have jailed Galileo for the heresy of saying that Planet Earth wasn't the center of the solar system, but that was clear back in 1633; they'd long since eased their ways over the worst of their intellectual speed bumps, leaving medieval thought in the Middle Ages. "So you don't just mean that your ex goes to church a lot," I said. "You're saying that she's making a thing out of it, and that she's taking Brendan with her."

Fritz's face crumpled with misery, but he said nothing. Sometimes the biggest, strongest men do not have a clue what to say or do.

"Why didn't you tell me?" I asked.

Fritz leaned forward and put his hands over his face. "I didn't realize how bad it had gotten until just recently," he said. "And I—I just sort of hoped it was a passing thing."

I turned and watched the force of concentration with which Brendan was kicking at the ground on which he stood. His mother had remarried and had moved away, taking the boy with her. It had taken some doing to get her to let him come on this trip. Fritz had campaigned long and hard, and had finally agreed to give up more than a commensurate portion of Brendan's summer visitation time in exchange for this extended spring-break time with him. It always sickened me to see a failed marriage continue its battle on the shared ground of parenting, but there was almost nothing I could do here but offer my best and overall, keep my nose clean. But did that now mean that I couldn't teach the kid about what I did for a living?

As I gazed at the pudgy curve of his shoulders, Brendan quit kicking at the sand and left the beach and waded into the river. The cold, opaque waters swirled higher and higher, taking from our sight now his ankles, now his calves, and finally his knees and thighs, much as his soul was disappearing into the turbulent world of adolescence.

❖

A little farther downriver we came to Vasey's Paradise, a spring-fed oasis on the right bank of the river. There, in the middle of the desert, waters trickling down from the heights of the Kaibab Plateau far uphill to the west, concentrated together at a particularly porous stratum in the Redwall Limestone, and spilled down the face of the rock. Groundwater had trickled along fractures and through cavities, opening them up into an extensive cave system, and here at the foot of the cliff the water made a short run as a happy little creek, then tumbled into the river. The wet red cliffs hung with intense greenery.

I took Brendan for a walk along the path, admiring cattails and a rich growth of scarlet monkey flowers against bright green leaves. A survey party from the national park was there. We struck up a conversation with their botanist, a tall, fair-haired woman named Susanne Mc-Coy. She had twinkly eyes and an easy smile and quickly took a shine to Brendan. "Are you interested in botany?" she asked him.

"I'm on independent studies from my school so I can take the whole month off and go rafting," he said importantly, "so yes, I'm interested in everything about this place!" He reached a finger out toward a shiny green vine.

Susanne prevented him from touching it by gently taking his hand in hers. "Watch out for that one," she said. "That's our old pal poison ivy. Here, step over this way and get a look at this little sweetheart, this maidenhair fern. I love that, don't you?"

Brendan smiled at her like he wanted her to sit down so he could play kitten and curl up in her lap.

"What work are you doing here?" I asked, making a mental note of her gentle way of protecting him in the hope that I could be a better guardian.

"We maintain a database on the riparian plants to see how these little ecosystems are faring," she said.

"Is global warming an issue?" asked Brendan.

The botanist lavished another smile on him, her bright blue eyes disappearing into creases etched by happiness. "We're watching for that impact, but we're also studying some influences here that are more local, such as water levels. Before the Glen Canyon Dam was put in, the river level varied a whole lot more. Spring runoff shot floods high up the walls and brought a renewal of sediment. The beaches at the campsites were much larger, and there wasn't any tamarisk along the banks," she said, referring to the thick belt of skinny trees that raised great sprays of scalelike leaves into the desert air forming a hedge along the river-bank wherever it found an inch of soil to drive a root. "It isn't even from this continent, and it didn't get to Grand Canyon until the 1920s and '30s."

"Then where did it come from?" Brendan asked.

"It's native to the eastern hemisphere," she replied. "It was brought to North America in the nineteenth century to stabilize soils, and it does do that, but it has become very invasive, disrupting the structure and stability of our native plant communities and degrading native wildlife habitat. It competes with native plant species, makes the soils salty, soaks up limited sources of moisture, concentrates salts in the soils and increases the frequency and intensity of fires. We have to cut the tammies and apply herbicide to them so that these more delicate plants can survive."

"How can you hope to pull it all out?" Brendan asked. "There's so much of it!"

"There's a huge volunteer effort to rout it out, so far mostly in the side canyons. In other areas in the Southwest a beetle has been introduced that's got a huge appetite for it, and that may come, but for now we're trying stoop labor."

Brendan said, "Are there any endangered species here? I mean, this little ecosystem is so . . . little."

"Yes, there are." Susanne bent to examine the stream bank. "I'm looking for . . . Yes, here's the little darling." She held aside a leaf so we could admire a small spiraling shell.

"It's a snail," Brendan said doubtfully.

"Yes, the endangered Kanab ambersnail. It thrives here, but see how isolated it is? And as you so rightly obseved, in so small a territory."

Through Susanne's eyes Brendan and I were beginning to see the delicacy of the canyon, a tenderness that lay in stark contrast to the bulwarks of rock and brash expanse of desert sky.

Susanne took us farther up the short trail and pointed out a bank of watercress. "And do you like orchids?" she asked. "There's a lovely big one here if I can find it, *Epipactis gigantea*—though I don't suppose it will be blooming just now."

"Orchids?" asked Brendan, incredulous.

"Why, yes, orchids are one of the largest and most diverse plant families in the world. Arizona is home to twenty-six orchid species. Ten species occur in the park, and three can be found in the Inner Canyon, always down near the river, as you can imagine."

Brendan beamed at her, imagining.

I could hear Mungo rattling his oars. "Time to make miles, river rats!" he roared.

"Sorry," I said. "We have to leave."

"I've greatly enjoyed what you've shown us," said Brendan, offering her a little bow.

"I'm sure we'll meet again," she said. "We'll be working our way down the river as part of this survey."

"Now!" Mungo bellowed.

"Coming!" I said, and we were off.

We rowed only another mile before making a stop at Redwall Cavern, a broad, arching recess in the otherwise unrelenting face of the limestone. Here the river had cut deep under the cliff wall, creating a spectacularly wide arch and a deep bank of sand that begged us to land. No camping was permitted here, but one could land during the day and gallop across the shaded beach.

We all beached our craft and ran up the sand, hooting for an echo, flopping this way and that, like a bunch of golden retrievers looking for sticks to fetch. Someone produced a Frisbee and tossed it; others ran out to catch it, purposefully crashing into each other. Wink leaped at the Frisbee as it sailed past but he missed it. An odd glint of anxiety flashed across his face. He turned abruptly toward Brendan, grabbed his arm, said loudly, "I'll show you some judo!" and gave the boy's arm a hard twist.

With horror, I watched as Brendan crumpled to his knees, neck arched backward in pain. "Stop!" he shrieked.

I closed on the scene quickly and without thinking bellowed, "Let him go!" in the most commanding voice I could muster.

Wink said, "Aw, we're just horsing around."

"*You* are horsing around. Brendan is telling you to *stop*. Let him *go!*"

Wink released the boy's arm as if tossing away a rag. His face tightened with frustration, and as he turned to face me, his eyes narrowed ever so slightly.

Brendan folded the offended arm across his belly and began to rub it, pulling into a sulk.

I stepped between man and boy and glared, wondering where Fritz was. Had he seen any of this? I glanced around just in time to see the elegant, athletic splendor of my husband's body arch as he leaped to catch the Frisbee at the far end of the cavern. Had I embarrassed the lad by stepping in? What did a mother do at times like these?

Ignoring me, Brendan gave Wink an evil look and slunk away. I trailed along behind the boy at a respectful distance, wishing I felt confident enough to put an arm around him. Instinct told me that a thirteen-year-old boy who'd just had his dignity impugned by a show-off nitwit needed his space. When it became clear that he was trending in the general direction of his father, I veered off his track.

I found Jerry and Danielle sprawled on the beach, enjoying its dry warmth.

"You look like you're doing much better," Jerry said.

"Who, me?" I asked, joining them on the smooth, soft sand.

"Yeah, you," she told me. "At the launch, you looked as nervous as I was the first time we ran this river. I'm so afraid of water that I couldn't stick my head under a shower to wash my hair. Don almost didn't get me to come along, but he was bringing most of our family, and I didn't want to miss the fun of being with our kids and grandkids, so I swallowed my fear and climbed onto the highest part of the raft behind the oarsman, just like you did. I tell you, by the end of that first day I was down in the bow leaning into the suds with the best of them!"

Danielle said, "And how do you wash your hair now?"

"In the sink, like any sane woman!" Jerry threw back her head and laughed. "Heavens, but I do love it here. There's nothing like getting out into nature!" In a tone she might use for suggesting that I put on more sunscreen, she added, "But you'd better keep an eye on that Wink fella, so he doesn't injure your stepson."

Danielle laughed. "Compulsive bastard."

"I thought I was the only one who noticed," I said stupidly.

Danielle's laughter tightened. "His behavior is pretty hard to miss."

I glanced over my shoulder. Wink had gotten his mitts on the Frisbee and was making a simple game of disk-toss with Julianne into a contact sport. The man had annoyed me at first, but that annoyance was now turning to worry.

We passed another hour at Redwall Cavern in relative peace, then loaded back into our various vessels and headed a short distance downriver in search of that night's campsite. As I climbed back aboard our raft from the safety of terra firma, I decided that Jerry was right about my growing confidence. I only had to run my mantras through my head once. Impulsively, I took a seat in the bow next to Brendan and gave him a hug.

Olaf paddled by in his kayak and spoke to Fritz. "We're not camping at Little Redwall, are we?" he asked.

"I was thinking we would," said Fritz. "Why?"

Olaf shivered. "Mice!" he said. "All over the place, mice. They have a little highway up against the rock wall at the top of the sand beach. It's a narrow campsite, so you can't get away from them, and all night long they're scurrying back and forth just inches from your tent."

Mungo rowed his raft up close to join in the discussion. "Grow a pair," he said simply, then pulled hard on his oars toward a rather narrow beach against an abrupt rock wall, chuckling all the way.

Youth has its own way of dealing with stress. "Yeah, Olaf!" Brendan called, and held his hands up to the sides of his head like a pair of mouse ears, wrinkled his nose, and squeaked.

Diary of Holly Ann St. Denis
April 3

Dear God,

I am writing from the banks of the Colorado River in the Grand Canyon! I always wanted to go here and now here I am! Praises be to You, Lord! And I see Your love in every turn of the river, twig, and face of rock. This will be my very special baptism. We launch tomorrow and will float on this river for TEN DAYS!!! This is the best Spring Break from school EVER!!!! Mom said life gets better after you turn fifteen, and SHE WAS RIGHT!!!!!

Mom wasn't too interested in taking this trip, I could tell, but "Uncle" Terry got her to come. I thought things were going to settle down after "Dad" Amos died, but Terry picked right up where he left off in oh, so many ways. But more about the river. We'll be floating on the river for ten days! Camping!!! Singing by firelight in Your holy canyon! Terry says we will see direct, incontrovertible evidence of Noah's Flood. Wow! I will be so close to You!!!

Okay, gotta go Lord, Mom's calling. She says we have one more night in the motel up the road to "get our pretty on," then it's ten days with no hot showers. She says that we'll all be in those thin tents packed so tight that there will be no privacy. She thinks that's awful but I think it's GREAT! "Uncle" Terry will have to, as Mom says, "keep it in his pants" for TEN BLESSED DAYS!!!

APRIL 4:
CHAMBERED NAUTILUS

An early stop the next morning was Nautiloid Canyon, so named because the shells of wonderful, cone-shaped chambered sea creatures lay fossilized in the limestone there. They had been eroded smooth with its surface, fortuitously sliced open end-to-end so we could see their insides. I couldn't spot any at first, but then Don Rasmussen dripped water on them from his canteen and they stood out plain as day. He led Brendan, Mungo, Jerry, and me about the area pointing out one fabulous specimen after another, greeting them like old friends.

Brendan peered at these creatures with suspicion. "What are they?" he asked.

Don was a kind, nurturing sort of guy by nature, tall and smiley and all rounded at the edges, and he took to the task of educating Brendan with gusto, settling his gaze on the lad with the eyes of a loving granddad. He said, "They're close cousins to the modern squid, but the squid doesn't have this external shell. This animal had long tentacles that would have stretched out here." He traced imaginary appendages, dangling from the wide end of one of the cones along the rock.

"You mean, like the giant squid that ate the whaling ship in the movie?"

Jerry, who was standing near her husband, smiled at the image.

Don nodded. "Well, I haven't seen that particular movie, but yes, the nautiloid's tentacles would have had sucker discs on them, much like the modern-day squid, I imagine. We don't get to know exactly, because those soft tissues were not fossilized. But we can see a lot from the hard tissues that tell us that their anatomical structures were much like modern nautilus shells, except that instead of being straight, the modern ones spiral up. On this one you can see the casing along the siphuncle, which was a long strand of tissue. You can see that it stretches all the way back here to the narrow end, where the animal first lived. As it grew, it repeatedly moved forward and secreted new shell and built a partition walling off the earlier part. He left the siphuncle back there so he could empty the water from the empty chambers as he built the new space."

"Sort of like a soda straw?" Brendan asked.

"Not exactly. He sucked the water out, but not like you and I suck on a drink. He used the suction of osmosis. He would increase the saltiness of his blood in the siphuncle, and that made the water move from the more dilute chamber into his blood. At the same time, gas diffused from his blood through the siphuncle into the emptying chamber."

"You mean like he was farting?"

Mungo chuckled appreciatively.

Don smiled, understanding the workings of the thirteen-year-old male mind perfectly. "I could go into a dissertation on how farting works, and what it does for you—you wouldn't want to hold on to that pressure!—but what's important is that when you fart you are releasing pressure, while what this critter was doing was lowering his overall density. He was making his shell into a flotation device."

"Did he pop to the surface?"

"No, the idea was to maintain the exact density of the depth of water in which he lived, so he could swim effortlessly."

Brendan suddenly stood up and glanced around at the scattered fossils as if they had begun to squirm. In a small voice, he said, "Were they bad?"

Don straightened up, surprised. "Why do you ask that?"

"Because they're fossils. They died."

"We all die," Don said softly.

"But I mean, God killed them."

Mungo closed his eyes as if he'd suddenly developed a headache.

Don said, "I'm afraid you're going to have to explain what you mean by that, son."

Brendan launched into a tumble of words. "Mom says that fossils are these creatures who were sinners and God killed them all with the Flood, and so maybe this one was nasty and ate his brothers or something, and so he had to go, see? And that one over there, well . . . I mean, God had to have his reasons. Mom says there's a reason for everything!" He slapped the knuckles of his right hand into the palm of his left for emphasis.

Don said, "Oh, I see. You're talking about the Book of Genesis and Noah's Flood. These creatures died a long time before then."

"How long? I want to know!"

"These nautiloids were alive during the Paleozoic Era of geologic time," Don said soothingly. "Paleozoic means 'old life.' Specifically, the Redwall and all the fossils in it were deposited during the Mississippian Period of the Paleozoic Era. Round numbers? Three hundred fifty million years ago."

Brendan stared at Don as if he were a face on a television set.

From the beach where the boats were tied up, Danielle's voice rose to a holler. "Luncheon is served! Sandwiches! Dried fruits! Prompt, courteous self-service!" I glanced her way. She had laid out breads and cold cuts and sliced tomatoes and probably the last of the romaine lettuce we would see until we could resupply at Phantom Ranch ten days into our trip. She leaned forward and wiggled her arms as if they were squid tentacles with which she would snatch up her food.

Don reached out to put a hand on Brendan's shoulder, but the boy turned and headed down toward the beach.

As one person, Don, Jerry, and Mungo turned to me. Jerry said, "What's the story there, Em?"

Now I opened my mouth and words tumbled out, just like Brendan. I said, "It's tough. He's a good lad—bright, intellectual, caring—but he's not like either of his parents. You can see that his dad is smart, but in a different sort of way, a doer instead of a thinker. And Fritz is built on heroic proportions, and he flew jets; imagine following in those footsteps."

"And his mom?" Mungo asked.

I winced. "She's all about the looks. No, that's not fair. She cares about social position, and looking good is part of that, and she really is a dish just the way nature made her, and when she throws on the afterburners, she is a knockout! But Fritz did not walk the path she expected of him. She was an officer's daughter, and she married an officer herself, expecting the same life."

"A life she knows how to live," said Jerry kindly. "She's a practical woman."

"In a manner of speaking. Anyway, she wasn't happy when Fritz quit the military and launched into a less predictable life, so she dumped him and found someone else, but she acts like she was the injured party." I took a deep breath, feeling a little like I had told a secret that wasn't mine to tell.

Mungo said, "She's religious, I take it."

"Yeah, well, I guess she's all about the church now. She was always a little on the pious side, but when she remarried it was like a suit of armor she climbed into. She wears the Bible the way some vets wrap themselves in the flag."

Mungo asked, "What denomination?"

"Something . . . Christian . . . I don't know exactly. To be honest, I can't keep them sorted out. I try to stay out of it."

Mungo said, "Some denomination of Christian fundamentalist, then. The other brands have names that are easier to keep sorted out, like Presbyterian and Episcopalian."

Jerry said, "And Fritz?"

I said, "His religion is flying."

Mungo said, "So Brendan's caught in a crack between his parents' points of view."

I said, "I'm sure they disagree on a lot of things, and I don't want to judge."

Don said, "We've heard about Fritz's flying. He runs an air charter business, am I right?"

"Yes."

Jerry said, "It's great that he could get enough time to take a nice break, then. And to bring his son! It's the perfect time for a father and son to have a nice manly experience together."

I looked down the shore toward the line of boats, where Brendan now sat alone, straddling the bow of his father's raft, tossing pebbles into the water while his father played at rock climbing with Olaf and Gary. Togetherness seemed to have its limitations.

APRIL 5–6: NANKOWEAP

THINGS SEEMED TO IMPROVE WHEN BRENDAN ROWED HIS FIRST RAPID—a glorified riffle, to be precise, but not in his eyes—on the morning of our fifth day on the water, officially becoming a boatman. Fritz was deliriously proud, and the lad about broke his face grinning.

It was a lovely day of cobalt blue skies and brick red cliffs reflected dark upon the waters. I watched swallows flit above the river and heard the long, spiraling call of the seldom-seen canyon wren. We told jokes and swapped stories, calling out punch lines from one raft to another, and lunched on peanut butter and jelly sandwiches, pretzels, and beer.

Later in the day we made landing at Nankoweap, a broad beach formed where a large side canyon leading in from the west had created a delta. We'd been on the river for five days getting into the groove of the daily loading, rowing, and unpacking, and it was nice to make a break in the rhythm and set up camp knowing we did not have to grunt all our gear back onto the rafts the following morning. We would lay over for a day and just relax and explore.

It was our turn to cook, and I did my best, but mostly Fritz gave me directions, like "chop these veggies" and "fill this pot with water." Halfway through the job of cooking, a storm whipped up and crashed down on us. Clouds had built during the afternoon into a steep, dark cumulonimbus that chose our position in time and space to open up with an astonishing microburst, a sudden and fierce downdraft that grabbed our folding cook table and the stoves on it and hurled them against a tree. I counted myself lucky that I had not yet turned on either stove and thus the water that splashed across my legs was not boiling, but one of the stoves was broken beyond repair, and we were all doused with huge drops of rain as we grabbed equipment and ran for our tents.

"I'll break out the sat phone and get Faye to order a new stove," Fritz said, as we huddled together inside the thrashing tent.

"I'd like to say hi to Faye when you're done," I said, remembering her plan to report any dirt she had dug up on Wink.

The storm soon abated, and in spite of my shortcomings, we served up a dinner of smoked beef sausages with sautéed vegetables on a bed of creamy polenta. No one complained, and none was left when it was time to wash the pots. After dinner Fritz dug out the rented satellite phone from the ammo can in which it was housed and stretched out across the starboard tubing of our raft to watch for a satellite. "There's no reason to switch this thing on until I see one," he told me, as I found an equally comfortable lounge spot across the bow. "The rental company gave us two batteries, but on close inspection here one of them is already half used up, so I have to husband our use of it in case we have a real emergency."

"Scoundrel rental company," I said.

"I'm sure it was just an oversight."

"An oversight that could render the sat phone useless, you mean."

"There's one," Fritz said and switched on the phone.

The satellite was a pale, luminous dot in the sky moving from east to west. By the time we spotted it, it was already halfway across the narrow slot of sky that stretched between the soaring canyon walls, and it would take only a few minutes for it to transit to the other side.

"Faye!" Fritz said when she picked up. "Get Hakatai Mattes to buy us a new stove and bring it to us when he joins us at Phantom Ranch, okay? You got it?"

The satellite had set. Fritz began to pack away the telephone.

I said, "I'll wait for another satellite and call her back. You know, make sure she got the message."

Fritz smiled. "It's a nice enough evening for satellite watching," he said, sliding over toward where I was resting. He bent and gave me a kiss that said that gazing at the heavens was the last thing on his mind.

I lay on my back softly tickling his neck, momentarily forgetting all about moving dots in the sky, but the image of Wink's assault on Brendan flashed in my mind, popping open my eyes just in time to spot a satellite as it appeared over the rim. "There's one!" I said and switched on the phone.

Faye answered right away. She said, "Your guy Oberley should be jailed for false advertising. He did matriculate at Princeton—he must be bright to have gotten in—but he's not going to get any kind of a doctorate there. The scuttlebutt my cousin was able to get for me was that the department 'urged him to find like-minded people elsewhere.' That's code for he was off the rails somehow. He was trying to prove some kind of gooney ideas, and he got into a fight with his thesis committee over them."

A pattern began to click together in my head as I remembered Wink checking the list at the launch ramp and searching the access road. "Anything to do with 'creation science'? That's code for—"

"No, his research wasn't into evolution, it was the age of the earth. And tell Fritz I've already got a stove here on the Internet. It looks—"

The little dot of light had set over the opposite rim of the canyon, taking Faye's voice with it. I handed the phone back to Fritz. "She says she's got a good stove on order."

"Good. But what's that got to do with creationism?"

"Don't ask and I won't trouble you with the answer," I said.

Fritz gave me another lingering kiss, put away the phone, and then got up off the raft. He took me by the hand and led me on a walk through the tamarisk along the shore, letting the quiet power of the high rock walls and the brilliant stars of the night sky above them embrace us. "Enjoying yourself?" he inquired.

"This is wonderful." I gave his hand a squeeze.

A network of trails led through the tamarisk brush that grew thickly near the shore. We had chosen the campsite farthest downriver and had placed our portable toilet at the extreme end, for the sake of privacy, around a bend in a small path. Short pathways led to more secluded tent sites. I noted that Julianne had set her tent farthest upriver from our gathering space, and quite close to the stretch of beach where the rafts and dory rode the current. Two of our party had been sleeping on their boats: Mungo because he snored, and Wink, whose connection to his dory was almost that of an umbilicus. Julianne's tent faced out onto the water overlooking Wink's craft.

Fritz held firmly to my hand, drawing me along a path that curved parallel to the river, and presently we came within earshot of another campsite. The party there was getting pretty rowdy. Feeling mischievous, we took a seat on the fallen trunk of a boxelder tree where we could secretly both listen and watch.

The group had gone primitive and were dancing and chanting around a fire that had been built to leap high. I supposed that their utterances were meant to sound like Indian chants. Some staggered, evidencing intake of strong spirits. "Grease bomb! Grease bomb! Grease bomb!" they grunted. One put on a pair of oven mitts and lifted a long pair of tongs high over his head as if enacting a great ritual. He made some noises, then marched over to a camp stove, where he used the tongs to lift a pint beer can the contents of which had been heated to smoking hot. He carried the can over to the fire pan and set it in the center of the open flames. The crowd let out a roar.

"What's in the can?" I wondered out loud.

"Bacon grease," said Fritz. "These wackos are going to light the whole beach on fire if they don't watch out." He chuckled.

I glanced sideways at him. "So igniting the beach is a good thing?"

"Their biggest problem is going to be cleaning up the sand afterward. That's if they don't manage to burn their own whiskers off."

"What the hell——?"

He was grinning. "Just watch," he whispered.

Now the man who had set the can of grease into the fire picked up a long pole. In the light of the leaping flames I could see that a cup had been duct-taped to one end of it. The man marched to the river, dipped the cup into the water, and hup-hup-hupped it back up to the fire pit. As his mates brought their chant up to fever pitch, he swung the cup over the fire and decanted several ounces of the cold water into the can, atomizing a shot of roiling hot grease.

As the atomized grease ignited, a ball of fire burst up over the pit. The crowd roared with approval.

"How do you know these things?" I asked Fritz.

"Boy Scouts was very educational," he murmured.

Another ball of fire bloomed, and another.

"Let's get out of here," Fritz said, bending his great frame to slither off through the brush. He kept hold of my hand, drawing me after him.

"Where are we going?" I asked, as I realized that he was not steering me back toward our camp.

"I'm just trying to find the blanket I hid out here," he said. "Ah," he purred, "here it is, my love."

Finding privacy on a river trip is difficult, but entirely worth the effort.

◆

In the morning, we had a leisurely breakfast of pancakes and bacon. It was our first rest day, so we all looked after homey rituals that involved heating a little water. Molly Chang and some of the other women and I found a private stretch of riverbank and took turns lathering our hair with castile soap and pouring water over a friend to rinse it off. We crouched over the river to scrub the rest of our parts, avoiding dipping into the bracing chill until we were so soapy that the idea finally appealed. After that, it was back to the tenting area for a clean pair of skivvies and shirt. My biggest problem was finding them in the deep darkness of my dry bag. Some dry bags opened end to end like a duffel, but the waterproof zippers made those bags expensive. I had opted for the type of bag that opened at one end and rolled and cinched shut, creating a waterproof seal through compression of the folds. Life on the river was simple but had its chores.

Wink pulled a tool kit out of one of the covered compartments on his dory and proceeded to do a little maintenance. Julianne made a fuss out of offering assistance, so he handed her a paintbrush and a small can of paint and had her give the dory's trim a fresh coat.

"You don't want me to paint over the name, do you?"

"Yes, I do," said Wink.

"Oh, but I think *Wave Slut* is such a cute name. It's kind of like me," she said, tipping a hip toward him.

Wink reached over and gave her bottom a pat. "I'll repaint it later. I don't have the right brush and paint along for that."

"Oh really, let's leave it. It's so cute."

Wink took the brush out of her hand, dipped it in the paint, and slapped it across the name, all but wiping it out with one stroke. Before handing the brush back to Julianne, he dabbed it to her nose. "Now you're cute," he said.

She grabbed the brush and tried to hit him with it across the chops, but he grabbed her arm forcibly and said, "Hey, I just shaved!"

With a bit of a jolt, I realized that this was true: For the first time since we had first seen Wink, he had actually bothered to shave. He had washed his hair, too, and had even combed it, slicking it back like he was trying out for a remake of a movie from the 1950s.

As the day meandered through lunch and on into an otherwise lazy afternoon, Fritz and Brendan made plans to hike up to the ancient granaries above the camp, and invited me to join them. "You'll love this," Fritz told me. "We'll need water bottles and a snack."

The path to the granaries led through the low trees and brush that grew at beach level up through sparser and sparser scrub as we climbed the ramp of alluvium that spread like an apron along the foot of the Redwall cliff. The river had cut down more than three hundred feet closer to sea level since the put-in at Lees Ferry, carving through the Muav Limestone and into the Bright Angel Shale below. The trail led us up from the shade of the trees at the riverside and out into the naked heat of the desert air and, as it grew steeper, began to switch back and forth up through the crumbling red desert soils. Fritz set a mercifully leisurely pace, stopping here and there to admire a wildflower so that those of us who were relatively short-legged could keep up with him.

At one turn in the trail we came across Wink Oberley. He was standing still on the trail peering upriver, watching, looking for something in particular.

"Have you lost your dentures?" Fritz asked.

Wink kept his pose as if ignoring him, then abruptly swung toward him, flipped up his sunglasses, forced a smile, and said, "Oh, I get it. Flyboy talk for have I lost something. Very funny. Ha-ha." He lowered his expensive sunglasses back into place and took a couple of steps past us, ending the interchange.

I looked back at him from the next turn in the trail. Clearly, he was scanning the river for something. Or somebody. Just like on the day he arrived at the river, he was looking for something he expected to see. Why had this man chosen to come on the river with us? What was he up to? Tiny had said that Wink had taken great interest in the fact that

Molly Chang, a geology department chair and thus a potential employer, would be on the trip, but so far he had chatted her up but not in earnest, and as far as I knew Molly didn't have any jobs to offer.

At the top of the trail the cliffs overhung a long, narrow shelf of rock. Tucked into this slot, a row of storage compartments had been built of the native stone. Fritz said, "The people who lived here then—around a thousand years ago—came to the Nankoweap delta to raise crops. Then, after harvesting, they stored some of the grain here."

"Where are their houses? Did the Flood wash them away?" Brendan inquired.

Fritz shrugged his shoulders. "I don't know. I suppose it's a lot like farming by a river most anywhere: You have to consider that at times, the river is going to rise and come over the bank, maybe wash the dwellings away. Isn't that right, Em?" he asked. "Em's the geologist. Ask her."

Brendan turned a piercing gaze my way.

I wanted to kick Fritz about then. I didn't care how big a fight he had going with his ex-wife; it just wasn't fair to divert all of these questions to me. "Well, it's about as your dad says," I said, buying time. "Early cultures had to deal with floods just like we do today, but they didn't have all the machinery we have to build dams to try to control them. On the other hand, because they weren't fighting nature, the rivers were free to carry in the annual layers of rich sediments and organic matter that made deltas like this one really good places to farm. The Egyptians had some of the richest soils for farming in the Mediterranean until they built the Aswan Dam and turned the lake it made into a settling basin."

"But some floods are a whole lot bigger," said Brendan. "Like Noah's Flood."

I took a breath, let it out. "Sure, there are stories of huge floods in most so-called primitive cultures, and even today we have some that overwhelm our best predictions and planning. Like Hurricane Katrina and New Orleans, or . . . or sure, take for instance the stories of Noah's Flood. Those floods were devastating, downright traumatic, and maybe the stories grew to fit the impacts of the events."

Brendan's gaze shifted. He now studied my face as if I had become something abstract and poorly understood, like the granaries. "My mother says that God sent the Flood to punish us," he said.

Fritz's eyelids slowly slid closed.

I thought sourly that Fritz's reluctance to engage with such issues was one reason why his first marriage had broken up; in fact, a greater puzzle was that it had ever begun. And I was sick of her games. It wasn't so much what she believed that bothered me, it was the way she used those beliefs to torment everyone around her. To punish *us*, not some people who lived a long time ago. Emphasis on the punishment, one big fat control game. The message was that everyone—including this wonderful young man, her son—should feel bad, and in the odd moments when we hadn't screwed up in her eyes, we should be kept on tenterhooks that our next screwup was only moments away.

As I looked down the steep slope at the splendor of the canyon, at the rose pink walls of stone and the zigzagging strip of chocolate water below, I realized that I had the power in this moment to offer Brendan another way of thinking about himself, and that if I failed to use it, I would be derelict in my duty to him as a fellow human being. So I said, "Brendan, I don't know much about that one particular flood they talk about in the Bible, and I don't want to have a debate with your mother about it because for one thing, she isn't here. I will say, however, that if you study geology you can find evidence of absolutely *huge* floods here and there, like the Channeled Scablands of Washington and Oregon, where water built up behind an ice dam during a glaciation and then let go all at once. Actually, it's thought that this happened repeatedly, so in fact the effect was not just one huge rush of water but several, and there's Lake Bonneville, and—"

Brendan said, "You're losing me, Em."

"My point is that floods aren't unusual. There's evidence of a lot of really big ones, and here in a place like this, flooding would happen almost every year. Local tribes have their own flood stories about the carving of the Grand Canyon. So they wouldn't want to go to the trouble of building a permanent residence too awfully close to the river because it would just be swept away in the next spring flood. Like your dad said, it makes more sense to build up there on the Kaibab Plateau and then just come down here and camp seasonally in this warm place where there's easy access to water, so you can grow your crops."

Brendan nodded. "Okay . . ."

I let the bit about Noah rest. I considered saying something about the difference between Stone Age recountings of traumatic events and scientific examination of evidence, but I figured that it was tough enough that Brendan was stuck shuttling between a Bible-thumping ma, and a dad who didn't want to talk about things. The poor kid didn't need me putting any more bricks on his load.

Brendan turned back to me and said, "So you believe a different story from what my mom says."

I ransacked my brain for an answer to his question, which hadn't really even been stated as a question. Finally, I said, "As a scientist I try not to believe things per se, which means 'in isolation.' The idea of science is to gather a whole lot of evidence to try to find out what is so, to eliminate things that can be proven wrong and see what's left. When you talk about religious beliefs, that's a different thing altogether. Science and religion are like apples and oranges. Science tries to uncover physical laws, while religion deals with moral laws. Science examines physical, rational phenomena, while religion tries to cope with the unknowable."

"Mom says that if it's written in the Bible, then it's true."

For the moment, I let go of trying to be Brendan's stepmother and just spoke to him as one human to another. "Okay then, take Noah's

Flood: That's a story from the Bible, which is a book that was written down in bits and pieces a long time ago by a bunch of different people in languages that are no longer spoken. They are stories, and stories have a special place in our lives, and each their own purpose. Sometimes we tell a story to teach history, other times it's to try to explain something, or maybe in the case of a flood big enough to drown most of your family and friends, you tell a story to try to cope with something horrifying and sad. What I'm trying to say is that I don't want to argue with what your mother says, because I choose to stick with those few stories that I can read in this big book of rock that's all around us. Though sometimes it's darned hard to interpret. Like your mother's Bible, this one was written a very long time ago, and no one alive today was there when it was happening, and some of the information has been lost."

"Mom says the Bible is the Word of God."

I felt my dander beginning to rise. "Well, and maybe it is! But for crap's sake give me a chance here to tell you where I'm coming from!"

Brendan turned away and stared at the ground.

I felt mean for yelling, and stupid as hell, because I knew that the kid wasn't trying to piss me off, he was just trying to deal with a big, whopping ambiguity that was making his young life messy. I said, "I'm sorry to get angry. It's not your fault. The thing is, as a geologist I get this a lot, especially living in Utah, where about every other Mormon is a fundamentalist. There are folks who insist on arguing with me about these things, but you know what? The truth is just as important to me as it is to them. Science is all about trying to discover what is true while staying humble enough so you don't jump to conclusions, so it kind of gets under my skin when someone . . ." I let it trail off and thought a moment. "Brendan, I am tempted to say, 'You're at an age when these questions start to come up,' but I won't. Because I'm here to tell you that they keep on coming up indefinitely unless you . . ." I almost said. *Unless you acquire a rigidly held system of beliefs like your mother.* It was incumbent on me not to load more fight onto this battleground. "You're a smart person, Brendan. You'll be okay."

Out of the corner of my eye, I could see that Fritz was staring at the broad palms of his hands, and that he was smiling.

◈

Back at camp, Molly and Nancy were playing a portable game of Boggle, and Julianne was starting dinner. "Have you seen Wink?" she inquired.

"No, I haven't," Fritz told her.

"He's supposed to help me," she explained, in a tone that suggested that she was very eager that this should happen.

"He's down at the next campsite talking to another party," said Brendan. "Those grease bombers from last night took off this morning, and now there's another group there."

Never forget, I reminded myself: *Nothing gets past this kid! Nothing!*

Just then Wink popped into the clearing from one of the trails that snaked through the tamarisk. With a flourish, he removed his sunglasses and closed on Julianne. "I am here to assist you, my sweet," he told her.

Julianne blushed prettily, and as Wink sidled up to the folding table where she stood, she curved her spine toward him, meeting his body with hers.

Oh, so it's gotten that far already, I noted, guessing that ol' Wink wouldn't be snoozing on his dory tonight.

After dinner, folks pulled folding camp chairs up around the fire pit and swapped tales of rapids ridden on earlier trips and other adventures. It was a mellow evening under a night so black and an arch of stars so crisp that each satellite stood out clearly as it slid across the heavens. Jokes were told, a bottle of single-malt Scotch made a circuit, and

Brendan did his math homework. I leaned back in my chair enjoying the stories and camaraderie.

"This sure is nice tonight," I said to Nancy Skinner, who was sitting next to me. "Folks are in great form."

Nancy snickered. "You mean because Wink has found his way somewhere else."

"Why would that make the difference?" I asked.

"He interrupts the stories," she said. "You know how it is: Some people tell stories to entertain, while others tell them to hear their own voice. I've noticed that each time someone starts a story he goes on the alert, not because he's interested but because he's cuing up one that's meant to top it, and he's just waiting for the guy to take a breath so he can barge in." She shrugged her shoulders. "His stories are okay as far as they go, but I suspect they're just that."

"Just what?"

"Stories. What a liar the man is."

I was just opening my mouth to ask her to say more when our conversation was interrupted by an unusual sound: the singing of a hymn.

Mungo Park roared, "What the fuck is that? We got angels landing on the beach?"

Jerry said, "It's probably that church group in the next campsite."

"Church group?" echoed Mungo. "What flavor?"

"I don't know," said Danielle, "but did you catch the style? Lots of short haircuts on the men, woven cloth shirts rather than T-shirts, and not a pair of blue jeans in the place. And one chick was wearing high-heeled sandals!"

Mungo elbowed Molly in the ribs. "You think it's God's Voice, that Young Earth group we heard about?"

"Young what?" asked Dell.

Molly raised one shoulder and dropped it. "A lot of Christian fundamentalist groups have a literal view of what the Bible says about Creation. Like it took six days roughly six thousand years ago to make all of this."

"Is that a fact?" asked Dell.

Molly laughed. "Well, not if you ask me it isn't. We're down below the Redwall now, below the Temple Butte Formation and the Muav Limestone, and into the Bright Angel Shale. That's Cambrian Period; you're looking at strata that are over five hundred million years old, and by the time we get down to the Inner Gorge, we'll be looking at granites and schists that formed almost two billion years ago."

Dell said, "You never know who you're going to meet in this canyon. I don't know, Mungo, maybe a bunch of holy folks aren't as dangerous at the oars as you are."

"Praise the Lord and pass that bottle of whisky," said Mungo, to round of appreciative laughter.

The hymn was a familiar tune accompanied by some lovely guitar strumming, but I couldn't catch the words. It sounded like one that my grandmother used to hum, but I couldn't quite tell; the tempo had been kicked up a bit, which took some of the gravity out of it. Led by my curiosity, I wandered to the edge of our clearing so I could listen.

As I stepped even farther away from our fire, Julianne crept out of the shadows of the path that led to her tent, clutching a fleece sweater around her bony shoulders. "Have you seen Wink?" she asked. She sounded lost, inconsolable without her paramour.

"He's not up here by the fire," I said, leaving out the next words that came into my head, which were *I thought he was with you.*

As if reading that thought, she said dolefully, "He said he'd drop by . . ."

"If I see him, I'll tell him you're looking for him."

"Oh! Oh no, that's okay!" she said and scampered down the path toward her tent.

The music pulled at me like a shepherd's crook. I was particularly intrigued by the instrumental pieces between verses, when only the guitar carried through the dry desert air, filling it like a row of questions that called for answers. I strolled slowly down the trail toward the box-elder tree where Fritz and I had sat spying on the group that had camped there the evening before, wanting this time to see the hands that were releasing such notes from the guitar. But when I arrived at that vantage point, I saw something that surprised me so much that I barely noticed the guitarist: Wink Oberley was standing with the congregation of churchgoers, hands folded humbly in a way that rounded his stout shoulders, voice lifted in song with the others. He had swapped his sagging T-shirt for a short-sleeved plaid shirt that looked most of a size too small for him. It gaped slightly at the buttons, straining to reach around his meaty chest. Seeing him with this group, was such a shock that I gasped.

Wink's head snapped my way. He squinted into the darkness.

I froze.

After a moment, Wink settled back into his pose, and I turned my attention to the guitar player. It was a young girl, not very many years older than Brendan. Her face was round and plain, but her hair shone like gold in the firelight, and her eyes were soft with the flow of her playing. At the end of one last exquisite phrase in her music she caressed the strings as if the vibration made her heart keep on beating.

The hymn complete, a tall, angular man with a big Adam's apple and a conservative haircut raised his right hand, squeezed his eyes shut in concentration, and offered a benediction: "Oh Holy Father, we ask that you guide us in your light and smile upon the work we humbly do here in your name. We who gather in your sacred canyon ask that your blessings be upon us. May we rest in your grace . . ." The prayer rolled onward, meandering through sprinklings of beseechments and requests for guidance while the gathered flock waited quietly for grace to descend upon them. Twice during this monologue Wink opened an eye and peeked, glancing across the gathering at a woman who was, indeed, wearing sandals that had something of a heel to them. They didn't appear to be true ankle-breakers, only an inch and a half at worst, but not what I had expected to see at the bottom of the Grand Canyon. Footwear on this river was a stiff challenge: The water was cold, so we wanted something that would insulate. At the same time, stepping in and out of the water and dealing with waves that splashed into the foot wells of the rafts kept our feet uncomfortably wet, making it important that whatever we wore drained and dried quickly. River sandals had heavy rubber soles with little or no heels, and the straps across the top had to be waterproof and tough enough to take grit and other abuse as equals to the bottoms. This group had hired a commercial rafting company to do all the cooking and carrying, but still it would be preferable to have something that would withstand walking around on the sandy floor of the campsite. This woman's sandals had soles so thin that they must have acted like little shovels, scooping up grit between her skin and the skinny leather straps. These pretty little numbers had beads sewn across their tops, and the woman had painted her toenails a luscious bright red, the better to show them off.

Above the ankles, the woman looked equally out of place: She wore her bottle-blonde hair in a style that must have required ample applications of hair spray and fancy brushing, she was heavily made up, and her aging (though still curvaceous) figure was packed tightly into white capri pants and a stretchy halter top. As she shifted her fingers to adjust their prayerful pose, I could see that the fingernails matched the toenails, and a row of bangle bracelets glinted in the firelight.

There was the problem of stowage space for clothing worn in camp, even if a person did not find it necessary to wade into the water repeatedly during the evening to get supplies or equipment out of one of the boats. Many in our group had brought a pair of hiking boots or running shoes, but such an item took up a lot of room in the old dry bag.

For a moment I was less interested in why Wink had decided to catch an evening prayer meeting than how this creature had managed to maintain this effect during her travel down the Mighty Muddy Colorado. How long had they been on the river? I tried to remember what it had said on the bulletin board at Lees Ferry about this group. Our group would row for twenty-one days, the maximum time permitted to transit the 226-mile navigable stretch of the Grand Canyon from Lees Ferry to Diamond Creek, but we were oar-powered, and this commercial trip used motors, and thus could run the distance much faster. Either way, this woman had been on those rafts and camping on the riverbanks for at least three days, and yet she looked like she'd just stepped out of a salon onto a nice stretch of concrete sidewalk. I was downright impressed.

I couldn't help but wonder if Wink's interest in her duplicated my own amazement, but the fourth time he sneaked a look, I noted that he was gazing rather adoringly at her face and not downward at her feet. What exactly was he doing there?

As the prayer ended with a hearty round of amens and praise-the-Lords, the group stretched and wished each other well and began to stroll off toward their tents. Beyond them I could see their row of boatmen, who had arrayed themselves on the rafts at the foot of their beach. The contrast between the clean-cut church people and their scruffy river guides was more than a little bit comical. Certainly Wink fit in with the river trash rather than the church folk. Had he simply wandered over to visit some old rafting chums and gotten sucked into prayers by happenstance? The man sure was a puzzle.

Wink said his good nights and began heading my way, so it was time for me to skedaddle. I didn't want a collision, not with the marvelous Wink Oberley. Flexing my own unlovely river sandals, I stepped quietly off into the tamarisk, but got caught in a prickly bush. As I worked to free myself, a hand closed over my head. I jumped.

"Snoopy, snoopy," Wink cooed into my ear, and then, with a mean snicker and a little shove, he let go. "See you in the morning," he added and brushed past me, heading off in the direction of Julianne's tent.

It was several long minutes before my pulse settled and my breathing returned to normal. I did not like being touched by that man, not one little bit.

Diary of Holly Ann St. Denis
April 6

Dear God,

We've been so busy marveling at the majesty of Your Creation that I haven't had time to write to you, so I'll try to catch up! We've camped for four nights now on beaches in Your canyon, singing hymns of praise to You each and every night. Lord, how I thank Thee for Thy kindness in giving me the gift of music! I feel You in each and every note I play on my guitar.

The rafts we ride on are these big inflated things with motors on them so we can go a long way or a short way each day as we choose or to get to all the places our geology consultant says we've got to see. One of the boatmen—this real cute guy named Dan—says we'll "throw it in gear" after Phantom Ranch if we're going to make the whole 226 miles in the 10 days "Uncle" Terry paid for. Dan says there's "big" water to come in the next few days and he bets I'll like it! So far we've been over lots of what he calls "little" rapids and God you wouldn't believe—oh, silly me, of course you would, you made them—how "big" "little" can be!!!

The thing I like best so far is all the colors and shapes of the rocks and the flowers and lizards and also the Indian ruins. Nankoweap is especially pretty. While our consultant was showing everyone the layers of rock that settled out of Noah's Flood I sneaked up and looked at the granaries where the Indians stored food in these little storage units they made out of stone. Mom said it was bad to go there because these Indians were probably bad people who were killed in the Flood, but I think she just says that. The Indians must have lived here after the Flood waters receded carving the canyon, because otherwise the waters would have swept away the granaries, right? So they were good people, right? Besides, I think anyone who lived here looking on Your glory every day would find the goodness in them.

E-mail from Mohave County Coroner Ernest Crowder to USNPS Chief Ranger Gerald Weber

DATE: April 18, 5:52 P.M.
SUBJECT: Body now identified as George Oberley, aged 39, late of Rocky Hill, N.J.

This 175 cm tall white male showed no gross signs of physical illness that would have contributed to his death. As you know, the eyes, parts of the facial flesh, throat, and areas below the life vest had been scavenged by vultures. I observed postmortem lividity on the dorsal skin consistent with the resting position in which it was found. The fronts of the legs and middle abdomen underneath the life vest displayed scraping, suggesting that the body had been dragged across a rough surface. As regards cause of death, I observed two traumas that would cause it, one slowly and the other abruptly. The first was an impact wound to the back of the skull that caused fracturing to the skull, bruising, and bleeding to the skin, specifically the parietal and occipital bones bridging the lamboid suture, slightly to the right of the central dorsal line. This blow had set off bleeding in the brain, which stopped when the second trauma occurred.

The second trauma was a narrow but deep puncture wound between the fifth and sixth ribs to the left of the spine. The wound terminated in the heart. If this cat didn't die of massive hemorrhaging caused by this wound I'll eat my hat, but I'll run the usual tox screen and examination of internal organs just in case.

Now, what you really want to know is this: Neither of these wounds would likely be caused by accidental collisions with fixed or floating objects in the river, i.e., in my professional opinion both traumas were delivered by man-made objects that you don't find floating in the Colorado River and likewise would not find in any of the mats of flotsam that get thatched onto the banks. The puncture wound to the heart appears to be a tidy little knife wound. Blade 3 cm wide and 10 cm long. I realize that doesn't help you much, as anyone on that river could be carrying such a blade as a pocketknife. The head wound, however, has a more distinctive pattern to it. It is a perfect 3 cm square, delivered by a heavy metal object. Judging by the angle of the blow, my guess is a square-headed tool like a mineral hammer. So that narrows your search to geologists carrying pocketknives. A very tall geologist, judging by the angles of the wounds.

Have fun, you old coot; this looks like a hot one. Keep me posted,

Ernie

APRIL 7: KWAGUNT RAPID

I'LL HAVE TO ADMIT THAT IT WAS RANK CURIOSITY THAT LED ME TO RIDE for an hour in Wink's dory. He may have caught me eavesdropping on that church group, and eavesdropping is, yes, a mild form of spying, but I figured I didn't have much to apologize for; or at least, nothing worse than the cheek he had displayed by walking right into that campsite and making himself to home with the parishioners. It occurred to me that another hypothesis might also fit the evidence: Piecing together what Faye had discovered at Princeton and Wink's dalliance in the other camp, perhaps he was one of those scientists who had left reason and the rigors of slowly gathering evidence behind for a literal interpretation of the Bible. So I had an itch to know more, but I should have known better than to try to scratch it.

It took a little finagling to get a seat in that dory. Julianne had become all but a permanent fixture there, fussing around helping Wink bail because his pump wasn't working. I dare say that I was not the only one in our group who had noticed that she was receiving him in her tent at night, but as long as she didn't make a spectacle of herself no one really gave a damn who she slept with, and so far I was the first to argue with her over a chance to ride in that glorified leaking wooden shoe box with pointy ends.

Wink seemed pleased enough to have me aboard his boat, or perhaps he was just better at the social fake than I gave him credit for. Our conversation started out easily enough. I asked him about his doctoral work: What was the subject matter of his dissertation, and what did he hope to do when he finished it (knowing that he would not)? He launched into an overly technical riff on something to do with Precambrian biostratigraphy (which is the study of what can be deduced from the combination of sedimentary rocks and the fossils within them), all of which sounded reasonable enough, but soon he began to gripe about his professors. "They want to argue with me over this, suggesting that I'm taking too big a risk with my interpretation. Well, I say they should grow a pair. Just because I've come up with a new idea that none of them had considered, what gives them the right to tell me to take a less controversial track?"

"Got me," I said, doing my best to sound like I believed his bullshit. "You're kind of outside my expertise there."

"I mean, I know I'm older than a lot of their students, so maybe they see me as a threat."

That sounded downright paranoid. I peered at him through my sunglasses, deciding that it would be ill-advised to confront him directly with the information Faye had dug up for me. "So tell me about what you did before you started graduate school," I suggested.

"Well, I was a boatman here on the river while I did my undergrad, so that took a while," he said.

"And before that you were in the army?"

"Yeah. Yes, I was." He let that float away.

"What was that like? Did you do any specializations? I think Tiny said you were in the Airborne Rangers, but maybe I misunderstood."

"I was in the Rangers, yes."

"Hey, well, that's some pretty cool stuff. Did you make a lot of jumps?"

Wink rearranged his face from jolly boat boy to martyr and said, "I wasn't able to get that far. I had an injury." He spoke this last word with a sepulchral dip to his voice, to indicate that something very grave had happened.

"So if you didn't jump, then you weren't an Airborne Ranger exactly."

"I gave them everything I had, but they set me up." He headed off into a well-practiced screed on the cruelty of army sergeants. He had taken a fall, poor him, blah, blah about his pain and suffering.

"Well then, at least you were able to get home safe and sound to your wife," I said, probing another corridor of the circus fun house in which he seemed to dwell.

Wink's little-boy pout grew even more pathetic. "Life can be very difficult with a woman like her," he began, and in the next few sentences he managed to suggest (but never actually state) that his marriage was a thing of the past and that the woman was being a real tyrant, demanding that he get a job to support her and their two daughters.

I was quickly growing annoyed with his pity-me attitude and decided to change the subject at any cost. "What's underneath these hatches?" I asked, reaching for the foredeck lid that I hadn't been able to open on the launch ramp.

"Leave that be!" Wink ordered, all trace of the sad little boy instantly vanished.

My curiosity was now up double-good, so I grabbed the hatch with both hands and tugged.

Wink's hand slammed down on it. "There's nothing in there you need," he growled. "All the veggies and other communal gear are in the after hold. You just stay the fuck out of there!"

"Oh, gosh," I said innocently, "I was just hoping to get a look at your bilge pump."

Wink flipped a switch by his knee, and a grinding sound emerged from under the floor of the cockpit. "Satisfied?" he asked.

"I thought Julianne said it wasn't working."

"I got it running fine," he said calmly.

I studied his face with care, fascinated by how quickly he now rearranged his expression from pissed-off Kabuki to a mask of placid indifference. It was downright scary. I let things ride for a while and watched the canyon walls slide by.

He said, "I understand you studied with Molly for your master's."

"Yes," I said. "So you're thinking that she might get you a job at the U?"

"Oh, that would be terrific!" he said, his tone suddenly gushing with naive enthusiasm. "I can't think of anything I'd like better than that! I love to teach. I tell you, what I truly want in life is to make a contribution as a geologist. Consider this canyon, for instance." He let go of one oar for a moment and lofted that arm in an arch that eloquently took in the sky, the rock walls, the river, and every plant and animal that lived there.

I thought, *Does he really think I'm buying this?*

Wink now widened his eyes to indicate amazement. "I overheard you talking to Brendan about Eddie McKee, the park ranger from the 1930s. Published on everything he saw. A brilliant man. Brilliant, just plain brilliant. Everything he touched, magic. That's who I want to be like: Eddie McKee. If I could lay down everything I had to walk in his shoes for an instant, I'd do it. I just can't think of anything greater to aspire to. He took over as chief naturalist here in 1929. The park's first naturalist drowned in the river, so the job just opened up for Eddie McKee. Everything he did was like that, almost like it was magic." His jaw tightened now, and his tone took on a edge of sour grapes. "Life just dished things up for him on a platter. He went on to chair the Geology Department at Arizona and then went to the USGS in Denver."

I had heard about enough. I said, "I don't suppose it was as easy as all that for him. I've heard that he did all his geology fieldwork on his own time, on his days off."

"Oh, I'm sure he worked really hard, I'm not saying he didn't, but, you know, it was like things sort of fell into his lap. He led a charmed life. I mean, they have his ranger hat in the museum collection up at the

South Rim, and there's an amphitheater named after him. Imagine! So I'm thinking if I worked with Molly I could be like him. Now, my life hasn't been that easy, but really, I'd like to be exactly like him. So if you'd like to put in a kind word with Molly . . ."

I tried to imagine a freeloading slob like Wink accomplishing half of what McKee had. Fed up, I said, "Maybe the first thing you'll need is a new philosophy."

Wink's neck stiffened.

A low rumbling began to crowd into my conscious awareness. There was a rapid coming, much sooner than I had reckoned.

Wink suddenly began pushing much harder on the oars, accelerating down-current, and I saw a mean glint in his eyes.

I looked around at the other boats. Fritz was a quarter mile farther down the river, just pulling over to the right bank so that he could climb out and scout the best route through the waves. That meant that this was a big one, not to be trifled with. "What rapid is this?" I asked.

"Kwagunt," he said. "It's a six on the scale of ten, just a little fella. Seven-foot drop over the run. Nice big waves." He began to laugh.

We had closed half the distance to the rapid, but Wink was not rowing toward river right, where the others were now beaching their rafts. He stood at the oars, scanning the water.

I said, "You are going to scout it, aren't you?"

"No need to do that! I've been down this river *how* many times is it?"

"This is your forty-third trip, or so you *claim*," I blurted.

Wink grinned into the opening maw of the rapid. "You just relax, missy," he said, letting the last word hiss from his innards, like a snake.

I glanced around at Fritz. He stood with his back to us, gazing downriver along the run of the kicking water. Mungo and Dell were clambering up over the rocks to join him. Only Brendan was looking upriver, and as he saw what Wink was doing, his eyes grew wide and he began to shout, but the roaring water swallowed his words. He was running now, jumping up over the rocks to reach his father.

I twisted around to face the waves. The smooth lip of water formed a downriver V pointing into the churning rapid. We were one hundred yards away, fifty—

Fritz turned. I could see his eyes go round, his mouth open wide. He was pointing, jerking his arms to indicate a hazard, his face growing dark with rage.

Wink pulled hard on one oar to ferry out into the V, tapped the other to swing the bow back into the current, and shot the splintering dory smack into the tallest wave in sight.

The bow of the dory leaped into the air. I held on tight as the boat rocked and pitched, bounced and bucked through the waves. Then suddenly it was over, the sound of the water was quieting, and the raw cackle of Wink's laughter was all.

E-mail correspondence to and from South Rim Dispatcher Cleome James

FROM: Cleome James
TO: Chief Ranger Gerald Weber
DATE: April 19, 8:22 A.M.
SUBJECT: Of possible interest RE: body found at Whitmore Wash

Hey Ger—Word is getting around about what Seth Farnsworth found at Whitmore, the South Rim being a small town after all. I know you want to keep a lid on this, but if I heard something that might possibly have a bearing on how that body got to be a body, I should forward that to you, right?—Cleome

FROM: Gerald Weber
TO: Cleome James
DATE: April 19, 8:40 A.M.
SUBJECT: RE: Of possible interest RE: body found at Whitmore Wash

Yes, send it.

FROM: Cleome James
TO: Gerald Weber
DATE: April 19, 8:42 A.M.
SUBJECT:FWD: you ain't gonna believe this one!

Okay, what I've got is a somewhat embarrassing note on my private e-mail from Bryson Borowitz down at Phantom. Here it is.—Cleome

(begin forwarded message)

FROM: Bryson Borowitz
TO: Cleome James
DATE: April 10, 5:31 P.M.
SUBJECT: you ain't gonna believe this one!

Cleome, you won't believe this one! Midmorning this chick named Lisette St. Denis Carl (I remember the name because she said it three times, like I should maybe know who she is) demanded that I "fetch that muleteer" for her because she was "in urgent need to get out of this hell-hole of a ditch." Hell-hole ditch! That was a new one for me! Add it to our list, would ya? I explained that mules aren't for hire from Phantom. When I suggested that it was an enjoyable hike, she pointed at her feet, like wasn't I paying attention? They were swollen and bloody with broken blisters, not surprising considering that this little pistol was wearing sandals like you shouldn't see this side of Rodeo Drive.

The divine Ms. Carl was followed immediately into the room by a tall, angular man with a large Adam's apple who ordered her to get her sorry butt back to her raft. I didn't think her butt was all that sorry (forgive me, but it's been a while since you and I got together!) though what he probably meant was that her butt was a little old to be loaded into such tight pants. Anyway, I pretended like I wasn't listening, and really meant not to,

until a familiar name came up in the middle of their arguing: George Oberley. So I'm thinking, could they mean ol' Winky-poo?

Anyway, this Oberley fella they were spitting about was apparently in
their hire, but not as a boatman! No, you're gonna love this, Mr. Adam's
Apple was saying that the "geological consultant" Ms. Carl hired wasn't
worth what she was paying him and she was shrieking that Mr. Apple
should stay out of her personal business. Okay, so here's where it gets really good: Mr. Apple notices that I'm listening and starts laying words on
her about how the Lord didn't mean her to do this or that but instead she
should be a good camper and get back in the raft so that their Ministry—I mean really, the way he pronounced that word, you knew he meant
it to have a capital *M*—would not be disrupted.

About then the dime dropped and I realized who this chick is. Okay,
so have you Googled her already and you're thinking what a backwoods
hick I am? Yeah, she's that Las Vegas showgirl who found Jesus! I'm talking about the wife of the late but great Reverend Amos Carl. He's that
televangelist who famously keeled over dead a couple months ago in a fit
of religious fervor right in front of his whole congregation. I mean not just
in front of some folks who were sitting in his church building, but in front
of all the millions of good folks who were watching on the TV from the
comfort of their living rooms. Remember? Hell, that made such a splash in
the tabloids that I heard about it clear down here at Rock Bottom.

Then things got even weirder. Totally ignoring me, the chick turns to
the Apple and squeals words to the effect of, "Dr. Oberley's life is in dan-
ger!" Oh, baby, you should have heard the drama she loaded into that
one! And I'm thinking, well, old Wink's life has always hung over the edge,
because he's always pissing someone off, or he has it stuck where it just
don't belong, or he's trying one scam or another to get a regular meal
ticket. He's been fired from half the commercial rafting companies that
row this river, and a man's gotta make a buck to pay his alimony and child
support if he ever gets around to divorcing his wife, but really, "consulting

geologist" to a fundamentalist evangelical outfit? Really? *Really?* I'd like to know what the Discovery Channel crews he's wooed into interviewing him about the history of Planet Earth standing there with the Grand Canyon as dramatic background would think about that!

So I'm thinking that this must be some other George Oberley they're talking about, but then Sandals tells Apple she overheard an argument the night before between our man and a big guy from Oberley's rafting party and I'm thinking that sure sounds like our Wink. Noticing that I'm listening, Mr. Apple hisses that she should keep her dramas to herself, but she's really insistent, saying that last night at Cremation Campground she overheard this big dude outright threatening Oberley's life, something about, "You put your hands on my boy one more time and you will have drawn your last breath!"

Mr. Apple finally takes her rather firmly by the arm and hauls her out of there. But that's not the end of my tale. I was trying to figure out how the Winkster could be consulting to them but rafting with someone else, though come to think of it that sounds like his kind of scam. Then half an hour later, who should walk in but guess who, Wink himself! So I ask, "Rowing the churchy types these days, Wink?" and he kind of gives me one of his blank looks, and says, "What in hell you talking about?" So I tell him there's been this babe in tight pants in there worrying about him (I'd figured out who she was by that time, but didn't mention her name, just baiting him to tell me, because you know how he does love to brag), but he didn't go there. Instead, he said, "No, I'm with the Fritz Calder party, private trip." He enunciated the name very carefully, like he wanted me to remember it. Then he sticks his middle finger up his nose to let me know I'm still number one with him and finds his own way back out of the room.

Fritz Calder. I wrote the name down as soon as he left the room so I could look him up on the river manifest. He's got a 21-day private trip going and the church group is God's Voice, a 10-day run. Judging by the launch dates, they've likely been leapfrogging for the past few days, but as God's Voice has only a few days left to run the rest of the canyon they'll be pouring on the muscle and making for Diamond Creek.

I know this will make your day, you sitting up there on the rim, oh, so far away from me, my lovely! Answering all those boring radio and sat phone calls and such, I figure you'd need a little intrigue to keep your day going. We can have a wager here: I'll put five dollars on the line that says this time someone's actually gonna drown that jackass. Are we on? We can meet at Indian Gardens to settle up . . . you, me, a nice bottle of wine . . . say yes, my sweet peach!

Lotsa love, to you, my dove, Bry

FROM: Gerald Weber
TO: Cleome James
DATE: April 19, 9:01 A.M.
SUBJECT: RE: FWD: you ain't gonna believe this one!

Cleome you got any other critical information you've been sitting on?

FROM: Cleome James
TO: Gerald Weber
DATE: April 19, 9:02 A.M.
SUBJECT: Additional info

G—You might want to come listen to the voice recordings I've got of the call made by the Calder party to report a man missing.—C
PS: Thanks for not puking over Bryson's e-mail.

FROM: Gerald Weber
TO: Cleome James
DATE: April 19, 9:04 A.M.
SUBJECT: RE: Additional info

Appreciate any and all information, regardless of source, but as regards communications, advise that you not use language you don't want to hear read back to you should you find yourself on the witness stand in a court of law.

> FROM: Cleome James
> TO: Gerald Weber
> DATE: April 19, 9:07 A.M.
> SUBJECT: RE: Additional info

Are you saying that Oberley's death will become a matter of prosecution?

> FROM: Gerald Weber
> TO: Cleome James
> DATE: April 19, 9:15 A.M.
> SUBJECT: RE: Additional info

I require official transcripts of all calls even remotely related to this case, and you know what that means. AND KEEP THIS ON THE QT DAMN IT.

> FROM: Cleome James
> TO: Maryann Eliasson <private e-mail address>
> DATE: April 19, 9:21 A.M.
> SUBJECT: YOU WERE RIGHT!!!!

Maryann—You know that little old bit of river carnage down at Whitmore that Seth Farnsworth scraped up? Well, I think you win the pool on that one. I slipped the name OBERLEY into e-mails back and forth with Weber and he didn't deny it or correct me. Maybe he assumed I knew who was dead from catching the sat phone call from the poor suckers who got stuck with him this run. So you're right, it's Wink! Is that one gigantic collective sigh of relief I'm hearing or is it just me? It's like Christmas and

Birthdays rolled into one for every woman whose path he ever crossed! But here's the kicker: WINK WAS MURDERED! I know this because Weber said it was going to court! That's no surprise, I guess. The only thing about this that does surprise me is that it might be a guy who killed him, not a woman! Weber wants a transcript of that call, so I played back the tape of the call made by the Calder party reporting the stupid shit missing and this Fritz Calder guy sounded entirely too calm. What can you tell me about him, and when are they pulling out at Diamond Creek so I can be there to shake his hand?—Cleome

APRIL 7: LITTLE COLORADO RIVER

FRITZ DID NOT SAY A WORD TO ME WHEN, AT THE FOOT OF KWAGUNT Rapid, he pulled over to pluck me from the place along the riverbank where I had ordered Wink to drop me. I stood shivering even though the air temperature was nearly eighty degrees and I had on a fleece sweater underneath my life vest, which was now cinched up so tightly that I could barely breathe. I suppose I did not look like I wanted to discuss my experience. Wink was already half a mile down the canyon, probably still laughing and even breaking into song.

I climbed onto the load in the back of the raft. Fritz sat in the bow and stared down the river. Brendan took the oars and pulled manfully, guiding us down through two small rapids and four miles of flat water.

At mile 62, the Colorado River was joined by the Little Colorado, which flows in from the east, and Fritz signaled for everyone to pull over at river left so we could play in the water there. He had to stand in the bow and signal to Wink, who was still leading, bouncing along on the riffles in his dory by himself. The jerk almost overshot the beach, and I wish he had.

The waters of the Little Colorado are much, much warmer than the Big Colorado and much, much, muddier. It was fascinating to watch the two waters meet: on my left hand the Little Colorado, rushing brick red from a recent rain, and on my right the big Colorado, cold and almost green by comparison, all its silt and sand having settled to the bottom of Lake Powell. I could see the two waters run beside each other for quite a distance, slowly curling together into one water. It goes to show how much the Glen Canyon Dam changes this river: The water upriver of the dam probably is just as warm and muddy as the Little Colorado, but when you dam a river into a lake all that sediment settles out, and the water out the bottom of the dam is forty degrees cooler.

Fritz told Brendan to keep his life vest with him. The two ran up the riverbank together, the tall father all grace and arms, legs pumping in a smooth, integrated unison, and the son chugging along on his stumpy legs doing his best to keep up. A hundred yards or so upriver Fritz turned and fell like a log into the water, pulled off his vest, and sat on it, and Brendan followed suit. Together, they floated down through the red waters, laughing and hooting. Mungo joined them for a second run, and a third.

"What are you looking for?" I asked Nancy Skinner, who had waded out into the water.

"I'm hoping to see a humpback chub," she told me.

"A who-backed what?"

"It's a fish," she said. "There aren't many. In fact, they're endangered. When the dam chilled the waters of the big Colorado and took the silt out, it about spelled the end for this creature. They couldn't compete with the trout. The trout love the cold, clear water because they're sight predators and because they need the higher oxygenation of the colder water."

"The trout were introduced, right?"

"Yes, to attract anglers. Did you see that fisherman up by Lees Ferry returning from a run upriver to the dam's outfall? He'd caught a fish that had to weigh ten pounds!"

"That's good eating."

"Yeah, but."

"You're preaching to the choir. So what do they look like?" I asked, wading into the river beside her.

Nancy pulled a copy of the river guide out of her vest pocket and flipped it open to the page that showed the confluence. "Here it is in all its fat-headed, narrow-tailed glory," she said. "This stretch is one of the few places you can still hope to see them. They need the warm water to spawn."

From the picture I could see immediately how the fish had earned its name. Its back puffed straight up from its eyebrows. Quasimodo had nothing on this creature. "That really is one ugly fish," I said.

Nancy turned and ran her fingers over the page. "Look at those fins!" she cooed. "They're beautiful!"

I looked again. She was right; it had enormous, lovely fins. I could imagine it gliding through the shallows.

The other members of our group continued to run up the riverbank and float down. When I saw Jerry and Don floating along holding hands just as easily as if they were sitting in deck chairs sipping drinks, I considered joining them. Surely it was time I completely overcame my fear of moving water.

"Want to try it?" asked Fritz, who had sneaked up behind me to apply one of his cradling hugs.

"Hey! You're wet and cold!" I squealed. "But don't go away, it feels good." I wrapped my arms across his and leaned back against him.

Brendan popped up out of the water onto the riverbank and ran back up-current for another run. Danielle ran after him, and Julianne, and now Wink, who was splashing along in the shallows next to Julianne, playing a little game of grab-ass. She shrieked with uncertain pleasure, then swung her arms into the water and splashed Wink. He splashed her back, missing widely and hitting Brendan instead.

"Hey!" shouted Brendan.

I stiffened and felt Fritz's arms tighten, too. "Let him handle it," he whispered. "He can do it."

Wink splashed Brendan again, purposefully this time, pouring on the aggression. Brendan waded into the water and smacked it hard, kicking up a rooster tail of spray. Wink set his jaw in a grim line and hit the water again. The fight deteriorated quickly into a rage of foam as the two battled toward each other. Wink charged forward in the water, closing the gap, then reached forward, grabbed Brendan's head, and pushed him down into the water.

I said, "This doesn't look like a game, Fritz."

I could hear my husband's breath in my ear coming in hard puffs, but he did not move.

Where was Brendan? Suddenly, the boy shot out of the muddy water several yards away from Wink, swimming hard to widen the distance between them. When he had gained a distance of about ten yards, he climbed out of the riffle of water and stood in a shallows with his back to all of us, shaking water from his small body.

Wink lifted his head and thrust out his jaw in victory.

Still Fritz did not move. The boy had to prove himself, and the father must not help.

I felt sick to my stomach. I disentangled myself from my husband's grip and stumbled away on the uneven trail.

Nancy was laying out lunch next to the rafts. She unscrewed a plastic jar of peanut butter and jammed a butter knife into it. "What a jackass," she said.

"Who?" I asked. I was so upset that for a moment, I thought she was talking about Fritz.

"Wink. He can't keep clear of that kid. I've watched him."

I wanted to cry, but even that was stuck. "Why does he do that?" I asked.

"Wink has a thing about authority figures, haven't you noticed?"

"Yeah, but . . ."

"So who's the biggest authority on this trip? That would be Fritz, right?"

"Then why not go after Fritz?"

Nancy laughed. "You think Wink has the chutzpah to go after the real thing? Hell no, he goes after a proxy, someone smaller or weaker than he is. That's why he ran you through the rapids just upriver, too, unless I miss my guess."

I bowed my head and rubbed my forehead. "The man is a problem," I said simply.

"The man is not a man. He's a boy, and I don't mean like Brendan. Brendan is already twice his age emotionally."

I sighed. "I guess that would fit with the fact that he was kicked out of the Airborne Rangers before he more than just got started with the training."

"The Rangers would make short work of a fool like him. He can't cooperate worth a damn. You have to be able to work as a team to do that job, be trustworthy and trust those around you. I had a chat with one of the commercial boatmen that camped next to us at Nankoweap, and he told me there's not a company on the river that will employ Wink anymore. You just can't have a loose cannon rowing your boats when you're trying to run a business down here. The guy told me they fired his ass years ago, and that's when he built that leaky dory."

I said, "He told Fritz that he built it so he could do fieldwork for his master's."

Nancy said, "And that would be how he's gotten permits to keep rowing here."

Jerry Rasmussen came down the path to the rafts. "Whose character are we assassinating here? Wink's?"

Nancy nodded. "It's easy pickings."

Jerry said, "Well, you can't blame a man for loving this place, but I am curious to know why Tiny invited him on this trip."

I said, "Tiny met him at a biking convention down in Vegas a couple months back and they got to talking about the river over drinks at the bar. I guess he knows how to make a first impression. Sometimes."

Nancy asked, "How did Tiny and Fritz get to be friends? They're kind of an odd match, the navy jet driver and the biker—though I guess when I look at it from that angle, they do have a bit in common."

Jerry slathered peanut butter on a slice of bread. "They both like wind in their armpits, you mean?"

I said, "They both love adventure, and like Fritz, Tiny has a big heart. A little too big this time, I guess."

Nancy said, "Or maybe his fecal filter was clogged."

Jerry said, "What I've been wondering is why Wink wanted to come with us. He doesn't really seem all that happy. The only thing that I can figure is that he wanted to impress Molly so she'd hire him when he finishes his Ph.D."

Nancy began to nibble on her sandwich. "*If* he finishes his Ph.D. How old did he say he was?"

I said, "Why would anyone behave like he does? I mean, where does it get him?"

Jerry said, "He gave Don a big sob story about how he was abused as a child. His dad—or perhaps it was one of his mother's lovers—was some kind of terror." She shrugged her shoulders as if to shake off a chill. "I just hate child abuse. It just ricochets down through the generations. He gets abused, so what does he do? Takes it out on whoever's smaller than he is. I feel sorry for his kids."

My mind was running like a fevered squirrel in a cage, trying to figure out a way to separate Wink Oberley from Brendan for the rest of the trip. Fritz might have other ideas about how to manage things, but the boy was suffering, and knew that I couldn't stand by and do nothing.

I grabbed the box that had the satellite phone in it and carried it up the slope above the river and dialed. Faye answered. Seldom had I been more relieved to hear her voice. After describing what had just happened, I said, "It's time to get someone to do a background check on him. Maybe he has a record of violence. You still have your contacts at the FBI, or maybe Ray at the Salt Lake police could help. I'll call back when I can," I said, just as the connection failed.

I hurried down the slope to stow the sat phone before Fritz caught me using it, so I wouldn't have to explain.

As if on cue, Nancy straightened up and shouted, "Hey, you bunch of crazies! Lunch is ready!" We stuffed our faces, then climbed back into our various boats and headed off downriver through the mixing waters.

Olaf, Lloyd, and Gary all played in their kayaks through the long riffle, spinning and bobbling. A modern whitewater kayak is impossibly short, a glorified extension of the kayaker's legs, and is shaped like a pumpkin seed. The union of kayaker to kayak is exaggerated by the spray skirt, which is a neoprene gaiter that fits tightly around the paddler's ribs and spreads downward to a tight gasket fit inside a flange in the cockpit of the boat. The three men wore helmets and life vests, and each also wore a paddle jacket, which is a water-repellent shirt that comes to a snug, neoprene closure at neck and wrists. The bottom of the jacket is cinched under the spray skirt. Two of the men also wore neoprene gloves, the better to deal with the cold water that was constantly soaking their hands as they dipped their double-ended paddles this way and that.

I enjoyed watching the kayakers spin around on the water, playing in the waves, and was comforted to know that were I to fall off my raft or, worse yet, be hurled into the water should the thing flip in a rapid, one of these men would be at my side to assist within a matter of seconds. So maneuverable were these little boats that these crazy men actually went looking for "holes" formed where the water flowed over submerged rocks. They liked to slip into the backward-curling waves kicked up by these obstacles and play at rolling over. I watched with amazement as they purposefully flipped upside down, practicing Eskimo rolls, frolicking in the foam. Better them than me.

Brendan turned to his father and asked, "When do we hit the big water, Dad?"

"Day after tomorrow."

"I can't wait!" said Brendan. "I hear the drop gets to twenty feet on

Tanner, then Unkar drops twenty-five feet, and Hance! I was reading the river guide, and it says it drops thirty feet!"

I said, "You don't mean drops like in a waterfall, do you?"

Brendan laughed. "Oh, Em, you're such a worrywart. No, that's how far the river drops over the length of the rapid. That can be as much as a quarter mile. Don't worry," he said, patting my shoulder, "I'll look after you!"

I wished I shared his confidence. It was good to see him grinning again, his sunburned face shining with excitement, and in that moment I saw what Fritz saw when he looked at him: a young man. His jaw was growing, and was that the beginning of a downy fuzz I saw along it? I took his hand and squeezed it, smiling my love to him. Having waited until I was past forty to marry, I didn't suppose that I could have a child myself, but in moments like this, when the three of us were together and happy and enjoying life, I got little glimpses of what it might be like to be a mother.

Fritz said, "Sockdolager Rapid is the real dog of the bunch. The drop is only nineteen feet, but it comes over a shorter distance, and the river narrows there as it carves down below the sedimentary rocks and we head into the Granite Gorge. It's like one long slide of waves. There's nowhere to eddy out until you get to the bottom." He was referring to the use of still pockets and back-currents as places to duck out of the waves during descent down a rapid. "Our safety kayakers won't be able to tuck in and wait mid-rapid. They'll just go for the bottom and hope we make it down right side up!" He grinned, sharing the joy of risk with his growing son.

Brendan grinned back as he flipped pages in the river guide. "Hey, Dad, that campsite we're just passing on river right? Why's it called Crash Canyon?"

Fritz's grin faded. "Two aircraft crashed up there in the cliffs back in 1956, a TWA Super Connie and a United DC-7."

"Really, Dad? Two planes crashed up there the same year?"

Fritz stared into the water in front of him. "The same day, Brendan. They hit each other. Both pilots had diverted from their assigned routes to show their passengers the canyon, and they collided. They found the left wing of the DC-7 tangled up with the Connie. I guess they kind of hooked together in midair."

"Whoa!" said Brendan. "That's really stupid, isn't it, Dad? I mean, to hit another plane like that?"

Fritz pulled on one oar rather harder than was necessary. "They never saw each other. Aircraft have rather large blind spots."

I thought, *Aircraft aren't the only things with blind spots.* How had Wink found his way through ours?

Brendan asked, "Was anyone hurt?"

Fritz nodded. "There were a hundred and twenty-eight people on board those two planes. All lives were lost. The Hopi and the Navajo consider it sacred ground, and the National Park Service has set it aside as a protected site."

"Why?"

Fritz stopped rowing. "Because they couldn't find everyone. Or all the parts of everyone. The Connie slammed into Temple Butte, and the climbers could reach parts of that, but the DC-7 hit Chuar Butte so high up they couldn't reach every . . . thing. They only recovered . . . well, only some of . . . like a third of what they were looking for."

Brendan's jaw gaped open in adolescent amazement. "So you mean there are human body parts up there?"

"Yes."

"Wow!" said Brendan. "This place is amazing, Dad! Those people died trying to get a look at the place, but did you know you can also die here just taking a leak? Mungo says that some people just fall into the river and because it's so cold they can go into shock and drown! Or you can fall out of your boat, I guess, and hit your head on a rock, or you could fall off a cliff, or . . ." He leaned back and stared up at the cliffs where the airliners had met their fate, and added, in a tone of amazement heard only from those who haven't lived long enough to understand their own mortality, "There are just so many ways to die in the Grand Canyon!"

Notes of Gerald Weber, Chief Ranger
Investigation into the death of George Oberley
April 19, 9:30 A.M.

These facts have been established:
  Deceased is George Oberley of Rocky Hill, N.J.
  Cause of death = blow to back of head by square-headed (mineral
    hammer?) object + knife wound
  Mode of death = murder
  Body found Whitmore Wash April 18 approximately 7:15 A.M.
    (reached beach well before that, judging by vulture damage)
  Oberley last seen alive April 15 Ledges Campsite @ 10:15 P.M.
  Absence reported April 16 at 9:45 A.M. by alternate private permit
    holder Fritz Calder

Background on Oberley, from conversations with Farnsworth and
  others:
  Highly experienced river guide
  Military service

At Princeton working on Ph.D. in geology

Something of a loose cannon

Questions:

How did body get to Whitmore?

Ledges to Whitmore = 36.5 miles

Maximum time between last seen at Ledges and first seen at Whitmore = 57 hours

River current = avg. 3 to 4 mph, faster over rapids

Ergo, theoretically floating object could make distance in ~10 hours

BUT: corpses and other flotsam usually get caught in eddies.

Why didn't this one get caught?

Of interest:

Calder overheard threatening Oberley

Calder's voice on dispatcher's recording surprisingly calm—why?

Calder had been awake since 5:15 A.M.—what was he doing for FOUR HOURS?

Steps that should now be taken:

Inform next of kin

Interview river ranger Maryann Eliasson re: Observations of party at Lee's Ferry

Track down and interview woman who overheard Calder making threat (need first hand testimony)

Arrive at decision re: culpability of Calder and party before scheduled take-out April 21

APRIL 8: THE VIEW FROM UNKAR DELTA

Beyond the confluence of the Little Colorado, the river made a huge turn from flowing south to flowing west. The canyon was particularly wide for a few miles, forming a bottomland, and we stopped on the broad, sandy delta formed where Unkar Creek flows into the river from the north and visited the ruins of stone houses.

Brendan was flabbergasted. "People lived here. Wow," he said, bending to examine a pot shard that still showed a fragment of decoration.

Fritz said, "It's been a while. These homes were last occupied eight hundred years ago."

"I wonder why they left."

Fritz smiled. "That's a good question. Maybe you'll become an archaeologist and find out."

"Or you can ask their descendants," said Mungo. "Their great-great-some-odd-great-grandchildren live not too far from here."

Brendan gave him a look that was hard to interpret.

Fritz had given Brendan a camera to use, and the lad put it to good use photographing groups of pot shards. "My independent study report is going to be awesome! So I'm thinking I should put in some stuff about the geology, too," he said, turning to me. "Like, for the report it doesn't matter so much what Mom says anyway, because they teach it differently in school."

It, I thought. *They teach "it."* And what exactly was "it"? Was he talking about earth history, religion, or what?

"Well?" he said. He had flipped his sunglasses down like a visor.

Fritz artfully took a stroll farther along the path until he had exited the sphere of our conversation, then stooped to examine a flowering bush as if it held his undivided interest.

So it was time to take another walk through Brendan's personal mine field. I fixed my own gaze on that which always anchored me—the rocks, the bones of Mother Earth—and said, "Sure, kiddo, what do you want to know?" Here the river had carved deeper into the earth, down and down, down below the vertical walls of Redwall Limestone that dominated the upper reaches of the canyon into more complex stuff below. At this wide place in the canyon the palisades of sedimentary rocks stepped away toward the horizon like a giant flight of stairs. The biggest step was the Tonto Platform, formed where the soft Bright Angel Shale had eroded back across a table of the more resistant Cambrian-aged Tapeats Sandstone, and the cliffs of Redwall and Supai and everything else above receded beyond it. Here beneath the Tapeats, the river had cut downward into older layers yet, into Precambrian rocks, strata that had been laid down almost a billion years ago, when life on earth was just beginning to evolve from simple cells to more complex forms. The splendor of the landscape soothed me, but how could I explain all of this to a kid whose mother believed that these bands of rock fell out of the waters of a forty-day flood and that the canyon had been cut in the weeks that followed?

"Why are those rocks so screwed up?" Brendan asked. Gazing at the cliffs, he put his left hand at the angle of the Precambrian strata, which were tipped to the north, and lined up his right hand above it at the angle of the younger rock layers, which lay relatively flat.

"Good eye, Brendan," I said. "That's called the Great Unconformity. So what do you think happened there?"

"Something big?"

"Yes, something big. How much do you want me to tell you, all in one bite?"

Brendan said, "Just tell me what you think happened."

What I think *happened; ouch!* Like a great trout, I rose to the bait of the debate, opened my mouth, bit hard. "Well, like I said, that's an un-conformity, which is the geological term for a place where the strata don't continue without a break. Unconformities tell a story."

"So tell me the story," he said, impatience seeping into his tone.

"Okay, that angle tells me that all those layers didn't just drop out of the waters of some cataclysmic flood, because sediments that drop out of flood waters lie flat. It also tells me that deposition stopped and tilting and erosion occurred before deposition started again. The crust of the earth got all busted up here and sections of it tipped as great big blocks, which made hills or mountains, which were then eroded flat across the top. After that the younger layers were deposited. All of that takes time, a lot of time. And there's a gap in time represented by what's been eroded away. Now this whole region has been lifted up and the river has cut down through the whole shebang and left us a nice cliff face where we can see the whole story in cross-section."

"Shebang. Story."

"You don't have to use fancy names for it. Geology is pretty straight-forward, pretty intuitive as sciences go. Seeing it as a story helps us put the events in sequence."

"What do you mean 'intuitive'?"

"Most sciences are very quantitative, which means by the numbers. For instance, in chemistry you take sodium and chlorine and combine them and you'll get sodium chloride—table salt—every time. This plus that at such-and-such temperature and pressure equals X. What happens in the lab is exactly what happens in nature. There are a lot of numbers in geology, too, but we have to deal with rocks that are missing because they eroded away, or because they're covered, or because they've been cooked and have transformed into something else. Geology is ultimately a physics experiment with a lot of chemistry thrown in, but the variables are extremely complex and some of them are, like I said, hidden or missing. So we have to approach geology more qualitatively, looking at patterns. We look at the overall story and make an interpretation, or a prediction if we're looking into the future."

"Aren't the stories written down?"

"Not on paper. Most of geology happened before there were any people to observe it, but in another way of speaking, it's all written right here. We have to read the rock. But like I say, some of the pages of the book have been torn out and recycled."

He pondered this for a while, then said, "You said there was time missing between the tipped rock and the horizontal ones. How much time?"

"About three hundred million years."

Brendan suddenly laughed, whether in scorn or frustration I could not tell. He said, "I can't imagine a hundred years, much less three hundred million."

"Most people can't," I said. "But geologists can. People vary in what they're good at. One person might be best at keeping the trains running on time, while another cooks a whole lot better than I do, another understands how to heal people that are sick, and a few of us are good at understanding this kind of thing. We call it 'deep time.'"

Brendan said, "You're kind of weird, Em."

"Yes I am, and you know what else? Being good at thinking in billions of years makes me suck at politics, because what happens all in the short span of human history seems kind of unimportant."

Brendan considered this a moment, then said, "I kind of like that idea. So exactly how do you know there's three hundred million years missing there?"

"Erosion happens kind of slowly; we observe that directly and can measure it, though again there are a lot of variables to it. Moving water is a powerful tool of erosion, but it's not just the Colorado River that's eroding this landscape. The river is only about a hundred and fifty feet wide here, while the canyon is probably a dozen miles wide from rim to rim, so what's grinding away at the rest of it? Well, I look at all the side canyons, each with a little creek that's carrying its own bits of grit and mud downhill toward the river. On the slopes where there's no obvious creek, still the rain falls there and you get what's called sheet wash. In the winter, the snow and rain trickle into little cracks in the cliffs and freeze and thaw and freeze and thaw, and each time that water goes from liquid to ice it expands, and that's both physics and chemistry. These expansions act like little jackhammers, helping to split the rocks apart into smaller bits that will fall down the slope. Everything wants to follow gravity downhill, both the water and the rocks, and that's physics, too. You can see tumbled blocks all over the place, and the action of rainfall and freezing and thawing and the wind—more physics. Animals digging burrows under the rocks and so forth, now we're into biology, all contributing to a process we call mass wasting. In aggregate, it's mass wasting that's kicked all the hundreds of cubic miles of rock that used to be here down into the river and carried it away. Each of these bits of the process we can observe directly and measure and back-calculate to interpret the story of what's happened here, and how long it might have taken."

"So how long did it take to carve the canyon?"

"Several million years. We don't know exactly, because again, some of the pages in the book are missing. But we can say confidently that overall, erosion happens rather slowly here. We've got photographs that go back a hundred years or more and we can take a picture at the same spot now and compare them and see how much has actually moved, and that's all part of how we learn the story of geology."

As I stood there waving my arms and trying to explain geology to Brendan, the rafting group that had camped near us the second night at Nankoweap pulled up onto the beach. As the passengers climbed out of the rafts, Wink trotted down the beach to join them. He had put on that ill-fitting plaid shirt again, and he lent a hand to the bottle blonde with the skinny sandals. The girl who had played the guitar that night took her other arm, and Wink guided them toward a trail that led up to a group of ruins.

Brendan was watching them, too. He asked, "What about the stories in the Bible?"

I shook my head. "I don't want to argue about that, Brendan."

The boy looked at me out of the corner of his eye. "Do you have a religion?" he inquired.

I laughed. "Sure. When I stand in places like this and contemplate such vastness of time and space, and witness how deposition and erosion and all the other parts and processes of geology work together, I see an astonishingly beautiful system that is . . . well, the word is 'divine.'" I took a deep breath then and shared my heart with him. "In its simplicity and complexity nature makes sense to me, Brendan. I observe it from the center of my being, and that experience is profound."

"Mom says scientists are trying to disprove the existence of God."

I don't work as a geologist so I can disprove anyone's religious convictions. I wanted to scream, or weep. I sat down on a rock and put my face in my hands. "Honey, some scientists are Mormons, and others will tell you they're atheists, or agnostics, or whatever variety of Christian, Jewish, Muslim, Hindu, Buddhist, or . . . I don't know, maybe pagan."

Brendan patted me on the shoulder. "I'm sorry to get so wound up about all that Bible stuff, Em. Really, I'll try to take a vacation from it today, okay? Just working on my independent study report here."

I leaned my cheek onto his hand. "Thanks, Brendan."

"So you were going to tell me how those rocks got tipped."

"Sure," I said. "Those rocks have got a name, the Grand Canyon Supergroup, and they got tilted when an old continent tore apart."

Brendan began to laugh. "Yeah, sure, like . . . rip!" He pulled his arms apart as if he were opening an accordion.

I nodded. "Just like that, only much, much slower and on an immense scale. Didn't you learn about Plate Tectonics in fifth grade?"

"Fifth grade I was home-schooled, remember? Mom and Dad were getting their divorce and Mom thought I was such a tender flower she had to keep me where I wouldn't get rained on."

I winced. "You don't watch PBS or Discovery Channel?"

"Mom doesn't go for that stuff."

I put an arm around him. "Well, continents move around, at about the speed your fingernails grow, and they rip apart or smash together, or sometimes just grind along past each other."

Brendan smiled. "Maybe you've been out in the sun too long, Em."

"That's what they told Galileo when he said the earth moved around the sun rather than the other way around. So yeah, the continents move; we've measured it using satellites, and the earth's crust—"

"Now you're telling me that the earth is like a loaf of bread?"

I gave him a squeeze. "No, it's more like it has a hard candy shell over hot jelly filling with a really hot nut at the center."

"How can you know that, Em? You've never been inside the earth!" Brendan tipped back his head and giggled.

At that exact moment at the ruin, Wink threw back his head in a similar gesture, but on him it was not playful or attractive. It struck me that some people who still behaved like children as they approached their forties were stuck on an emotional snag; instead of remaining pleasantly young, they withered into emotional pygmies. In Brendan, adolescence was right on schedule, but underneath his clowning lay a terrible tension; would he get caught on it and wither, or work through it and grow into a man?

I loved Brendan intensely in that moment and wanted desperately to give him something that would sustain him through his coming trials. I said, "Brendan, I *love* science, because it gives me a way to sort out what's knowable from what's not, but we each get to decide where to draw the line between what we see with our eyes and what we know with our hearts."

Fritz waved to us from the place where he waited on the trail. "It's getting late," he called. "We'd best get the group together and make some miles on that river."

Brendan said, "Tell me more about the candy shell on the hot jelly earth, Em."

I took his arm in mine and we began to walk toward the river's edge. "Maybe on another day," I said. "I'm getting sort of tired."

We passed close to where Wink still stood with his group from the other raft trip. Fritz told him, "We're launching in ten minutes."

Wink ignored him, shifting his footing so that he showed Fritz his back.

As we reached the rafts, Brendan asked, "What are you going to do about him, Dad?"

Fritz didn't answer, but I could see that his jaws had bunched up tight with rage.

Diary of Holly Ann St. Denis
April 8

Dear God,

   Yesterday we went past places where there is salt hanging out of the cliffs, sort of flowing down out of nowhere, it looks like. I'm not sure where it came from, but You work miracles every day! Anyway boat-man Dan was telling me that these were sacred salt mines that the Hopi Indians still visit today but "Uncle" Terry said the Hopi were not men of God so I should turn my face from this sacrilege lest I be turned to salt myself. Our geology consultant Dr. Oberley was rowing along be-side us then, and he heard that. When we made camp this evening at Nevills, Dr. Oberley walked over from where he's camping with this other group and when no one was listening whispered that I shouldn't worry about being turned to salt. He said that T was just trying to scare me and that it was easy to get scared when you see a pillar of salt and think it's a person who's been frozen but that things don't happen ex-actly like that. I liked that he called "Uncle" Terry "T." I asked if I could call him "Dr. O" and he smiled and said he'd like that.

God, is Dr. O right about this? I've been reading in my Bible where it says that Lot's wife was turned to salt because she disobeyed and looked back while Sodom and Gomorrah were being destroyed by the angels, and I apologize for always asking questions, but it says that the bad men came to Lot's house and said he had to bring the angels out so that "we may know them" but Dr. O says that in his version it says "so we can have sex with them." Is he right that "knowing" is a code word for "sex"???? Or does Dr. O have a fake Bible with errors in it? I like Dr. O. He's nice to me and speaks to me like I have a brain, and he seems to understand "how things are" for me. He says I play the guitar beautifully. And Mom likes him, too. And when we stopped for lunch at the Unkar delta today he showed us places where the Indians who used to live there left behind their artifacts. There are little bits of clay pots they made that are just sitting there on the ground! Surely the Flood would have washed them away.

Here I go questioning things again! There's sure a lot of places in the Book of Genesis where You got mad at people and destroyed them! And that says that "Uncle" Terry is right, not Dr. O.

Dr. O told me in our private talk here at Nevills that bad things can happen to you when you're a kid and you don't have much control over what the grownups around you are doing, but that when you get older, you have a little more control over things.

While we were talking a woman named Ms. Hansen from the other camp walked by with her stepson Brendan and Dr. O introduced me to them. He told me that Ms. Hansen is a geologist, like to say, See? Girls can be geologists, too, and that really amazed me. I asked her if she knew that the rocks came from Noah's Flood and she looked at me a long time like she was really thinking about what I'd said, and then she told me that all nature was very beautiful to her. In that moment I saw Your Love in her eyes. She looked at me from Your great calm and said, "This is where I look to see God." Then she said she hoped I was having a good visit to this very special place and she and Brendan continued on their way down the trail. I'm meeting such interesting people here, people who know a whole lot!

Well, God, it's time for me to say my bedtime prayers and put out this light, so I'm going to say good night and then say my prayers to You. Mom's here and she looks tired and worried, but she won't tell me why. I know that her feet hurt her where she's gotten blisters. Well, like I said, good night!

APRIL 8: NEVILLS

ACCORDING TO OUR RIVER GUIDE, OUR CAMP AT NEVILLS STOOD AT about 2,760 feet elevation. That meant that we had ridden the river down about 450 feet closer to sea level over the seventy-six miles we had traveled from the put-in at Lees Ferry. The nearest point on the rim of the canyon was at 7,000 feet, over three-quarters of a mile higher. The canyon was not called Grand for nothing.

Brendan asked me to go for another walk with him, so I said okay and we grabbed some dried fruit from the kitchen box and headed down through the brush toward the river's edge, chatting about the rapids his dad had let him row that day. As we stepped out from the thicket of tamarisk, our conversation was abruptly interrupted: There stood Wink Oberley and the girl from the church group who played the guitar so beautifully.

At the sight of us, Wink stopped talking.

The girl looked our way and smiled. She was very pretty and blond and wore what I'd have to call a cute print blouse and a pair of jeans that looked like they'd just come out of a laundry room. "Hi!" she said, addressing herself to Brendan. "It's nice to see another kid down here."

Brendan returned her smile uncertainly.

Wink cleared his throat and introduced us. "Hey, what do you think of this? Ms. Hansen is a geologist! She works for the Utah Geological Survey, and you know what she does? She solves crimes sometimes, using geologic evidence."

The girl's eyes widened. "You mean like on TV?"

"Sure, just like that."

I smiled. "Except my hair and makeup aren't as good as the women on TV, and I never wear high heels if I can help it."

Holly Ann tipped her head like a chickadee that was examining a seed. She didn't say anything for a moment, and I was afraid that I had offended her, but then she stared deep into my eyes and said, "Well, if you're a geologist, then you must know that these rocks came from Noah's Flood."

Well, that stopped my clock. I looked from her to Wink and back again, waiting to see if he'd correct her, but he did not. I wondered how the whole Young Earth thing jibed with getting his doctorate from Princeton. Geologists disagreed, but there was a difference between disagreeing and stepping off the curb into I-read-it-in-a-book-so-it's-true.

I turned back toward Holly Ann and returned her gaze, reaching as far inside her soul as she was reaching into mine. There was something very special about this girl: strength mixed with vulnerability. I can't remember how I answered her question, so stunning was her gaze.

Brendan had gone from silent and nervous to just plain silent, so we continued on down the trail. Thirty yards or so along the way, he whispered, "Nice."

I gave his hand a squeeze and said, "Thanks. Let's just enjoy the sound of the river."

Fritz came down the trail and met us then. As we strolled back to our campsite we came across the tall man with the prominent Adam's apple who had led the prayers at the fundamentalist campsite at Nankoweap. He strode up to Fritz and said, "You're with Oberley's group, right?"

Fritz said, "He's with us, yes."

"Well, maybe you can tell him that we don't need his help anymore."

Fritz let his words slow almost to a drawl. "I'm sure you can tell him that yourself."

The man narrowed his eyes. "Who do you think you are, Chuck Yeager?"

A corner of Fritz's mouth curled in a smile. "A fellow pilot, are you?"

The man jerked his head back in surprise and blurted, "SuperCobra."

Fritz said, "A-6," brushed past the man, and continued along the trail.

"What was all that?" I asked, as I caught up with him. "Was that code for something?"

"He flew helicopters in the marines over Iraq," said Fritz.

Fritz was usually very polite to people he'd just met, so I was surprised that he had taken any of the man's bait, much less felt the need to let him know that he had zoomed overhead in a fast jet while the marines were grunting along with their flying eggbeaters. Under his breath, he said, "Crazy jarheads get dropped on their punkin heads in boot camp, each and every one of them."

Transcript of telephone call from Ranger Gerald Weber to Heather Oberley,
wife of George Oberley, late of Rocky Hill, New Jersey
April 19, 9:45 A.M.

Mrs. Oberley: Hello?

Weber: Hello, am I speaking with Mrs. George Oberley?

Mrs. Oberley: Who wants to know?

Weber: Ma'am, this is Chief Ranger Gerald Weber at Grand Canyon National Park in Arizona. And ma'am, for your information I am recording this call.

Mrs. Oberley: Oh. What's he done now?

Weber: Excuse me?

Mrs. Oberley: Wink. He's got hisself caught again, huh? All right, where do I gotta go to bail him out?

Weber: Ma'am, are you confirming that you are his wife?

Mrs. Oberley: Yeah, that's me, ol' lucky Heather, the idiot that married Mr. Wonderful.

Weber: [pause] Oh. Well, Mrs. Oberley, I'm afraid I have some bad . . . well, some news for you. Are you sitting down?

Mrs. Oberley: What is this, some kind of a joke? Who did you say you are?

Weber: No, I assure you this is not a prank call. I am chief ranger at—

Mrs. Oberley: So cut to the chase. What is it you've got to tell me?

Weber: Ma'am, your husband has been found dead.

Mrs. Oberley: [long pause] Dead? [another pause] You're shitting me!

Weber: No ma'am, I assure you I'm not—

Mrs. Oberley: How?

Weber: How did he die? Well, we have an investigation under way to try to determine exactly what happened, and—

Mrs. Oberley: Wait a minute! You say you're calling from the canyon?

Weber: Yes.

Mrs. Oberley: Then . . . and you're telling me he's *dead*?

Weber: Yes.

Mrs. Oberley: Where?

Weber: His body was found at a place called Whitmore Wash. It's at the bottom of the canyon, river mile—

Mrs. Oberley: I know where Whitmore Wash is! You're telling me that bastard has been in Arizona all this time?

Weber: Were you . . . you didn't know he was here?

Mrs. Oberley: Hell no! I haven't seen him for weeks! A month, almost! A month *this* time. He's been out there gallivanting around for how long?

Weber: His party launched from Lees Ferry on April first.

Mrs. Oberley: And this happened when?

Weber: His body was discovered on the eighteenth. He had been missing for two days. The information on the roster we had for that raft trip was incomplete . . . inaccurate where it came to your husband, so it took me a while to trace you, and—

Mrs. Oberley: Yeah, I'll bet he didn't exactly leave a forwarding address!

Weber: Has he done this sort of thing before?

Mrs. Oberley: Not more than half a dozen times. [starts to cry]

Weber: Ma'am, I'm sorry for your loss, but I have a few more questions for you if you can—

Mrs. Oberley: I loved him, no matter what!

Weber: I'm sure you did. Now, we are trying to determine exactly how he died. He was found—

Mrs. Oberley: My poor Georgie!

Weber: Here's the thing, ma'am: We think he was murdered.

Mrs. Oberley: [pause] Oh.

Weber: So we need to determine who might have done this.

Mrs. Oberley: [nervous laughter] Well, get in line! I mean, that's a long list, you know what I mean?

Weber: Did he have any . . . Well, are you aware of anyone in particular who would want him dead?

Mrs. Oberley: No . . .

Weber: Ma'am, are you acquainted with a Fritz Calder of Salt Lake City?

Mrs. Oberley: No . . . never heard of him. Did he kill my Georgie?

Weber: We do not at this time know who was responsible for your husband's death. Calder is the leader of the rafting trip your husband was on. He was the alternate, actually, standing in for one Albert "Tiny" Lewis. Are you acquainted with him?

Mrs. Oberley: Never heard of either of them. But that don't mean nothing. Georgie's kind of a schmoozer. He'd talk his way into anything, especially a raft trip!

Weber: Okay, that's helpful.

Mrs. Oberley: I just recall him saying he might have a lead on a job. He took off from here one morning saying he was going on an extended job interview, was all. See, he's been working on his

Ph.D. here and, well . . . okay, so I've been the breadwinner for the whole while, and our kids have to have new shoes, you know?

Weber: I get the picture. Ma'am? I'm afraid I've got a request for you. It is customary that we get the next of kin to identify the body.

Mrs. Oberley: Well now, how am I supposed to get myself to Arizona? You think maybe plane fares grow on trees? I'm living in a one-bedroom apartment over a bar with two kids and a missing now *dead* husband and I've got no car! I go downstairs and work for tips, you know what I mean? And who'd look after my children? Come to think of that . . . [again breaks into sobbing]

Weber: I'm sure this is a terrible shock.

Mrs. Oberley: No, in fact it is not. Or it's a shock, but no surprise, know what I mean?

Voice of child in the background: Mommy?

Weber: I . . . It's important, ma'am. Can you help us in any way to identify the body?

Mrs. Oberley: [angrily] Sure, I can help you with that! Roll him over and look at his left butt cheek. You'll find the name of that damned leaky dory of his right there in a lovely little tattoo! I sure had to look at it enough!

Voice of child in the background: Mommy? Is something wrong with Daddy?

Weber: And . . . and what was the name of that dory, ma'am?

Mrs. Oberley: [to child] Honey, run along. Mommy's got to talk to a man about . . . Just run along, please.

Weber: I'm sorry, ma'am. Do you need some time?

Mrs. Oberley: No. No, it's okay now. [sound of door closing] You were asking me something . . .

Weber: You were telling me about a tattoo. It was the name of his dory?

Mrs. Oberley: Yeah, *Wave Slut*! It was his love name for me . . . and for half the other women in Coconino County! So ask one of *them* to identify him! Me, I'm the sucker who followed him to New Jersey, and if you think the Ivy League was any cure for what ails that man, well . . .

Weber: Could you name someone in particular?

Mrs. Oberley: Sure, try Cleome James. Does she still work in your damned park? Yeah, ask Cleome to look at his damned corpse! I have better things to do, like raise his children! Good-bye!

Connection ended by called party.

APRIL 9: THE BIG DROP

FRITZ WASN'T KIDDING THAT THE RAPIDS GOT A WHOLE LOT BIGGER.
Hance was a monster.

Rapids tend to occur where a side canyon has shot a large tumble of boulders into the river. Sometimes the rocks are big enough (or the water is low enough, because the guys upstream at the dam have "turned the river off" again) that they stick up through the waves they create. Fritz calls this a "rock garden." Other times the rocks are fully submerged. I'm not sure which I like better—or less. Even the most experienced rowers scouted the larger rapids before they ran them, because not only did the water level vary due to changes at the dam and runoff from side canyons, but, Fritz explained, those big rocks did occasionally shift, changing the dynamics of a rapid, and such simple things as the sun angle could make the water "read" differently. I supposed also that by scouting the larger rapids they could exult in how terrifying it was and prolong the pleasure of swamping themselves in adrenaline.

Mungo told me one evening over the campfire that he didn't like to get wet as much as he used to, so he "sneaked" most rapids over to one side of the biggest waves. Fritz and Brendan liked to run right down the biggest line of waves laughing and screaming. I worked my damned fool mantras as hard as I could, and I'd gotten to the point where I enjoyed the rhythms of the waves on the small-to-moderate-sized rapids, but the trauma that underlay my fear still lived in my nervous system like a weird parasite, shooting adrenaline into my bloodstream and releasing intrusive memories. The flash image of my brother's face would erupt in my mind. He floated wide-eyed, just beneath the waters, like he was down there in some other world trying to see into this one.

I shoved these visions firmly into another part of my brain and instead studied how the water formed up at the top of a rapid: Dammed up by the jumble of rocks, it pillowed up to a pour point, forming a V of eerily smooth water that pointed downstream. I watched for "holes" formed by submerged rocks, and mapped places where the curves in the river and rock-strewn disturbances in flow might pull our sixteen-foot rafts off into eddies, jam them against walls, hang them up on rocks, or suck them into holes. I began to create over each rapid a moving diagram of success, a sort of space-time solution to the puzzle presented by rock and water.

The art to rowing a rapid began with "ferrying" the raft from the launch point out across the current to an optimum position relative to that smooth throat of water that was forming up over the spill point. The oarsman must present the side of the raft to it like an offering, and then, at the perfect instant, pulling on one oar just hard enough to swing the bow of the raft downriver, aiming it down the throat of that V. The oarsman had to continue to row, creating forward momentum with those oars to maintain maneuverability lest the raft begin to turn or spin and become the wrong kind of toy. The train of waves kicked up by the rocks was seldom straight. Some lay in opposition to each other, and sequences of rocks farther down a rapid presented additional problems.

The oarsman sits about two-thirds of the way back in a raft, facing downriver. A second person sits up in the bow, usually kneeling just behind the forward roll of the flotation tube, hanging on for dear life as he throws his weight, "punching" into the waves to keep the bow from kicking straight up and maybe flipping the boat ass-over-teakettle backward. "Keep it straight in the big stuff and don't hit the hard stuff," Mungo liked to say.

Fritz had promised that on the day we went over the first big rapids at Hance, I should plan on getting soaked. I had put on a waterproof paddle jacket underneath my life vest, and, as the weather was looking to turn rainy toward the end of this big day, I had struggled into a set of neoprene "farmer John" skintight overalls, a sleeveless form of wet suit that I had borrowed from a friend in Salt Lake City who liked to go scuba diving. For good measure I wore a fleece shirt under the paddle jacket to keep my arms and neck warm. Thus, as I scrambled over the rocks and sand at the mouth of the side canyon that fed Hance Rapid, I was moving stiffly and beginning to overheat.

Hance was rated at a 7 to 8 on the scale of 10, serving up a thirty-foot drop over a run of a quarter of a mile. It arced slightly to the left, curling around the rocky debris pile that had accumulated at the mouth of the side canyon. The safety kayakers were already out in it, splashing and flipping like a bunch of funny-colored dolphins, making sudden moves with their double-ended paddles to steer this way and that.

"Are you ready for this, Em?" Brendan asked, appearing at my side.

"Sure," I lied. "Bombs away."

Fritz had wandered farther down the bank of the river with the other oarsmen to discuss some particulars. Wink lagged behind them, heading to where I stood with Brendan. Over the pounding of the waves, he hollered, "They should just shoot it, right, Brendan?"

Brendan tried to ignore him.

Wink threw a couple of fake punches his way like a shadowboxer, then snapped forward, grabbed the kid's arm, and twisted it hard, his expression changing from ha-ha-I'm-playing to the intense focus a hawk displays when he is about to hit a sparrow in midair.

Brendan shot sideways to evade getting flipped, but in the process managed to twist an ankle on a loose rock.

"Let's get a snack before we take this rapid," I said loudly, giving

Brendan an excuse to follow me. I began walking, very quickly, up the beach, and Brendan lurched after me, limping. There was raw anxiety in his eyes, and I saw a glint in Wink's, frustration mixed with rage that his prey was being taken from him.

Fantasies of smacking Wink with a paddle or, better yet, one of the nice long oars from Fritz's raft, began to bloom in my head. The man scared me, but much more than that, I was beginning to feel a visceral hatred of him. *How dare he come on this trip?* I wanted to know. *How dare he live and breathe?*

It startled me that I felt so strongly. *Is this how mothers feel about their children?* I wondered. *Is this what it feels like to be a mother?* I hadn't children, but given much thought to having suddenly, it didn't matter that I was childless, because I had Brendan and I was damned well going to keep him safe, at least from this kind of harm.

I turned and faced Wink, standing with my arms crossed like an angry schoolmarm, giving Brendan a chance to get ahead of me while I glared at the damned fool of a bully who pursued him.

Wink stopped, smiled, and tipped his head to one side as if to charm me.

I gave our staring match a ten full seconds, then turned and continued to our raft, and loaded Brendan into the cockpit. I tried to examine his ankle, but he refused to let me look at it.

The boy stared across the river. After half a minute or so, as if by afterthought, he silently slapped me a crooked high five.

Yes, this was definitely what motherhood must feel like: We were in this together, and he loved me just as I loved him.

I shot Hance Rapid in the bow of Fritz's boat, singing out my joy of being with the people who made my world complete. I weathered the raging waters right there next to Brendan, grinning at the lad, taking in the grin he offered in return. We splashed and crashed through the water, the big raft bucking and rising on the humping waves and at the bottom of the waves, we shared a hug. Life was good—no, it was great!—as we continued downriver, the first traces of the Vishnu Schist and Zoroaster Granite appearing along its banks. Over the next mile and a half of water I was happy. I was exultant. Then we reached the next big drop.

Sockdolager Rapid.

Fritz called it "Proctologer." I didn't like the sound of that.

We beached our boats and climbed out to scout it—everybody came, even the safety kayakers, and even Wink; everybody, that is, except Brendan. He stayed in the raft.

"Why aren't you coming?" asked Fritz.

Brendan said only, "I gave my ankle a little twist back there at the last scouting and thought maybe I'd soak it here in the river a bit."

"Good idea," said Fritz.

Brendan turned his back to us, peeled off his sandal and fleece sock, and worked his way over to the far side of the raft, where he could bobble his feet in the current. I said a silent prayer that the ankle was only bruised and not sprained or anything torn.

Fritz double-checked the bow line of his raft, which he had cinched with the other boat lines around a large boulder, then headed up the slope to the scouting overlook. I clambered up the rock-strewn slope to the left of the rapid, turned, and looked down along the chasm we must now descend. The chute of whitewater was tight and churning, a heaving thatch of waves.

The walls of the canyon had narrowed considerably in the last mile as the river bit down into the dark granites of the Inner Gorge. The orderly layers of the sedimentary rocks were a cliff-top memory now as we descended into the open maw of these most ancient rocks. "It's a full-assed nine out of ten today," Mungo pronounced cheerily. "God help us all."

Fritz slapped him on the shoulder. "Looks like we need to run it right down the middle," he said.

"You mean, because there aren't any side parts to it?" Nancy Skinner asked. "That hole there at the beginning looks big enough to swallow a bull elephant!"

Olaf spoke. "I heard this one guy tell me how he went into a hole here that pulled him down so hard that he had to shuck his kayak and dive rather than fight his way to the surface. Luckily it spat him out at the bottom."

The group stood silently for a while, mapping the holes and heaves as best they could, laying out plans. Mungo squinted and moved one hand in a dance, mentally rehearsing the route he would take.

Fritz broke the reverie. "The weather is beginning to deteriorate," he said. "I've been watching the clouds all morning, and now the temperature is beginning to drop and there's a wind coming up. We'd better get on down the river."

Wink peeled off and headed back toward his boat, but Julianne had stayed behind, staring awkwardly at her feet. Had she chosen to stay on one of the big, wide-bottomed rafts rather than chance this size water in the leaking dory?

Fritz deployed the kayakers next, saying, "If there's anything out there you think we haven't seen . . . well, pray for us, okay?"

"See you at the bottom," Gary said, as he headed down the slope. He pulled a beer out of the drop bag on Fritz's raft and stuck it down the front of his life vest, then joined Lloyd and Olaf as they climbed into their kayaks, snapped the neoprene spray skirts in place, saluted us with their paddles, and heaved off into the current. There was little playing this time as they traversed the rapid, only tightly concentrated efforts to get their tiny craft down through the giant waves without being sucked under.

I watched them go and next saw Wink in his dory, bouncing over the waves, his years of experience coming to the fore.

"No!" Nancy shouted. She grabbed Fritz's arm and yanked, directing his attention to a place just above the V, where the weirdly smooth part of the water was beginning to undulate over the rocks hidden beneath. I saw then what she was pointing at, something that stopped my heart: our raft, floating sideways out into the current, with Brendan still on it.

The boy scrambled to gain a seat at the oars, but his naked, injured foot became tangled in an oarlock and he fell. Racing to gain control of the raft, he pulled himself up and heaved himself into the rower's seat, but he was too late. The raft slipped sideways into that elephant-sized hole just as the fierce hydraulics of the Colorado River heaved the wave beyond it into a mountain. It grabbed the raft like a leaf and flipped it upside down. I stared in horror at the underside of the boat as it continued to plunge down the rapid.

"I don't see Brendan!" Nancy shouted. "He didn't get out!"

"He won't have the strength to push his way out from underneath the boat!" roared Mungo, as he ran toward his raft.

Fritz was already halfway down the slope, leaping from rock to rock with his long legs. He had the line to Mungo's raft in his hands now, untying it. Mungo shoved the raft from the bow, backing it into the current. The two men sprang into the craft, Fritz taking the oars as Mungo braced himself in the bow, ready to grab the boy if he came up. Fritz pulled hard, straining out into the current as fast as he could get the heavily laden raft to go.

A panicked thought shot through my head: *Please, God, don't let me lose both Fritz and Brendan!*

Nancy was beside me now, shouting to the rest of us to slow down to make sure that nobody was left behind. Quickly and efficiently, she pointed each of the displaced passengers into positions on the remaining two rafts. Molly and I loaded up with Don and Jerry Rasmussen, while Julianne climbed in with Dell, Nancy, and Danielle. "We're more heavily loaded, but it will have to work," she said. We untied the lines, pushed off, and entered the current.

Molly climbed up onto the load behind Don and grabbed hold of a pair of the wide blue cam straps that held down elements of the load. I sat in the bow with Jerry, who reached over and patted my arm. "Just hang on tight to the safety straps," she said. "People have swum this rapid on purpose, so Brendan will be fine."

As I scanned the waters for any sign of him, my mind held only one single dark thought: *Please, don't let him die like my brother.*

Don ferried our raft out into the current, spun its nose into the V, and kept it aimed.

The water began to roll like a row of ocean swells. A great boil of opaque brown liquid spread out before me, larger than the raft. The nose dipped and rose with the mounting swell, dipped and rose, and now we entered that hole. The water heaved straight up, jumped, arched, and landed hard on us, blinding me, ripping my sunglasses from my face and twisting their retaining strap tight around my neck. As that wave drained away, the next hit us, and the next.

"Sorry!" Don shouted from the oars. "Sorry!"

"To heck with the waves, keep an eye out for Brendan!" Jerry called.

The raft rocked and pitched, bouncing over the water like a toy. My hands went cold with the effort of holding the straps. The water sucked us to the left now toward a huge flat slab of rock, then mercifully let us go right before we hit. I strained to search for Brendan, but the water ran sunscreen into my eyes, blinding me. The rapid pitched on and on, the waves slowly diminishing in size, and now, a quarter mile downriver, Don pulled hard to the left, straining to steer the craft into the eddy where the runaway raft now floated, the underside of its broad rubber floorboards still turned heavenward. I grabbed a handful of water from the hold and doused my eyes, still straining in my search for Brendan. Where *was* he?

Mungo's raft and two of the three kayaks had pulled alongside the overturned raft. Gary and Olaf grabbed its sides, using it to steady themselves as they rolled head down into the water to look for the boy. Fritz snatched at the raft, shouting his son's name.

Suddenly Brendan burst up out of the water gasping, dazed, his hair flattened wet against his forehead. Fritz was in the water beside him now, grabbing his life vest by the shoulder, towing him toward Gary's kayak, which he gripped with his other hand. Gary flipped upright and paddled them toward Mungo's raft. Using the huge strength of a man shot full of terror, Fritz grabbed the float tube by one arm and heaved himself aboard, dragging his son with his other hand. The boy scrambled to follow, still sputtering and coughing.

At last the two were inside the safety of Mungo's raft.

"Shit!" said Gary. "I was sitting there in that eddy having myself a nice beer when I saw that raft coming down the river with its butt in the air! What came over you, boy?"

Brendan began to shake.

"I need a sleeping bag," said Fritz. Mungo dug one out of his load and Fritz wrapped it around his son and held him clutched to his chest.

It was a mess getting Fritz's raft right side up. There was no nice comfortable beach to stand on at the foot of Sockdolager, the sky was gray, and the wind had grown cold and now blew upriver, straight into our faces.

"Where's Wink?" asked Julianne. "He's so good at turning rafts back up."

"Not here," said Nancy. "He didn't stop at the foot of the rapid. He rowed off down the gorge by himself."

"Let's get on with it," said Fritz. "We've still got eight miles to row today, and the wind is getting stronger."

◆

It was a long, hard row down through three more sizable rapids, miscellaneous riffles, and too many miles of flat water in a mounting wind and threatening rain. Fritz put Brendan beside him on the raft so they both could row, the better to fight against the wind, warm the boy, and help him work off his terror of floating down that rapid trapped underneath the boat. We dragged into Cremation Campground at 6:00 P.M. tired, cold, and cavernously hungry. Wink was nowhere in sight, but his dory was tied up on the opposite bank of the river.

"What was it like under there?" I heard Mungo ask, as the two hefted their dry bags up the steep slope from the bank where we had—*extra* carefully—lashed the rafts and kayaks.

Brendan was very quiet for a while, then said, "It was dark under there, and all the loose ends of the cam straps were dangling in the water, and—" There he ran out of words.

I suppose Mungo didn't need to hear more. The man gave the boy a swat on the shoulder and said simply, "You're a blooded warrior now, lad."

Fritz said nothing. He was staring across the river at Wink's dory with a glare so intense I thought it might bring the water around it to a boil.

Interview of Cleome James, Dispatcher, by Chief Ranger Gerald Weber
April 19, 10:05 A.M.

Weber: Cleome, just so you know, this is a voice recorder. I am recording our conversation.

James: Oh.

Weber: Now Cleome, are you aware that George Oberley is dead?

James: Well, yes. You kind of told me that, right?

Weber: I suppose I did. Or I didn't deny it. Well now, I've spoken
with his wife, to advise the next of kin and all. I asked her to
come out here to identify the body but she's suggested that someone else do that for her. In fact, she suggested that you do it.

James: She . . . did?

Weber: Yes, she did. Now, this is a bit personal, perhaps, but she
asserted that you would be aware of certain identifying marks on
his body. So can you tell me what she meant by that?

James: Oh . . . gee . . .

Weber: Could you be a bit more specific?

James: I suppose she was referring to a tattoo.

Weber: Could you describe it, please?

James: It's on his bottom. We . . . Well, as you know sometimes when you're on the river, well . . . People have to bathe, you know. Yeah, and well, so I, uh . . . saw his tattoo, was all.

Weber: And can you describe this tattoo?

James: Yeah . . . it's the name of his dory: *Wave Slut*. In fancy script lettering. With a rose. He said he got drunk in Vegas one night and when he woke up the next day it was there. That's what he said.

Weber: I see. On which buttock?

James: On the left side.

Weber: Well now, I've called the coroner, and that tallies with what he's observed on the body that was found at Whitmore Wash. So now, do you have anything to add to this statement?

James: Maybe you could get ahold of that woman who overheard the man threatening Wink. Have you done that? She's probably off the river now, so you could call her.

Weber: Yes, I've tried, but her number isn't listed, and though I've left a message with the man who booked the trip, he hasn't returned my call, so I need you to think, Cleome. Is there anything you need to add?

James: They were that church group. The one where the televangelist died right in front of his whole TV audience, coast to coast. It was a heart attack or something, remember? And she was his wife, and they had her crying on camera week after week saying how everyone should keep on making their donations because their ministry was gonna carry on. Then the brother, the dead televangelist's brother, he started coming on the air with her and oh, man he was oily! What was his name? Terry Carl, that was it, and—

Weber: You're getting off the subject here, Cleome.

James: But is that who booked the trip? This Terry Carl guy? I mean, maybe you could call him and ask if he heard that man make the threat, and then—

Weber: That's enough! [pause] I'm fishing here, Cleome. Help me. I know you've been right up here on the rim the whole while, so you're not a suspect in this case, but the deceased's wife suggests that you were familiar with him, so . . .

James: I think I shouldn't say anything more, sir.

Weber: Cleome?

James: He . . . I'd prefer to leave it at that, sir.

Weber: I'm not accusing you of anything. We're just trying to find out—

James: He just had a very bad reputation. You can ask anyone. Ask any of the river guides, or ask Maryann, or anyone! There were a whole lot of people who were mad at him, and I'm not going to say another word unless I've got a lawyer, because he was a real jerk and he had a way of starting trouble and sucking everyone else down with him, and I'm damned if I'm going to fall for it twice!

Weber: [pause] Okay, I'll have to respect that. For now. But if you change your mind, you know where to find me, right? And get that lawyer, because there is due process to be looked after, and while I might sympathize that there are troublemakers in this world, there's also a thing called obstruction of justice, and no matter how many people disliked this man and aren't sorry to see him gone, I've got to find who killed him and bring that person to justice.

James: [undecipherable]

Weber: Take a deep breath and try again, Cleome.

James: It's just so embarrassing.

Weber: What is embarrassing?

James: I'm not sorry he's dead but if somebody killed him then they had their reasons, and that's all I'm going to say.

End of interview.

APRIL 9: CREMATION

WHEN WE REACHED CREMATION CAMP IT WAS SPITTING RAIN AND ALmost dusk. It was a tight, steep, and rocky place clinging to one side of the inner Vishnu Schist gizzard of the Grand Canyon. We had to crowd our tents together, tying their guy lines to the stunted trees that grew among the rocks, a compaction made even tighter by the division of the campground into accommodations for two parties.

"Why is the camp called Cremation?" Brendan asked, as he limped up the slope carrying his sleeping gear up from our raft.

I said, "It's named after Cremation Fault, a big crack in the earth that crosses the river here."

"Why's the crack named that, then?"

"The fault was named for Cremation Creek, which carved its little side canyon by following weaknesses made in the rocks when the fault moved. And before you ask the next question, the creek was named after what some former Native American residents of the area did with their dead." I turned to Fritz as we arrived at the tent . "Why are there two groups crammed in here?" I asked.

It's the midcanyon switch-out place," said Fritz. "Phantom Ranch is just across the river and around that bend, so these spaces are reserved for one-night use by people who need access to the trails that come down here from the rims. Danielle and Julianne will hike out tomorrow morning, and we'll have two replacements come in—Glenda Fittle and Hakatai Mattes. Hakatai will be joining us this evening, and I understand that Glenda is staying at one of the cottages across the river and will join us in the morning. As regards the other group that is staying on the other side of this crag, I have no idea what their plans are."

Jerry Rasmussen called to us from her tent, where she and Don were tapping stakes into the ground with my borrowed mineral hammer to tighten their rain fly. "Do you want to visit Phantom Ranch?" she asked. "It's really sweet. There are old cabins you can rent there that were built in the 1920s, and a campground for hikers. If you need any supplies like sunscreen, they'll probably have it, though nothing's cheap there. Everything comes in by mule train down the South Kaibab Trail from the South Rim."

Don Rasmussen asked, "How is it that you know Glenda Fittle?"

Fritz said, "I don't. She's a friend of Wink's. Tiny said that Wink found out we were one person light for the lower half and sweet-talked him into inviting Glenda. Hakatai Mattes I've met; he's a friend of Tiny's from his biker life. There he is now!" He pointed across the river at a big man—all shoulders and girth, a cross between a linebacker and a couch cushion—who was just then hefting his dry bag into the cockpit of Wink Oberley's dory.

I had not seen Wink since he pulled out from the top of Sockdolager Rapid. Julianne anxiously awaited him our side of the river, at the landing where our rafts were tied up. She clutched her hands to her chest in the cold, then raised one to wave at him, shyly at first, and then really starting to move her arm in a big arc, racking her frame with the effort. "Oo-hoo! Wi-ink!" she called across the waters. "Oo-hoo, Winky-poo!"

I was embarrassed for her. She would on the morrow be hiking up the trail toward the rest of her life, where, hopefully, she would find a bedmate of firmer moral stature. She was a foolish woman, but even fools deserved not to be used.

As Wink and our new crewmate pulled up on the campground side of the river, Julianne hurried to catch the bow of the dory and waded into the cold water. "Give me a kiss," she tittered. "I have to walk out tomorrow morning," she said. "My last night in camp, huh?" She leaned close to him and said in a stage whisper, "I pitched my tent right up there by that tree; see it?"

Wink said, "Now, remember what I said. Discretion, right?"

I heard Nancy banging a metal spoon on a pot lid to call us to dinner then, mercifully distracting me from this scene. I wanted to know how Wink Oberley got away with what he was doing. I wanted him to stop. I wanted most of all for him to take his vulgar, bullying, confounding act most anywhere else.

I headed up to Jerry and Don's tent and asked, "Do they have a real live telephone at Phantom Ranch?" I hoped that Faye had discovered something so damning that we could kick Wink off our trip before he managed to kill somebody.

Jerry said, "Sure. We'll stop there in the morning."

"Good."

I pulled on a waterproof parka and headed toward the kitchen area. Danielle and Olaf had polenta pie ready, a thick stew of polenta with fried hamburger, black beans, stewed tomatoes, black olives, salsa, and a whole lot of cheese. I heaped my plate and stood up to eat, cramming in the calories in an effort to warm up. It was beginning to spit rain. I hurried through my meal so that I could climb into our tent and avoid hypothermia. I preferred to live.

Julianne slunk up to the kitchen table. She grabbed a plate but appeared to have trouble deciding what to do next. Following her gaze, I noted that Wink was rowing back across the river.

Danielle said, "Fill your plate and chow it down, Julianne; you'll need the carbs to make it up that trail tomorrow."

"Huh," said Julianne. "Yeah, nine miles, right? Huh. Nine miles, is it?" She burst into tears.

Danielle heaped polenta onto Julianne's plate and dragged her away toward her tent, saying, "Nine miles is nothing!"

"I don't want to be that far away from him!" bawled Julianne.

"Nice stove," said Nancy, changing the subject.

Hakatai had brought a replacement for the stove that broke the night up in Marble Canyon when the wind blew so hard, fetching down the Bright Angel Trail strapped to his back. "It was nothing," he said. "A camp stove doesn't weigh that much, and my dry bag was strapped to one of the mules. I thought about loading my backpack with rocks just to add weight." He laughed. "And I'd forgotten to give the stove to the man at the mule barn at the South Rim."

After helping with the dishwashing after dinner I poured a cup of cocoa for Brendan. I then made one for Fritz but couldn't find him. As I scanned the hillside for him, I spied Wink, moving upriver.

"Looks like he's heading for his nightly prayer meeting," said Molly.

"Needs to get some more of that old-time religion," Nancy agreed.

"Got his Sunday-go-to-meetin' plaid shirt on," said Jerry.

"You'd think he could have bought one that fit him," Nancy said. "Or give it a bath now that he's spilled polenta on it."

"Oh, he didn't buy that shirt," said Jerry. "He pinched it off that guy who drove his dory down to Lees Ferry."

"How d'you know that?" asked Molly.

"I asked him," Jerry replied. "He was quite proud of himself. Imagine."

I wondered if Wink was headed out for another chat with that pretty young thing who played her guitar for the church group, and wondered, too, what the nature of their acquaintance was. He had seemed a different person when I came across the two of them the evening before, when we were all camped at Nevills. Why couldn't Wink have shown Brendan the same care he had shown the girl?

I spotted Fritz then, tracking Wink around through the trees. "What's he up to?" I asked Brendan.

Brendan's face was full of storms. "I told him not to say anything," he muttered. "I can handle this myself."

"Handle what?"

"Damned Wink. *Damn* Wink!"

"*Tell* me!" I insisted.

Brendan walked to the edge of the clearing and turned his face toward the trees. "I told Dad not to do anything, but he was so upset when he asked how the boat got loose, and I said I didn't know. He asked if I'd done anything to the lines, like touched them or anything, and I said no, because I hadn't, but then he asked if Wink . . ." He hung his head in shame, as if the whole horror of the experience were his fault.

"Wink untied your line, Brendan? *Really?*"

Brendan sighed, the sound wind makes when it rustles dry leaves. "The raft began to drift just after the dory left, and Em . . ."

I waited, letting him speak when he was ready.

Another sigh. He said, "I heard him laughing."

Diary of Holly Ann St. Denis
April 10, Phantom Ranch

Dear God,

Lord, why is this all so difficult for me? Do You test me? I am here, Your humble servant. I know that my trials are as nothing compared to what Jesus Your Son suffered on the cross. When I play my guitar for You, I feel Your Love raining down from above. Then "Uncle" Terry looks at me and I see the devil, Your fallen son. I know that we're all Your children and like Jesus Your Son I should love him. Why do we make life hell for each other? I'm not afraid to speak straight to You, Lord. WHY DO YOU ALLOW THIS? What would You have me do?

PRAISE God!

Lord I believe; help thou mine unbelief!

I thought I was safe from him last night at Cremation Campground because the tents were so close together, but he found me on the trail to the latrine and he said I looked ill and did I need him to lay on his hands and heal me and I said no I was fine. I had my period was all, but I didn't tell him that, because Mom says he thinks such things are the sign of women's sin. Then he insisted, and put his hands on me in that way that makes me feel sick like I'm going to throw up. Is there something wrong with me, Lord? He says I'm not receiving his blessing correctly. He whispered that I'm a growing woman now, old enough to serve him in the ways You designed me to serve him. Is that true? Just then Dr. Ober-ley came down that path and started to sing one of Your holy hymns, real loud, and of course "Uncle" Terry had to let go of me and move away, like it was all a lie that he was going to heal me in the first place. Dr. O just stood there looking all friendly and "Uncle" Terry slithered off like a snake.

I like Dr. O. He gave me and Mom a ride in his dory between the big rapids yesterday so we could have some privacy from everyone, and he told us stories about the rocks and all the creatures that lived in the waters before the Flood killed them. Dr. O treated Mom really nice and made her happy. When it got colder because the wind came up and the clouds came over he let us wrap up in his sleeping bag, and it was just so jolly riding along over the waters like we were in an old-fashioned sleigh. We laughed and told jokes and we all sang silly songs like before Mom found Jesus. It felt a little naughty, but Mom looked years younger and Dr. O told her so and that made her even happier. I like thinking of these things much more than what happened at Cremation.

I was still standing there on the trail to the latrine with Dr. O when Mom came down to use it and found us there. I told her that Dr. O was just keeping me company while I "recovered" from "Uncle" Terry's lay-ing on of hands, and she asked what I meant by that, sort of angry, but Dr. O said in this real calm voice, "You know exactly what she means, Lisette," and she looked from him to me and got real quiet. Then Dr. O said, "I'll just leave you two here so you can have a chat," and he wan-dered up the path. So Mom didn't seem to have anything to say to me then, and I couldn't figure out what to say either. We moved in behind the screen of leaves that gives us privacy when we're using the latrine and suddenly we heard a man's voice we didn't recognize. He was talking really angry at Dr. O. He said, "I am ordering you to keep your hands off my boy!" and Dr. O said, "What are you talking about?" The man said, "You're a filthy coward! If you have something to say to me, say it straight! Leave my son in peace! If you go anywhere near him between here and Diamond Creek I will kill you!"

Heavenly Father, this really frightened me, the idea that there was someone out there who could hate a man like Dr. O. So I peeked between the leaves so I'd know who said it. It was a big man, very tall, and he had one hand out like he was going to reach for Dr. O's throat. I was so scared! And now here we sit at the riverbank at Phantom Ranch because Mom took off before we could launch saying she had to make some phone calls from the ranger station.

Please, Lord, don't let anything happen to Dr. Oberley. He is the one kind man in this place.

APRIL 9–10: THE OVENS OF THE EARTH

Fritz was unwilling to discuss what he had said to Wink with me when he returned to our tent at Cremation Campsite. Brendan was already waiting, curled up in his sleeping bag trying to look like he was doing his math homework. Fritz was clearly upset, but he just shucked off his sandals and jeans and climbed into his own sleeping bag and rolled over and faced the wall of the tent. It was a long time before I slept, but I am sure that Fritz was still awake when I did.

In the morning Wink encouraged Julianne to get an early start up the trail to the South Rim: "I see weather building," he said, pointing at the single tiny cloud that remained from the day before. "Really, take your breakfast in your pockets and eat on the way. You don't want to get caught out there."

Danielle told Julianne that this was probably a good idea. "I'm going to run parts of it, so you get started and I'll catch you up, okay?"

Wink took Julianne across the river to Phantom Ranch and returned with our final new passenger, Glenda Fittle. She was breezy and confident and chatted us all up, explaining that she was acquainted with Wink from an earlier trip down the canyon. Her father had drawn a private permit for that trip but had made some off-the-record deal with Wink to help them out. She and Wink had become "friends," she informed us, letting the word roll out just a fraction of a second longer than might have been entirely necessary, but she wanted us all to know that more than anything she was just delighted to be back down in this big, gorgeous canyon.

Self-assigned ferryman Wink had rowed one girlfriend across the river to fetch another. I had to admire his finesse.

Glenda immediately set to work and helped clean up the breakfast dishes. She had hiked down to Phantom Ranch several days earlier and had stayed at one of the cabins, she told us. I envied the fact that she thus was up early, showered, freshly coifed, and ready and rearing to go at 7:30 A.M.

After loading up at Cremation we stopped at Phantom Ranch to receive Glenda and Hakatai's personal gear and stow our shipment of fresh vegetables that had been brought down by mules. Fritz told us we could take an hour to admire the rustic allure of Phantom Ranch and use the "real live flush toilets," and make any calls we needed to make.

Fritz and Brendan and I hiked up to the cantina, which was built of large granite cobbles that were no doubt pulled straight out of Bright Angel Creek. Brendan had lost a sandal when the raft flipped, and as he ambled into the little shop in the cantina to see if they had a new pair for him to wear, I drew Fritz aside. "What happened last night between you and Wink?" I asked.

Fritz scowled. "I'd rather not talk about that."

"And I'd rather you did. Really. I'm worried, Fritz."

"Well, don't be."

"But that idiot untied the raft with Brendan in it!"

"He denied doing that."

"I don't care what he said, I care what he did!"

Fritz's jaw muscles tightened. "I took care of things. Put it out of your mind. Relax." Fritz stared away from me, keeping an eye on his son through the doorway.

Giving up, I hurried around to the side and found the pay phone that was mounted near the toilets. "It's me, Em," I told Faye when she answered my call. "Have you found out anything?"

"Nothing unexpected," she began. "That address in Rocky Hill is an apartment over a bar on a side street. He has a medical discharge from the army, which won't surprise you, but it's for a back injury, not anything psychological. He's got one prior for indecent exposure, but it was some kind of a party weekend in Princeton and the judge let the whole lot of them off. Beyond that it's mostly misdemeanor stuff. No DUI, no drunk and disorderly, no wife beating, or at least none has been reported. There's one record of being hauled in for a bar fight in Flagstaff, but he was let go on his own recognizance. There is no car registered to him. There's a civil suit pending because he borrowed someone else's car and left it near the Philadelphia airport, where it was vandalized and collected parking tickets. That's interesting because he doesn't currently have a valid driver's license, having let his Arizona one lapse several years ago. Sorry, that's all I've gotten so far, except for this: He hasn't been seen around the Geology Department for several months. Oh, and he's in bad with the department secretary because he used her phone for long distance calls without permission."

"Where did they say he's been?"

"My cousin managed to find the guy who shared an office with Oberley at the university, and the guy had no idea where he was and made it very clear that he was not the least bit interested to find out. So how are things going? Has he kept his hands off Brendan?"

"No." I recounted the tale of Brendan's ride down Sockdolager Rapid.

"Shit!" said Faye. "And Fritz hasn't sent him packing?"

"They had some kind of a come-to-Jesus talk last night, by the looks of it, but all I could get out of Fritz this morning is that Wink denies untying the line to our raft. Wink is a slippery little snake, a fluid liar, well practiced at wiggling out of things. Sometimes I'm not sure if he knows when he's telling the truth or not. And you know Fritz."

"Yeah, Mr. Honorable."

I sighed. "That's why I love him. And he puts up with me into the bargain."

"You don't give yourself enough credit, Em. So where do we go from here?"

We. Where do we go. Until Faye spoke that word I hadn't realized how alone I felt with this problem. "For now, it seems like we're stuck with him, because once you're on this river with your equipment, there's really only one way off it, and that's to row your boat all the way to Diamond Creek and pull it out by truck or trailer. But the thing that gets me is that I really can't figure out why he's here."

"What do you mean? Does he have anywhere else to be?"

"No, but he's not getting along with us, and as near as I can figure, he's not even trying. One of the other women on this trip trotted out her theory about his having issues about authority figures, but would he come on a trip with a bunch of people he doesn't know just to play with that kind of demon?"

"I'm with you, Em. If you think there's something going on under the surface, it may not be just another hidden rock. Meanwhile, best of luck, and if I think of anything, I'll leave a message in your voice mail at home so you can retrieve it. Will that work? And if you think of something, call."

"Thanks for the stove," I said.

"That was easy. Make sure you give Fritz lots of sex so he stays as calm as possible."

"You think of everything."

We signed off after that, and I headed into the bathroom. It was indeed a delight to use a proper porcelain potty after nine days with the portable pit toilets we were required to use, and as I washed my hands at the sink afterward and splashed clear water on my face I noted what a novelty it was that the wash water wasn't carrying a load of silt. I was startled to see my own reflection in the mirror. It was strange to realize that in just nine days I had gotten so far away from civilization that I wasn't even worried about what I looked like anymore and didn't even entirely recognize myself. I stood and stared for a while, contemplating this. So many things had shifted. I was loving life on the river, at least when I wasn't preoccupied with the threat Wink posed to Brendan, and when I wasn't turning good energy into bad by disliking the man so intensely. I stared at my browned face, deciding that my dislike was a matter of distrust and was therefore quite reasonable, but did I have to let it sour my experience of this magical place?

I took a walk a little way down Bright Angel Canyon to the mule pen and admired the plucky little animals. Day after day they trotted up and down next to the sheer drop-offs along the South Kaibab Trail heavily laden with supplies and equipment and tourists. One of them lifted his head long enough to stare at me, as if to ask, *Why are you humans such a strange species? Just look at the hassles you create! Can't you just be happy feeding on some nice grain?*

For a moment I felt overwhelmed by the great cluster of longings and wishes and wants and needs that came with being human. I wanted to run up the trail that led up Bright Angel Canyon to the North Rim and keep on running. *You can deal with this*, I told myself firmly. *Don't be so emotional. Get going. Fritz and Brendan are waiting for you.*

Emotional. Why *was* I being so emotional? Usually being out of doors was a tonic for me, but over the last few days I had grown unusually tired. I told myself that big water was a stressor. And it had been cold and windy, and maybe that was why Fritz was so testy, too. Having thus rationalized most of my worries into a small smear, I said good-bye to the mules and headed back toward the bathrooms for one more experience of modern plumbing.

As I rounded the ranger station, I bumped right smack into some sort of domestic squabble. I recognized the woman with the fancy sandals and Holly Ann, the teenaged girl who played the guitar, and the man with the big Adam's apple who had led them all in prayer when they camped next to us at Nankoweap. The man didn't look very prayerful now; in fact, he looked very angry. He was leaning close to Ms. Sandals with his face all red, giving her a dose of words, struggling to keep his voice low so that he wouldn't be overheard. The woman looked to be in a full-on state of drama about something or other, and Holly Ann's eyes were round with fright. There was something downright ugly about the Adam's apple guy's manner, so I slowed down and put on a big grin and said, "Hey there, Holly Ann, so how's your trip coming along? Did you like the big rapids yesterday?"

As the girl turned toward me I could see the relief flush down across her body, but her eyes stayed wide with anxiety. "Hello, Ms. Hansen," she said, and added, "It's really nice to see you again," in a tone that suggested that she'd like me to stick around.

The man reached out one of his large hands, applied it to the woman's arm, and tugged her toward the river. Pulled off balance, she lurched toward him and had to swing out one foot to catch herself. The action of landing hard on that foot yanked a gasp out of her.

I looked down to see what had made her gasp and saw that her feet were badly torn up in those dainty little sandals. "Jesus!" I exclaimed, immediately sorry for my choice of epithet, and quickly followed it with "Wow, is there anything I can do to help you with those blisters? We've got a good first-aid kit on our rafts, which I'm sure are parked right next to yours. I mean really, let me help you!"

The woman gawked at me wild-eyed, as if paralyzed by my offer.

I stared back at her, amazed to see that much eye makeup this far from civilization.

"Mo-om!" Holly Ann urged. "Really, that's a *good idea!* Let's let Ms. Hansen *help* us!"

"I'm sure that won't be necessary," said the man, suddenly courteous to the point of effusiveness. He smiled sweetly at me, but tightened his grip on the woman.

Finally the woman spoke. "It's all right, Holly Ann," she said, her voice heavy with resignation. Suddenly her eyes focused on me and she said, "You're with Dr. Oberley's group?"

I almost gagged on the idea of calling Wink "Dr." and I wanted to assure her hotly that he was in my group, not the other way around.

She said, "Please tell Dr. Oberley that Lisette says . . . to have a nice trip, and . . . to, er, stay in touch."

At her words, the man's face clouded an ugly red, and he twisted the woman's arm so fiercely that she winced.

"Sure, I'll tell him," I said. As it was clear that by staying I was only adding to the woman's agony, I gave Holly Ann a sympathetic glance, excused myself, and headed toward the river. It was several minutes before Holly Ann managed to get her hobbling mother down to the rafts. Brendan trotted over to say hello. I cocked an ear to listen.

"Oh, hi!" said Holly Ann. "You're Brendan, right? Mrs. Hansen's son?"

"Em's my stepmom," said Brendan, unaware that I could hear him. "And she isn't *Mrs.* Hansen exactly. Our name's Calder, but she kept her name when she married my dad because she said she was so old already that she wouldn't be able to keep track of a new name."

"How old is she?"

"I don't know exactly. Forty-something. Really old."

"Does she have children from another marriage?"

"Nope. This is the first time she's been married. She told me that she had to kiss an awful lot of toads before one of them turned out to be a prince."

"So you're an only child?"

"Yeah."

"Me, too. My mom wasn't even married before. I was born in sin, she said, but now we've found Christ, and he's my brother, and our sins have been washed away." Her tone was matter-of-fact, just saying how things were in her everyday life.

I listened intently, amazed at the easy candor that could exist between two adolescents who happened to find themselves on the river together. It occurred to me then how lonely Brendan must be, and perhaps this girl was, too.

Holly Ann brought the subject of their discussion back to me. "Your stepmom's really neat. She's a scientist and all."

I thought, *Thank you for that!*

"Yeah, I like Em a lot. I kind of keep putting it to her about stuff my mom teaches me from the Bible, but she's real respectful and doesn't try to tell me what to think. She explains what she thinks but stays out of my stuff."

"That's really cool."

"Yeah, it's so complicated hearing one thing in school and another thing in church," said Brendan.

"I know what you mean. That's why my mom is home-schooling me. Or rather, why she let my stepdad home-school me. Only he's passed away now, so his brother is teaching me." Out of the corner of my eye I saw her make a face.

"Wow. My mom home-schooled me for a while, so I missed the part about how the earth has layers and stuff. So Em's teaching me that stuff now. I'm supposed to write an independent study report about this river trip, because Dad pulled me out of school to come here."

"That's pretty cool. So your mom was okay with you coming on this trip and being out of school and all?"

"Well, not really, but we made a deal that I'd do church camp this summer and join her church if she let Dad have me for this. I usually spend the whole summer with Dad, but because of this I'll have to do that."

This was the first I had heard of the deal Fritz had made to get custody of his son for the duration of this trip. My heart sank. I had hoped that Brendan's presence indicated a stage of conciliation between the divorced partners in parenting, but I had been wrong.

Fritz called to his son. "About ready to launch?" he asked. "Come on, Brendan! We've got to make some miles!"

We loaded up and pushed off from the beach and hustled on down the river. Glenda Fittle had settled right in on the forward seat in Wink's dory, her hair tucked up in a bun underneath a broad sun hat, holding herself with a prim upright posture and bearing. She reminded me of Katharine Hepburn in *The African Queen*.

Mungo rowed close by us to get a beer from the drop bag. "Looks like he got himself a new training mare," he mumbled.

Fritz pantomimed covering Brendan's tender ears, but the lad swatted his father's hands away, saying, "I know what that means, Dad!"

Mungo chuckled. "Well, let's hope this one runs him harder, so he stays out of mischief."

The day began to unfold with the rhythm of the oars. The narrowed chasm of the inner gorge framed a cobalt blue sky, and at the foot of Hermit Trail I saw another pair of California condors rising into its updrafts.

Brendan said, "I talked to the rangers about condors, and you know what they said? Everything we thought about how those birds mate for life isn't necessarily so. They don't even always raise their broods as a pair. They've got a trio of condors raising chicks here, a girl condor and two boys! And there's another place where they've seen two girls and a guy!"

"Ménage à trois," I said.

"What?"

"It's a French term, meaning—"

Fritz swung an oar sharply across the surface of the water, splashing me. I shut up. I still had so much to learn about parenthood.

It was a fine, sunny day, and though it was early enough in the year that the sun angle was still low and thus did not reach every corner of the Inner Gorge, bounced light caressed the fluted surfaces of the Vishnu Schist, which now rose like a strange, silvery temple above the riverbank. In places, the water had carved this ancient rock into fabulous arabesques, and here and there it was shot through with wide bands of pink granite. As our oars and the current carried us past, we pointed out our favorites, took photographs, and finally just stared quietly in awe.

"This is very different rock from that stuff upriver," Brendan said sagely.

"Yes, it is," I affirmed. "Schist is metamorphic rock. Remember when I was telling you about how the continents move around? And how they can rift apart or crash into each other? Well, all those tilted layers below the Great Unconformity got that way when the continents pulled apart, and here we see evidence of a collision."

Brendan opened his waterproof day bag and got out his notebook and pencil. "Draw me a picture of how it works, Em. Please?"

I took his notebook and drew the classic diagram that showed the engine of the earth, with its three major layers—the superhot core, the soft-solid mantle, and the cooled crust—all sliced open like an apple so I could draw in arrows showing how heat flowed from the center out to space. "There are convection cells in the mantle, just like in boiling oatmeal. As heat rises here, the cooled bits descend. But here's the key thing: This stuff that's rising from the mantle is mostly dense minerals, heavy in iron and magnesium, so it's just as happy to sink again as it cools, but there are also less dense minerals that tend to accumulate up at the surface, stuff that's rich in aluminum and silicon. So as the dense stuff rises, it makes basalts, which are rich in iron and magnesium, and that flows out underwater and becomes ocean floor. You're aware that the earth is about three-quarters ocean; well, under all that ocean are crustal plates made of basalt. Got that?"

Brendan nodded, staring at my drawing.

"Okay," I said. "So what do you think happens to the less dense stuff?"

"It stays at the surface?"

"That's what we see, yes. If you look at the continents, you'll see that they, too, are big crustal plates, but they're less dense, so they float like marshmallows in your cocoa."

Brendan smiled. "I like cocoa."

"So do I. And I like continental crust a whole lot." I pointed toward the rocks of the Inner Gorge. "Here we have schists and granites. The granites are made of feldspars, quartz, and mica which are mostly silicon and aluminum. In fact, quartz is nothing but silicon."

"So why did it come up as granite instead of basalt?"

"Brendan, you ask all the right questions. The deal is that it did not come all the way up from the mantle as granite. Instead, the lighter minerals slowly gather at the surface and accumulate on the ocean floors—silt and sand and dead critter bodies and what have you. Then, because those convection cells are sort of dragging the crustal plates around, the plates crash into each other. They slide apart where there's a big boil of new basalt coming up—we call those mid-ocean ridges, and every once in a while they open up on land, like in the African Rift Valley—but then there are places like this." I drew two convection cells rolling toward each other, pushing two crustal plates together. "What do you think happens there?"

"They crash!"

"Yes, they do, and if one of them is an ocean bottom plate it dives back down, because it's heavier, or colder, and the continent slides up on top." I added that to my drawing. "Then what happens?"

"I . . . don't know."

"Well, the ocean plate melts, see, because it's going back downstairs where it's so hot that it turns from rock back to soup."

"Really, Em: soup, marshmallows, cocoa? You're ruining food for me."

"It's just a handy metaphor. But the plate that goes downstairs is carrying a lot of crud that accumulated on it, right? All that silt and water and dead critters and so forth get squashed under unimaginable pressures." I pointed at the schist that formed the canyon walls. "So that's where this comes from. Think of a nice siltstone that's been baked in the oven."

"There you go again, thinking of food."

Fritz chimed in. "It's kind of amazing that she doesn't weigh three hundred pounds, eh?"

"Go ahead and mock me," I said cheerily. "Okay now, the descending plate continues to go down, and all of that crud that's riding on it has a cooler melting point than the basalt, so it melts first, and because it's less dense, it wants to rise up through fractures that have formed from all that smashing and crunching. A great big blob of rock pudding comes up and up and up until it finds its point of neutral buoyancy, and it begins to cool. All of this takes a long time, and it cools slowly because it's still down there several miles, and the rock above it is a good insulator. So it keeps finding its way into cracks in the crust above, and eventually some of it shoots up to the surface. Now, because the two plates are jammed together, they've made a thick spot in the crust, many miles thicker than it usually is, and it has that hot juice squirting out of it. We call those volcanoes."

"Like Hawaii?"

"No . . . Hawaii is sort of a special case. It's made of basalt that comes straight up through the ocean floor from the mantle. Think instead of Japan, with Mount Fuji. This type of volcano spews lavas that are rich in silicon and aluminum. The name for that kind of lava is andesite, like the Andes Mountains, but don't worry your head about the names, just know that this kind is full of quartz and it is connected down below to a big tub of hot stuff that's cooling into a granite, which is the same thing as andesite only it cools slowly. Are we good?"

Brendan gave me a thumbs-up.

"So here's the thing," I said. "As the oatmeal continues to boil and these rafts of less dense crust form, they start to bang into each other and fuse together into bigger and bigger platforms."

"Like lint," said Brendan. "Sorry, I couldn't come up with a food metaphor."

I nodded. "Lint will do. Like lint accumulating in a lint trap, building up and building up. These microcontinents, that's what we call them, get crunched together and bump up high, and the volcano parts on top are sticking up, so they erode down, dumping more silt and sand into the oceans that gets swept up into schists and melted again into blobs that become granites, continuing the cycle. Eventually we just get a bunch of granite that has rings of younger and younger microcontinents accreted around it."

"Like an onion." Brendan gave me a cheesy grin.

"Like an onion. And these older center parts are pretty stable, like marshmallows floating around—"

"On the oatmeal."

"On the oatmeal. Yeah, and eventually these marshmallows get big enough that they start to slam together, too. So now you've got ocean floor crust banging against ocean floor crust and arguing over who's going to go down, and continent banging continent and arguing over who's going on top. Can you name a place where two continents are slamming together right now?"

"No."

"Try Asia. India started out way south near Antarctica and has slammed into Asia, forming a big wrinkle in the crust that we call the Himalayan Range. If we had Google Earth on this raft I could show you how India is pushing so hard against Asia that it's kind of extruding a bunch of it down through China, or at least that's how it looks. But then there's a third kind of collision, and that's between an ocean floor plate and a continent."

"What happens then?"

"The ocean floor goes down, no argument, and you get the schist and the andesitic volcanoes and the granite. An example is the Andes in South America. Or the Sierra Nevada in California, only that's mostly done making volcanoes. The floor of the ocean was busy sliding underneath California, and it dragged a spreading center down under with it. For some reason the spreading center held together and it created a bulge that's now underneath Nevada and western Utah. So remember when you mimed that accordion? You were right, that bulge of heat is stretching everything apart from Reno clear east to Salt Lake City, and as that happens there are blocks of land that stay high and form mountain ranges and others that drop down and form valleys."

Suddenly Brendan's smile vanished. He mumbled something below our hearing.

"What's that?"

"It's something Mom's pastor says when he's talking about where the waters of Noah's Flood went. Something about the valleys going down and the waters receding."

I was quiet for a moment, then said gently, "I'd like to just round out my dissertation on plate tectonics if I could. There's one more kind of motion between crustal plates, and that's when they just slide past each other. So that place where the ocean floor was sliding under California? Well, the plates are actually sliding over a curved surface, and the turbulence of the heat convection can make them turn, so what was a collision zone turned and became a very long fault line, called the San Andreas Fault." I set down Brendan's notebook. "I think that's a lot for now, okay?"

"Sure," he said and put his book away.

◈

Life goes on, whatever mental cares it throws us, and on a river trip, the water just keeps on flowing down the canyon, kicking up into big, splashy rooster-tail waves whenever it flows over something that creates drag. Crystal Rapid was the next big one. It was another choppy run of waves, but the sun was shining, Brendan's ankle was improving, Fritz had him stay on shore while we scouted and tied the line to our raft in a way it could not possibly be tampered with, and all was good. Large as this water was, it seemed almost tame after hurrying through Sockdolager in search of a missing person, and I got my mantra back together and was actually beginning to enjoy myself again after the frights of that cold, windy day.

We made camp and had a dinner of boiled potatoes and sausages and cleaned up afterward, and by and by I noticed that I hadn't seen my husband or stepson for a little while. Figuring that they must have turned in early, I headed toward our tent, and sure enough as I walked up that path I could hear them talking. I was walking on soft sand, so they didn't hear me coming. I was just bending to open the tent flap when I realized that they were having a pretty important talk, the kind that I really shouldn't interrupt.

"But you and Mom got divorced," Brendan was saying. "Why, Dad? Why didn't you stay together if you love her?"

I froze, afraid to be caught overhearing these words, and because of that I was right there listening to his answer.

"Of course I love your mother, son. I wouldn't have married her if I didn't love her. We couldn't have made you if we didn't love each other. It's just . . . Well, there are many kinds of love, and sometimes you start out with one kind and it becomes another. Sometimes things don't go the way you need them to go to keep it together." He was quiet for a while, then added, "Even when folks get really mad at each other they can love each other just the same, but if that anger is covering up a great hurt, and you'd rather feel anger than pain . . ." He let it trail off, leaving a few things to his son's imagination.

I stared up at the stars, wishing I was most anywhere else, wishing simultaneously that Fritz would say something more.

Brendan spoke. "Was it Mom's church stuff? I mean, I know you don't go to church, and . . . well . . ."

"I don't think it's my place to talk about her religion. That's a personal choice, guaranteed by the First Amendment of the U.S. Constitution and has to be respected, just so long as no one is getting hurt?"

I winced, noting that his statement had ended as a question. *Was* Brendan getting hurt? Had his mother's beliefs—or perhaps her use of them in postdivorce politics—edged into a place where psychic injury might occur? Where exactly along the line of parenting did imposition of doctrine become, at minimum, abuse of power?

Brendan sighed. "She says that because I'm thirteen now I should join her church."

Should. The big conscience word. But *should* a mother's conscience, however well intended, dictate her son's beliefs?

Fritz murmured, "You've got to follow your heart's dictates there, son."

They were both quiet for a moment, and I was about to make a noise and head into the tent when Fritz suddenly spoke a flood of words very rapidly: "I don't know what I would do in your shoes. At your age I couldn't have made a decision like that to stand up in front of a whole congregation and say I believed *X* or *Y*. I've gone along with a lot of things, I suppose, but I've always tried to keep my mind open, because sometimes—oftentimes—I'm wrong about things, and it's important to have room to catch a mistake and change it. People differ; that's what politics are all about, and when they're done well, politics are civil. Your mom and I try to stay civil, because most of all we both love you in a way that will never change, and it's just not fair to let our differences mess up your life."

"Thanks, Dad."

I began to ease backward a few steps so I could make a noise a little farther away and thus, literally, cover my tracks. But they were not yet done with this conversation.

Brendan said, "You know that other group that's been camping near us? The one with the girl with the guitar?"

"Mm?"

"Well, she says her stepdad, who was this famous TV preacher, said everyone who didn't believe exactly as they did was going to burn in hell." He laughed briefly, the nervous kind that's supposed to say something's funny when it really isn't.

"Wow."

"Do you think God is really some guy that burns people for things like that? I mean, what about all the kids who don't have TVs, so they've never heard this rule? Do they get burned?"

Fritz chuckled. "Now you're talking about the difference between God and what a preacher thinks he's heard."

"What do you mean?"

"Well, maybe God's will is like a radio. The transmitter might be just great, but if your receiver's kind of weak you get a lot of static. When I'm flying an airplane I have to ask the air traffic controllers to repeat stuff all the time because I can't always understand what they've saying."

Now Brendan laughed. "Is that why there are so many religions that are all different but all think they've got the straight poop?"

"Could be."

"Well then, why do people follow preachers like that TV guy?"

"I don't know. I heard him once when I was flipping channels one morning, and he sounded kind of angry, but remember what I said about anger covering up hurt? The thing is, anger sounds more powerful than hurt, and it feels a whole lot more powerful than fear. It's this energy that gets you moving, while pain and fear can freeze you to the spot. So maybe people like to follow anger because they think it makes them strong, or they perceive an angry preacher as being strong. Or they see that anger as powerful. Or they feel like they've screwed up somehow and that guy is like a big mean dad who says, 'If you do this I'll forgive you and make it all better.' Or . . . I don't know, maybe the people who like to listen to that don't know how to make decisions and that angry preacher guy is willing to make them for them."

I stared up at the brilliance of the stars that danced across the heavens, marveling at my husband's wisdom. I felt privileged, even as an eavesdropper, to hear what he was saying. My heart rose with pride, and I shifted, ready to just jump into the tent and join the conversation, when Brendan brought up one more thing.

"Dad?"

"Yes."

"That girl I was telling you about?"

"Mm-hm."

"I saw her with that other man? That one she calls uncle? And he . . . um . . . well, they didn't know I was watching, and . . ."

When Brendan's pause stretched into silence, Fritz said, "It's okay, you can tell me."

"He was touching her, Dad, in ways I could tell she didn't like, and it looked . . ."

I heard things shift inside the tent as Fritz rolled toward his son. "He did *what?*"

"He said he was preparing her to 'serve.'"

Fritz's voice deepened into a growl. "Are they still near us on the river?"

"No. I think they motored ahead and were going to pull out soon."

"That's not only abuse of influence, that's molestation and child abuse. It's sexual assault. There is no gray area here. What he is doing is wrong and it's against the law!"

"But Dad?"

"Yes, son."

Brendan's voice was rising in pitch. "That uncle guy is running that church now. How's Holly Ann going to get away?"

Fritz was quiet for a long time, no doubt thinking through the complexities of his son's fears, the conundrum of his failed marriage, and the legal land mines these issues presented. Finally he said simply, "Son, that church is not above the law."

Notes of Gerald Weber, Chief Ranger
Investigation into death of George Oberley
April 19, 10:30 A.M.

Analysis of items found with body of George Oberley:

Shirt: Men's, size L, short-sleeved, plaid, manufactured by Cabela's. Appears fairly new. Shirt a size small, pulling at buttons across chest and belly.

Shorts: Men's size 38 (?) khaki cargo short, extremely worn, no label. Nothing in pockets. No underwear present.

Footwear: One rubber "flip-flop" sandal, men's size L showing heavy wear. Matching sandal not present.

Life vest: Extrasport B-22 Highfloat, dark blue, size L, marked as property of Canyon Rentals, Inc., serial number CR-452.

NOTE: Telephoned Canyon Rentals re: life vest. Jane Hickock in Supply Department checked records and stated that this item was rented to Fritz Calder of Salt Lake City, Utah, and delivered to him at Lees Ferry on March 31 of this year. Calder also rented their "oar raft package" which includes a 16-foot raft, two sets of oars, a full-sized cooler, drop bag, frame, and other rigging. Cross-check with sat phone communications shows a Fritz Calder first reported Oberley missing. Cross-check with list of rafting trips currently on river shows Calder launched April 1 as alternate trip leader for 21-day private oar trip.

NB: Calder party due to pull out at Diamond Creek in approximately 48 hours. FOCUS HERE FIRST.

APRIL 11: FISH AND VISITORS

IN THE MORNING I TOOK A BATH IN THE RIVER, REALLY JUST A LITTLE soap in the most critical places. I was, in fact, turning into a fine example of "river trash," having long since lost my hairbrush. I just ran my fingers through my hair each morning, and I had never been one to worry about a little dirt on my shirts or pants, much less my face. I was getting a fabulous tan across my nose and forearms, and during camp time when I could wear shorts, I was beginning to lose the shark-bait-whiteness on my legs, too, though my feet were turning strange colors from being packed into neoprene booties for long periods of time.

I had taken a long walk before I could hope to get to sleep after overhearing the conversation between Fritz and Brendan, pacing up and down along the dark nighttime waters of the Colorado River. The pain of children haunts me that way, wakening ghosts of my own. The girl with the guitar was far downriver now, where I could not help her, and that tied my stomach into knots, and I had my own small world to try to keep right side up, too.

Things actually seemed to have settled down within our own rafting party. By the end of the second day after the Sockdolager fiasco, I let myself hope that maybe Wink Oberley's tricks were over. Glenda seemed to be an excellent influence on him, and we had all cheerfully forgotten Julianne's embarrassing posturing as a thing of the past.

But then we floated by the foot of Bass Canyon.

There are trails from the canyon's rims that come all the way down to the river, and one of them comes down Bass, which sounds like the name of a fish but was in fact named for a fellow who built a tourist destination at this location in about 1890. There was a photograph of him in the river guide posing with his trusty animals, Joe the burro and Shep the dog. We did not see any remnants of Mr. Bass's tourist empire as we approached the mouth of that side canyon, but we did see someone we all knew: Julianne Wertz. She was standing there waving, calling to the man who owned her heart. "Woo-hoo, Wi-ink!" she called, now prancing from foot to foot to get his attention. "Winkie dear, I'm here!" There was tremendous excitement in her voice, and it rose to a crescendo of "darlings" and "lover boys" as the man, who was for once caught without words, floated by with his mouth gaping open and both oars out of the water. Glenda Fittle turned and gazed stone-faced through her dark glasses, her elegant spine growing stiffer yet.

Fritz pulled hard on the oars to get our craft out of the current and rammed our boat up onto the beach right by Julianne's feet. "How nice to see you, Julianne," he told her, "and . . . how unexpected!"

Julianne had stopped prancing. She did not look at us. Her body had gone strangely still, except for her neck, which swiveled as she tracked the progress of the dory, which now moved swiftly and with the obvious purpose of evasion down the river and toward the far side of the river.

The kayakers came to the beach beside us, and the other three rafts followed. "Hey, what's up? Are we stopping to look at the *Ross Wheeler*?" Mungo called, referring to a steel boat that had been abandoned on this shore by an unlucky crew in 1915. Then he recognized our former crew mate. "Holy shit, is that you, Julianne?"

The woman's face had grown an ugly shade of red underneath her tan. She began to tremble and was soon shaking with rage.

The dory continued down the river, disappearing from sight.

Julianne stamped a foot. She screamed. She snorted with rage. And words were not enough to express her feelings. Overwhelmed with feeling, she broke from her position and began to run into the river.

"Whoa!" said Mungo, lumbering out of his raft and blocking her progress with his body. "Settle down, woman! You got someone you need to visit with?"

"Yes!" she sputtered. "Yes! I need to talk to Wink! Now!"

Mungo gathered her into a bear hug and spoke soothingly. "No problem. I can row you right across this here river to where he'll be waiting for ya. We all had plans to camp tonight right there at Bass Crossing, just at the other side, and clearly you aren't gonna make it back up to the rim tonight, are ya?"

Hoping to avoid an ugly scene, Fritz directed everyone into taking a stroll over to see the abandoned steel boat. It was a flattened version of the modern Grand Canyon dory that Wink had built, but like it, it had a central cockpit and was decked over fore and aft, with a hatch opening into each compartment. I stared into it, contemplating the metaphor of all the lies Wink had stowed in the wrecked vessel of his life. I felt no pity or sympathy for Julianne, and neither did I feel scorn, I felt only a burgeoning embarrassment.

I was not happy about the prospect of taking her across the river. Even Mungo seemed to have thought twice by the time we had returned to the rafts. "Are you sure you want to go there?" he asked.

Julianne answered by climbing into Mungo's raft. Molly shifted to make room for her, and Hakatai took her backpack and lashed it on top of the load.

"Wait," said Fritz. "You can't go if you don't have a life jacket."

Julianne leveled a withering gaze his way. "Then I'll use the spare," she growled, yanking it out from under the tarp that Mungo had stretched over the top of his load. He had tethered it to the loose end of a cam strap, so she undid the knot and wrestled her way into it.

It was a short ride across the river, but it might as well have been miles. A pall had settled over our little group. Our surprise at first seeing Julianne on the riverbank had dissolved into a collective sense of loss as we watched this woman face her humiliation with such force. The otherworldliness of life on the river and what she thought was love had drawn her back down into the great, wide-open world of the canyon in search of more. She was an addict, and the attentions Wink had shown her were a drug. She would have it now regardless of its cost.

When we reached the other side and tied up by the dory, she hesitated only a moment before charging up the bank to the rock where Wink now sat waiting for her. Glenda Fittle had found herself somewhere else to be, strolling along a trail, admiring the flowers that bloomed there with the composure and self-assurance we had quickly come to expect of her.

Wink did not get up. He greeted his spurned lover with a slight raising of his eyebrows, not even favoring her by removing his fancy dark glasses to look at her with naked eyes.

She stopped five feet from him and again began to tremble. "Why?" she asked, her voice filled with angry, humiliated tears.

Wink tipped his head to one side and crumpled his eyebrows, as if confused by her question. "Oh, come on now," he said. "Everybody has a good time on the river, and what happens on the river stays on the river, right?"

About now I was wondering what Wink's wife might think of this scene, or if she might have viewed it often enough to find it simply tedious. And I wondered if either of his stories was true: that he lived happily with his wife and children in New Jersey when he wasn't out chasing women on the river or that they were separated but for lack of cash still living under the same roof. I now suspected that she had thrown his sorry ass out into the April rains, leaving him with no place to be but right here. Perhaps he had cozied up to the Christian fundamentalist trip because no one else would employ him. His life was a mess, at its tattered ends, and yet he was still scavenging what he could, from Don's granola bars all the way to this woman's fragile honor. How, I wondered, had we gotten so damned lucky as to have him hit rock bottom on our trip?

A standoff ensued, during which Wink kept his ass on that rock and Julianne continued to stand there staring at him, all decision-making power having finally leached out of her. Several minutes passed. The rest of us got busy emptying our nighttime gear out of the boats. We began to pitch our tents, and that evening's cook crew began to set up the kitchen. At last Julianne broke away from the confrontation and walked stiffly down past where Fritz and Brendan were setting up our tent, on down to the beach where the boats were tied up. Nobody was there when she arrived, and we all gave her the privacy of not staring. I could hear her scuffling around with the gear, and figured that she was kicking Wink's dory to work out her frustration. After a while, Mungo sidled down to where she waited, loaded her back into his raft, and rowed her across the current to a place where she could gain access to a spur of the Bass Trail.

The story came out after Wink and Glenda turned in that night, climbing into Glenda's tent like an old married couple.

"She told me her tale as we rowed back across the river," Mungo said, as he nursed three fingers of single-malt Scotch. "I guess he really swept her off her feet, or maybe her footing was a little dicey to begin with, but anyway he told her the whole yarn about being head-over-heels in love with her and so on and so forth, and she bought the whole goddamned lie hook, line, and sinker. He told her he was kind of shy and so he wanted to keep their liaison a secret as best they could, not show it around to everyone else. Then he started sneaking off of an evening to chat with the fundamentalists in the next camp and she got to wondering, but he'd told her it was a paying job, so she convinced herself that he was on the level. She said it was a long hike up the Bright Angel Trail. By the time she got to the top she'd rationalized the whole situation around to thinking this was never-ending true love. Danielle tried to talk sense into her, but no go. So Julianne took a shower at the South Rim and refilled her water bottles and packed her pockets full of snacks and had Danielle drive her to the head of Bass Trail on the hope that she could get down here in time to flag us down. She figured we were still one man short of our full sixteen allowed by the permit, and surely there was plenty of food to go around, and she would just eat less if there wasn't. You'll recall that she still had her sleeping bag here on my raft, because I was going to take it home for her at the end of the trip rather than paying for an uphill load with the mules. I told her it was nuts to start up the Bass Trail again by herself, but she said the hike would do her good, that there was still plenty of daylight and she had extra batteries for her headlamp and plenty of food, and I gave her some more. She seemed to have calmed down. I let her go."

We all listened quietly, as if he were telling us a story that had happened somewhere else or a long time ago.

"Did she have a backcountry pass?" asked Molly. "Do the rangers even know she's out there?"

Mungo hung his head. "I didn't think of any of that until I was all the way back here and it was almost dark. I feel bad letting her go."

Molly patted his shoulder. "She's pretty headstrong once she gets going, Mungo. She'll be all right," but the lines of worry on her face belied what she had said.

Interview of river ranger Maryann Eliasson by Gerald Weber via satellite telephone.
April 19, 11:54 A.M.

Eliasson: You wanted me to call you, sir?

Weber: Yes, Maryann. Report your location, please.

Eliasson: I'm at Stairway Canyon, mile 171. I climbed up to the Tonto when I received your message to call you, so we should have a connection for a while.

Weber: Good, because I have some questions regarding the Calder party that launched April first. You were the ranger on duty at Lees Ferry on that date, am I right?

Eliasson: That is correct.

Weber: Okay then, I have a few items of evidence I wish to discuss with you. First—

Eliasson: Evidence? Is this regarding the death of George Oberley, sir?

Weber: Yes, it is.

Eliasson: Right, go ahead.

Weber: First, the deceased was found wearing a PFD rented from Canyon Outfitters by Fritz Calder, the trip leader.

Eliasson: He was?

Weber: Yes. Why, does that sound odd to you?

Eliasson: Well, yeah, because he had his own gear.

Weber: You mean Calder had his own gear?

Eliasson: Who? No, Wink did. The deceased. I was there when he arrived. He had that old homemade dory of his on a trailer, and he had all his own gear, just like always.

Weber: "Like always." That suggests that the deceased had launched with you before.

Eliasson: Many times. He rowed for several of the commercial companies, and he'd been down the river a number of times with that dory, back when he was doing field work for [pause] oh, I forget what his excuse was. He was one of those guys who just couldn't stay off the river. He'd rig any kind of an excuse to run the river, see.

Weber: Then he was very experienced on the river.

Eliasson: Entirely so.

Weber: Okay, then he did have his own PFD and spare on his—this dory you describe.

Eliasson: Yes, he did. But you're saying he was found wearing somebody else's?

Weber: Yes, a rental checked out to Fritz Calder. Do you recall meeting Calder clearly?

Eliasson: Yes, I do.

Weber: You launch several parties each day, and it's been almost three weeks. What in particular was there about this man, that you remember them?

Eliasson: Well first, there are a whole lot more commercial trips than private, as you know, but he had Oberley with him, which didn't make a whole lot of sense, because Oberley is a pro, and Calder didn't look stupid enough to take Oberley as a friend.

Weber: So you were acquainted with Oberley.

Eliasson: Yes. Well, yeah, everyone knew him.

Weber: How would you characterize him?

Eliasson: What do you mean, sir? His abilities on the river, you mean?

Weber: That, and the man.

Eliasson: Oh. [pause] Well, he was very good at the oars according to anyone who ever saw him row, but he never rose in the ranks in any of the companies because he was sort of a loose cannon. He'd get crosswise with whoever was in charge and switch to another company, or he'd be let go for one reason or another. That was all a while ago. He quit showing up a few years ago.

Weber: But Cleome James was in touch with him?

Eliasson: Sir?

Weber: Cleome James, our dispatcher. There was a connection there.

Eliasson: I don't like to talk about people's personal stuff, sir.

Weber: I prefer to stay out of that myself, but here it is right in our laps.

Eliasson: Yeah, I see what you're saying.

Weber: So is there anything I should know?

Eliasson: About Cleome and Wink?

Weber: Yes.

Eliasson: [pause] Okay, they were involved personally for a short time a year or two back.

Weber: Please continue.

Eliasson: Well, there's not that much to say. It did not go well and it ended poorly. I'd say that Cleome bears some annoyance with the man, but apart from that, it's only what at least half a dozen other women in the area might have to report about him. Really.

Weber: Can you be more specific?

Eliasson: Oh hell, Cleome thought he really cared, but he didn't. But the worst part was that tattoo.

Weber: A tattoo. The one on Oberley?

Eliasson: No, Cleome's. Something about a lost night in Vegas, and she woke up with a sore bottom from a trip to the tattoo parlor she could not recall. It's hard to forget a guy when you've got his love name etched across your left glute. On top of everything she had to find her own way home. So that's the long and the short of it, and she was hurt and all that, but she wouldn't swat a mosquito if it was biting her, so if Oberley was murdered, then somebody else did it. What else can I help you with, sir?

Weber: You know, Maryann, it's kind of a giveaway that you're calling me "sir." Is there something you're nervous about?

Eliasson: Is there something you'd prefer I call you? You rank me, and—

Weber: Let's talk about Fritz Calder, the trip leader.

Eliasson: Yes, sir. Yes, he was the alternate leader of that trip and the permit holder couldn't make it for some reason, so he was it.

Weber: Do you recall anything about his manner around Oberley?

Eliasson: Let me think. Well, Oberley sort of arrived right in the middle of check-in, and I'd say that Calder was sort of annoyed.

Weber: Sort of? How about very.

Eliasson: Well, I remember that Calder had this rock hammer, and by the time Wink was done being a pain in the ass, Calder was banging it against his opposite palm in a way that sort of sent a message.

Weber: A rock hammer? You're sure of that? Not a different sort of hammer?

Eliasson: Yes, I'm sure. I took some geology in college myself, and I remember those things. They're like a regular hammer you'd use for building something, except that the metal head on them goes to a square face on one end and a wedge on the other. If it's a hard-rock hammer it goes to a point, but this was a soft-rock hammer, like you'd use on sedimentary rocks, so it had the wedge. They're mean-looking things, and heavy.

Weber: What was he doing with the hammer?

Eliasson: He just had it in his hand when he first came up to me.

Weber: Then why did he have it? The hammer.

Eliasson: I have no idea, except sometimes people have them on the river. They make a good camp tool. Maybe he'd been using it while rigging his raft.

Weber: Please describe the man.

Eliasson: Like I said, he's a big guy, really tall, but he didn't look like the kind of guy who would carry that kind of hammer, if you know what I mean. Geologists tend to be sort of nerdy guys, usually unshaven. They have beards, and they dress like they don't know what they look like. This guy was sleeker than that, and he had more the Eagle Scout look to him, less nerdy and more country club.

Weber: You found him [pause] presentable.

Eliasson: Yeah. Yes. Um, a good-looking man. Authoritative yet [pause] well, attractive is the word. Like he doesn't know quite how good-looking he is. But getting back to Oberley's arrival, the jerk all but missed check-in. He was undependable.

Weber: Did there seem to be bad feeling between them beyond that?

Eliasson: I couldn't say, sir.

Weber: Maryann, enough with the 'sir.'

Eliasson: Gerald, sir, whatever you want me to call you; I don't know. I just didn't get that big a take on it. I'll admit that the minute I saw Oberley I just wanted to get my job done and get out of there. The man is—was—trouble. Okay, now I've said too much, I suppose, but there it is. It's on the jungle telegraph that he was murdered, and I can't say that I'm the least bit surprised. Cleome's a close friend of mine and I was ready to yank his entrails out over the way he treated her, leaving her in the lurch with his name tattooed all over her [pause] posterior. But she didn't kill him. You know that because she was right there with you on the South Rim, not down on the river wherever it was this thing happened, and I am damned sure I don't know a single other thing about what happened down there, except it was good riddance.

Weber: Okay then.

Eliasson: Yeah.

Weber: Do you have anything else to add?

Eliasson: Nothing. Nada. Zip. Bupkis.

Weber: Thank you for your candor, Maryann.

Eliasson: Whatever you say. Sir.

Weber: Now I have one more request. Can you make Whitmore by tonight?

Eliasson: I've got a patrol raft, so I probably could, as long as I don't screw up in Lava Falls.

Weber: Oh. Right. Lava Falls. Are you alone?

Eliasson: No, I've got the botanist with me, Susanne McCoy.

Weber: Well then, please get yourselves down to Whitmore. The Calder party launched from Lower Cove an hour or so ago. They're either going to hit Whitmore tonight or stop somewhere short of that. Either way, this is what I want you to do: Do not let them progress past Whitmore.

Eliasson: Roger that. May I ask why, sir?

Weber: Because I want to talk to them directly, before they scatter from Diamond Creek, and I can get to Whitmore. I'll need confirmation from you of the time they expect to be at Whitmore, and I'll need transit across the river.

Eliasson: Roger that. See you there.

End of transmission.

APRIL 12–13:
GOING DOWNHILL

I'VE BEEN TOLD THAT THE FIRST TWO RULES OF PLUMBING ARE THAT SHIT runs downhill and Friday's payday. Those two rules seemed to apply the next morning as we prepared to launch. It wasn't a Friday, but it might as well have been, because Wink was paying for his little sins of opportunism, and everything sure was stinking and going downhill for him, and accelerating as it went. I guess that if you mess with enough people for long enough you'll eventually find one who will seek revenge, and that is what had happened. Julianne had sought revenge and she had used my mineral hammer to deliver it.

This is what happened: As she walked past the place where Fritz and I were setting up our tent on her way to cross back over the river, she picked up my trusty old rock hammer and took it with her. Fritz had brought it up from our raft to drive in the tent stakes, and when he couldn't find it when he was done tightening the guy lines he figured that I had already taken it back to the raft. In fact, I found it by the boats in the morning, not in the raft but underneath it, in the shallows of the river right beside the bow, getting rusty.

This is what she did with that hammer: She waded into the river to where Wink's dory was moored, leaned down below the waterline on the starboard side where no one could see what she was doing, and gave that rotting dory a couple of good whacks with it, enough to punch a hole into the forward bilge about the size of a silver dollar. The holes were big enough that Wink's jury-rigged pump would not have been able to keep up with the leak. If the pump had still been running. The pump was not working, however, because she crippled that, too. She accomplished this by reaching in through the hole and tearing the wiring right out of the pump and taking it with her, or at least, it could not be found anywhere around the camp or the boats. I guess that by riding in that boat for parts of nine days she had gotten to know it pretty well. I guess also that Wink should have shown her a little more respect, but the cheese had already slid off the cracker on that score, so we all just sort of stood there and kept our mouths shut and watched as Wink assessed the damage.

He was, understandably, quite upset. He did not notice the sabotage right away, because the boat was moored in the shallows and the river level had dropped a lot during the night, putting the dory and all of the rafts down on their bottoms on the riverbed. We had extended the mooring lines as far as they would go when we tied them up the evening before, but it had not occurred to anyone to move Wink's boat for him, which again was symptomatic of the degree to which Wink's shit was running downhill.

The rest of us were ready to launch. "Can it be fixed?" asked Fritz.

"Oh, sure, it can be *fixed*," said Wink. "You think these things never smack any rocks?"

"Okay then," said Fritz, "what needs to be done? The rest of us are ready to go, and time's a-wasting."

"Then you just get in your rafts and head on down the river," Wink growled. "I was running this river on my own before you ever even came here as a passenger. You just help me get this thing up out of the water and I'll fix it and catch up later."

"No you won't. We will help you fix it."

Wink stood up and glared at Fritz. "Like now you're the big hero," he said, finally confronting authority to its face.

Fritz stared at the man but said nothing. He wasn't going to rise to that bait. Fritz was a team player, the permit regulations said we had to keep together, and for better or for worse, Wink was on his team and he wasn't going to leave without him. The Winks of the world just didn't understand that kind of ethic, even when it stared them in the face.

Fritz said, "Okay then, let's get this thing unloaded so we can hoist it out of the water," and he leaned toward the forward hatch to pull it open.

Wink dove for the hatch and slammed his hands down on it. "You leave that be!" he roared. As abruptly he backed off the offensive and added, suddenly all charming, "There's hardly anything in there anyway, just my sleeping bag and clothes, so it weighs nothing. I can just lift the bow right out of the water, see?" He squatted and lifted, grunting to the point where I wondered if he was risking a hernia. After noisily letting go its suction on the bottom of the river, the bow came up.

Once the dory was beached it was decided that the kayaks and the other rafts should deploy a half mile down the river to Shinumo Creek, which had a lovely waterfall under which they all could swim. The Rasmussens offered to stay, but once it was clear that Wink would be able to patch his wounded nautical pride, Fritz sent them along, too, asking that they take me and Brendan with them. Brendan happily climbed into their raft, as did Glenda, who smiled cheerily, grabbed her day bag out of the dory, and told Wink, "You wouldn't want me to miss Shinumo Falls, I'm sure."

I didn't think it was smart to leave Fritz and Wink alone together, so I stayed. It took Wink an hour and a half to patch that hole, and while I wished I could be swimming in the creek at Shinumo with the others, it was rather fascinating to see how the patch job was accomplished. Wink applied two new slices of plywood to the hole—one inside and one outside—and held them together with rubber gaskets, some caulking, and a wing nut. The result was rough and crude, but it more or less kept out the water and after a little bailing the dory was once again floatable.

Wink launched the dory and climbed into it, and we followed him down to the mouth of Shinumo Creek, watching his waterline carefully, making certain that his patch was holding.

After beginning the short hike up to the falls just in time to find the others coming back, we all climbed into the various factions of our flotilla and continued down the river. Wink was again alone, Glenda having decided that it was a good morning to work on her skills rowing a raft. She had sweet-talked the Rasmussens into letting her row theirs.

We didn't get as far as we had hoped that day, but along with watching Wink bail, a good time was had by all. Hakatai Mattes got to row a raft through a rapid that bore his name, or rather, a rapid that had been named for the same person or feature in the canyon as he had, and he purred all the way through it, a real cool cat.

On our raft, Brendan was making a big day of it, rowing both Hakatai and Waltenberg Rapids, and any other riffles he could point our bow into. We made a lovely stop at Elves Chasm, where we found maidenhair ferns that grew there in the shade, cooled by the mists of water that splattered down over the rocks. All direct sunlight having by then long since left the Inner Gorge, we made camp a mile or so farther along at a site named Below Elves.

The next day, we were moving right along making miles, when we entered Dubendorff Rapid and things again went poorly for Wink. He had just bailed as much water as he could out of the cockpit of the dory, but as he was also taking on water in the forward compartment, he was riding a little low. Dubendorff is not a giant rapid—only a 5 to 8 out of 10, depending on the amount of water that's running over it, and only a fifteen-foot drop—but it's a messy one, with funny turns and lots of rocks gnashing at the sky.

Wink stared down into the tongue of water that welled up over the upper end of the rock garden, adjusted his stance on the water with a couple of quick dips of the oar, bringing the stern around to address the current so that he could ferry across the rapid to a place where the whole thing took that turn, and then started to pull with both oars, hard. He made the first part of the rapid fine but wallowed into that hole, broached, filled the boat to its gunwales with muddy brown water, and then, having lost headway, slammed sideways into that rock. I saw his head snap sideways. It looked ugly, and it was.

All three kayaks were needed to tow the wounded boat into the shallows, and after one look at the hole made by that rock, we knew we'd be there for the night. An area of plywood the size of a dinner plate had turned to mush, delaminating into shreds.

I shot a look at Fritz, who shook his head, and said, "Okay, everybody, let's get on down there and have some dinner."

We all set up camp while Wink worked on the dory, rumbling about under his hatches for additional pieces of plywood and rubber big enough to make the patch. We had a nice dinner of macaroni and cheese, and I played a few rounds of Boggle with Nancy and Molly while Brendan did his math homework and most of the rest of the party swapped lies over beers around the campfire, and once again Glenda Fittle received Wink in her tent as the stars glittered across the darkness of the night.

Notes of Gerald Weber, Chief Ranger
Investigation into death of George Oberley
April 19, 3:00 P.M.

Notes RE: Fritz Calder of Salt Lake City, UT:

Ran search on Calder through law enforcement network. No priors.

Ran search through Google:
    Owner/operator of an air charter company out of SLC. Phoned base
    of operations, no answer, left message on answering machine. Web
    page lists him as former USN, veteran jet pilot, served over Iraq,
    decorated. NB: PTSD?

Checked list of other passengers on Calder's trip, ran them through
Google. Three show up as geologists:
    Molly Chang. Teaches at U of U. No record with law enforcement.
    Donald Rasmussen, a paleontologist from Colorado. Clean record.

Emily Bradstreet Hansen. Utah Geological Survey, Geologic Information & Outreach Program. Title: Geologist, Public Inquiries, *FORENSICS*. Phoned office number for Emily Hansen, was informed that she assists law enforcement agencies with murder and other investigations that require analysis of geologic materials, and Hansen is on leave for three weeks rafting the canyon with her husband *FRITZ CALDER.*

NB: Calder has access to hammer and ways to cover evidence. *I don't believe in coincidences.*

APRIL 14–15: CIRCLING THE DRAIN

EARLY THE NEXT MORNING, TO EVERYONE'S AMAZEMENT, WINK AGAIN had the dory up and floating, and we launched and rowed on downriver, passing through the narrowest point of the river, a place where only seventy-six feet separates one rock wall from the other.

We made a stop to hike up the side canyon where Deer Creek enters the Colorado River from the right bank. The strata there formed lovely horizontal ribs of brown sandstone, and after chuffing up a series of switchbacks that led up the debris slope from the beach, we turned up into the narrow, twisting slot canyon the creek had cut. Light bounced and filtered down from the sky above, giving the chasm a gentle warmth.

Brendan asked, "What rock layer is this, Em?"

"This is Tapeats Sandstone again."

"How'd we get back into that? I thought the river was cutting down into older and older rock."

"It was, but this whole plateau is humped up in the middle, and there are faults here and there that drop a section of the rock down, so that here the Colorado River is carving through a younger part again." I tried to make a diagram by bending one elbow up and holding the other arm across it straight but it looked ridiculous. "I'll draw you a picture when we get back to the river," I said.

We caught up with Don and Jerry Rasmussen, who were examining a particular layer of the sandstone. When he saw that Brendan was interested, Don pointed at a network of squiggly shapes in the rock and said, "Trace fossils. These are burrowing traces made by worms when this rock was still soft sediment."

"Cool," said Brendan.

We made camp that night at a place aptly called the Keyhole. Concerned that we weren't making sufficient distance, Fritz got us up and moving early the next morning. We hadn't gone far before Wink snagged yet another rock, again slowing our progress to a crawl. We made an early lunch, and watched the ravens that hopped along the riverbank. Fragments of conversation held outside Wink's earshot told me that Fritz was not the only one who was beginning to feel hampered by the deterioration of the dory.

Mungo was the most outspoken. "I say we just sink the thing," he grumbled.

"Then we'd have to have him in one of the rafts," said Nancy.

"Children," Jerry warned, shaking an index finger at them.

Nancy said, "Hell, something's gotta give here. I've worked with plywood enough to know that when you leave a boat like that sitting on a trailer for a couple of years—how long is it he's been in New Jersey?—and then you put it back in the water, there are molds that grow in between the laminations. It is not good wood anymore, if it ever was. You saw what it looked like after that big rock in Dubendorff! Like shredded wheat! And now he's got patches on his patches."

We all talked in circles for a while, accomplishing nothing. What I didn't say was that my biggest concern was Fritz. Having drawn the line in the sand the two men had descended into a cold war at Cremation Camp, and Wink was not one to surrender if he had an ounce of fight left in him. He seemed almost to be baiting Fritz, giving him dirty looks and even taking little jumps toward Brendan, as if showing that he might still try to throw the kid with his jujitsu or karate or whatever it was, or just push him into the river.

Fritz had taken on the look of a caged lion, pacing up and down the beach while Wink was working, tossing rocks into the water, eating too many cookies, carrying two in each hand while still chewing on another, drinking beer before lunchtime, and sleeping little. His beloved trip was turning into a nightmare.

At last the dory again rose above the waves and we launched. Wink had sacrificed the hatch cover from his rear compartment in order to find enough wood this time. He had been able to cover the hatch with an old poncho, but he was running out of rubber and caulk. The dory was floating low in the water. He had managed to tinker the pump into working again, though he had to reach inside the hold to switch it on now, rather than push a button in the cockpit. "Let's get going," he said, as if in charge.

I glanced at Fritz. He stopped in midpace like he'd been hit by lightning. "Okay then!" he said, a little louder than he needed to, asserting his command over the group.

"We'll make the Ledges just great," said Wink, lifting up his T-shirt to scratch his belly in a gesture that showed Fritz his flesh in an insulting way.

Fritz turned and aimed his sunglasses at him.

Don said, "The Ledges? Is that where we're headed tonight, Fritz?"

Hakatai said, "I've never been there. What's it like?"

Mungo said, "It's pretty neat, actually, though it gives me the creeps that the rock you sleep on sort of slopes toward the river."

Bored to the point of irascibility from too much waiting, Nancy chimed in with her opinion of the Ledges, followed by Olaf and Lloyd. The cog wheels in Fritz's brain appeared to have jammed. I could almost see the smoke created by the heat of that friction pouring out of his ears. The loose cannon had rolled right across the deck onto Fritz's toes.

Fritz could see that his team wanted to go there, so he said yes, we would head for the Ledges.

We stopped briefly to admire Matkatamiba Canyon, managed to make it through Upset Rapid without further casualties, and pulled up to the campsite called Ledges and tied up for the night. That's when things went from wholly awful to much, much worse.

APRIL 15: LEDGES

LEDGES CAMPSITE LAY SO DEEP IN THE NARROWS OF THE CANYON THAT by the time we reached it, the sun had long since gone out of sight over the rim of the Inner Gorge, abandoning the campsite to an early dusk. Gnarled ribs of Muav Limestone crowded dark and steeply around it, forming a crude horizontal corduroy that rose to a first major step at least a hundred feet almost straight up. The strata that formed the ledges on which we would cobble together our camp sloped slightly toward the river. There was no beach, only the sloping rock, which stepped down and ended with a three- to four-foot drop-off at the water. There was limited space to tie up, and we had to lash the rafts to the rocks. It was hazardous to climb in and out of them to unload gear, and we had to rig the kitchen just a few feet from the water along one of the few stretches of nearly level rock. A thin coating of damp sand covered an active seep of water that ran out from the bottom of the cliff. Up against the canyon wall the sand was a bit deeper and thus mostly dry at the top, but it, too, sloped steeply and was crowded by willows, so there was only enough space to set up a few of the tents. Olaf defied his own convention by rigging a sleeping deck on one of the rafts, saying that no self-respecting mouse was going to sashay down across all that rock to bother him there, and Gary set up a cot just a few feet from the drop-off into the water. I suggested that he not roll over into the river during the night.

The dory was leaking badly, and there was no life left in the battery that ran the pump, so it was beginning to sink. It wallowed in the current, tipped heavily bow down, the aft compartment still relatively watertight, yet Wink seemed almost pleased with himself. He stood in the cockpit of his boat admiring the view.

"What are you going to do with this thing?" Fritz asked.

Wink turned slowly toward him and ran the middle finger of his right hand up beside his nose as if adjusting that expensive pair of sunglasses he wore.

Fritz's face darkened with rage, and he moved his fists to his hips. "It would serve you best if you straightened out your attitude!" he snapped.

This startled me. I had never heard him speak in that tone. Brendan grew extremely quiet beside me, holding his breath.

A staring match ensued. Slowly the current swung the dory around until Wink's head had twisted as far as it could go without unwinding off his neck. He could no longer maintain eye contact without awkwardly shifting his stance, so he let the boat move his gaze back to the river.

Mungo moved to distracte Fritz by asking his assistance with the fire pan. "Come show me where you want this thing," he said.

It was a grim evening. We ate quickly and washed the dishes in the buckets by the river and then just sat staring into the fire while Brendan did his math homework. Wink told a few stories, but no one seemed to be listening. People began to turn in early.

Dell Oxley sat by the fire nursing a beer, and Mungo, who was usually last to bed and early awake, produced a bottle of Scotch, which he had kept packed in bubble wrap in an ammo can. He offered some to Fritz, who muttered something about not needing it. Mungo said, "Well, I didn't bring it all this way to carry it home again." He poured himself a short one and set the bottle on the rock beside his folding chair.

"I'll have some!" said Wink. He grabbed the bottle before Mungo could retrieve it and splashed four fingers into a metal cup.

"Jesus!" cried Mungo. "Take it easy there, boy!"

"Aw hell, I can handle it!" said Wink, delivering one of his trademark one-eyes. He took a swig, said, "Nice!" and walked away along the edge of the ledge, heading toward the latrine.

"Where the hell is he going with that?" Mungo growled. "When a man pours that much single malt into a tin cup he ought to sit still and drink it, not take it to the crapper!"

"I'm just as happy if he finds someplace else to be," said Glenda. "I thought his stories were getting rather stale this evening." She got up and headed up the slope toward her tent.

Molly let out a low whistle and said, "Well, I guess everyone hits bottom eventually."

"Yeah," said Nancy. "Rock bottom. That's when your girlfriend finds your stories boring and your boat won't even float."

Mungo said, "And you can't even find paying work by dressing up funny and telling tales you don't believe to a bunch of fundamentalists. He probably thought you were going to hire him, right, Molly?"

Molly shook her head at the thought. "I couldn't do that to the rest of the department. He doesn't take responsibility for his actions. That would make a lot of extra work for everyone else."

"You're so reasonable," said Mungo. "I wonder how much farther that dory is going to make it."

Fritz said, "I'm done in. You about finished with your homework there, Brendan?"

"Yeah, just let me finish this one problem."

Fritz turned toward me and said, "Ready, my love?"

"Sure, I just need to take the usual stroll." I stood up and glanced toward the pathway through the willows that led toward the latrine.

Fritz scowled. "I'll walk you down there," he said and hoisted himself out of his chair.

Brendan closed his notebook. "I just need to use the river," he said. "See you at the tent."

Fritz took my hand and we walked over the damp sand and along the sloping stone toward the brush where we'd hidden the toilet. Trying to soothe my husband with humor, I said, "Hell of a way to get a little privacy together."

"I can't even think about that," Fritz said leadenly.

I squeezed his hand. I felt wretched that I couldn't do anything to make the torment stop.

We were halfway to the latrine when Wink lurched out of the willows swinging a now empty tin cup. When he saw us, he swung it high, adding a little flip to his wrist at the end of the arc. "A fine, smoky single malt!" he chortled. "Bet you can't handle this stuff, flyboy!" He ran his tongue around his lips, which bristled with a five-day beard. The effect was nauseating.

Fritz pulled me closer to him but said nothing in reply.

Wink planted his feet, blocking our way, and began to sing an obscene drinking ditty, the words slurring as if he was already feeling the Scotch.

Fritz said, "Get out of our way, man."

Wink put his fists on his hips, mocking Fritz's authority pose. "Little woman gotta go tinky?"

I tightened my grip on Fritz's hand.

Fritz's voice descended to a growl. "I've had enough of your behavior," he snarled.

Wink cocked a hip provocatively. "Well then, motherfucker, why don't you change it?"

Fritz took a step forward, but I pulled back on his hand. "He's not worth it," I said, though anger was rising through every nerve in my body. I steered my husband carefully around the doryman.

Fritz tracked along with me, but his eyes stayed on Wink.

Suddenly Wink careened toward the river, heading straight toward the brink where Brendan stood relieving himself.

Fritz yelled, "Brendan! Look out!" and lunged after Wink, nearly yanking my arm from its socket.

Brendan scuttled up toward the fire, hurriedly stuffing his penis inside his pants.

Wink threw his head back, and howled with laughter. "Oh, that's so ripe!" he roared. "You little piss-ant, I'll bet you peed yourself!"

Fritz's free hand began to rise toward Wink's neck. I held on tightly to the other one and yelled, "Don't! Look, he's *trying* to make you mad!"

Brendan called, "I'm okay, Dad! Please, Dad!"

"*Please*, Dad!" Wink mocked. "Please, Daddy, I am so *scared*!" There were daggers in his voice, saw blades, hatchets, all things sharp and lethal. He sauntered over to the pail of beers that were cooling in river water and bent to grab one, carelessly dropping his tin cup on the rock.

Mungo was on his feet now, hurrying toward Wink, calling, "Cut the crap, you worthless son of a bitch!"

Fritz leaned into Wink's face. "I've got you in my sights," he whispered. It was a small phrase, something that would have meant little had I not known Fritz's job in the navy: flying a jet into the night to drop bombs over Iraq.

Notes of Gerald Weber, Chief Ranger
Investigation into Death of George Oberley
April 19, 4:15 P.M.

Made repeated telephone calls to God's Voice Ministries of Las Vegas,
NV, in search of Lisette St. Denis Carl, the woman who reported overhearing Calder's threat on Oberley. Automated telephone answering
system did not yield a return call. Called back using "donations" line
advertised on their Web site and reached a live voice immediately. On
notification that I was calling as part of a law enforcement investigation, I was transferred to Terry Carl, brother of the deceased televangelist. Transcript of that conversation follows:

Weber: Who am I speaking with?
Carl: This is Terry Carl at your service. How may I help you, brother?
Weber: I am trying to reach Lisette Carl, who was recently a par-
ticipant on a river trip down the Grand Canyon. Are you—I see
that your name is also on the passenger list from that trip, am
I correct?

Carl: [pause] Yes, that is correct. How may I serve—ah, assist you, sir?

Weber: I wish to speak directly with Mrs. Carl. Is she available?

Carl: She is not here, sir. She is not an employee of this organization.

Weber: But you are in touch with her. You could get a message to her for me.

Carl: [pause] And what message would that be?

Weber: It is urgent that she contact me. Immediately.

Carl: Could you share with me the cause for this urgency? Is there perhaps some way that I may help?

Weber: Were you present when she overheard a conversation between George Oberley and another man at Cremation Campground on April ninth?

Carl: No. [pause] No, I was not.

Weber: Well then, you can best assist me by relaying my message to Mrs. Carl. Or better yet, give me a telephone number through which I can reach her directly.

Carl: She doesn't have one.

Weber: Excuse me?

Carl: She uses only a cell phone. [pause] And I don't have that number. She changed it recently. But perhaps I can reach her through other channels.

Weber: Where does she live? The address listed for her on the river trip manifest, I note, is that of your religious organization, which is highly irregular. So what is her home address?

Carl: That is not my information to release, sir.

Weber: Okay then, you can explain to me why this woman is so difficult to reach.

Carl: Mrs. Carl is a revered member of our church family, and as such is in great demand. If she were to make herself available to everyone who called—

Weber: This is official law enforcement business!

Carl: I [pause] hear what you're saying, sir, and will do my utmost to reach her and have her return your call. I can see your number on my caller ID and am writing it down.

Weber: Fine. Now, exactly how was George Oberley involved with your group?

Carl: Dr. Oberley? We are interested in God's word. He was loosely involved in assisting us with interpreting earth history in light of the Book of Genesis.

Weber: "Loosely involved." Exactly what does that mean?

Carl: He offered his expertise. I am given to understand that he was traveling with another river group and thus camping nearby on a few evenings. It was [pause] kind of him to offer, but he had little information that was of use to us. There are many who wish to serve God but take rather long paths in finding Him. Is there anything else? I have a lot to do, catching up with the management of our humble church after having been away.

Weber: Your name is Carl. Are you related to Mrs. Carl?

Carl: She is my sister-in-law. She was my deceased brother's wife.

Weber: And your brother would be?

Carl: The Reverend Amos Carl.

Weber: The one that died on TV?

Carl: [pause] We all greive his passing. Now, if there is nothing else. . .

Weber: Just get your sister-in-law to contact me. It is urgent that I speak with her. Remember that.

End of communication.

Summary note: Terry Carl seems an unreliable witness.

APRIL 16: MISSING MAN FORMATION

It was still pitch dark outside when I became aware that Fritz was already awake. I had heard him come and go several times in the night, checking the boats. All was quiet outside, the only sound the slight burbling the river made as it boiled over hidden rocks and slid past the blunt face of the ledge on which our camp rested. I slid to the edge of my foam mat and curled my body up next to his, sliding my hand up underneath his sleeping bag, which, in the warm air of the canyon bottom, he had left unzipped and simply thrown over himself like a quilt. "You're awake," I whispered.

Keeping his own voice low to avoid awakening his sleeping son, he whispered, "Go back to sleep."

"We stick together, Fritz."

He found my hand with his own and squeezed it. "I know."

"I love you, Fritz. Have I told you that lately?"

"There's been a lot going on."

I whispered, "You didn't ask him to come on this trip. It wasn't your idea, so it's not your failure."

He squeezed my hand again.

I put my head on his shoulder. "Really, the man's provocative as all hell, but if we ignore him, he'll find someone else to annoy. He's just got a thing about authority."

Fritz did not reply. He rolled toward me, and I nuzzled up under his chin and kissed the warm, bristly skin of his throat. I ran my hand up and down his belly in just the way he loved the most, but he did not respond to that, either. When I bent a knee and hooked my leg over his, he whispered, "I think I'm just going to get up, so you and Brendan can get some more sleep."

I did sleep after he left, though fitfully. As sunlight finally found its way down inside the fold of the canyon, I rose and shrugged my way into a fleece jacket and a pair of jeans, unzipped the mosquito netting, wiggled my feet into my sandals, and rose to greet the day.

It was a typical enough morning, though the strange setting of the inclined slab of rock seemed to have everyone in a quiet mood. In the kitchen area I found Fritz sipping meditatively on a cup of coffee while Molly Chang stirred a pot of oatmeal. Brendan had made a cup of cocoa and sneaked a shot of coffee into it. When the oatmeal was ready we all ladled it into bowls and added raisins, nuts, and reconstituted powdered milk. We'd all been together for over two weeks now, so little conversation was necessary. I was grateful that Wink appeared to have chosen that morning to sleep in, though I wondered if he would waken with a hangover, and worried that it would lead to even worse antics.

At half past seven, Glenda Fittle floated serenely down the slope from her tent arrayed in a gauzy nightgown topped by a fleece jacket in a vivid shade of orchid. Her hair lay wild about her shoulders. "Good morning, all," she said cheerily.

Mungo raised an eyebrow her way. "Is your companion feeling the aftereffects of strong drink this morning?" he inquired. "We haven't seen him yet."

Glenda knit her brow ever so slightly with curiosity. "I wouldn't know. I thought he was out here with y'all."

Mungo looked at Fritz, who in turn looked at Glenda. "He's not in your tent?"

"No."

"Then where is he?"

"I don't know."

"Was he there earlier?"

Glenda shook her head. "He tossed his sleeping bag in there when we first set up camp last night, but it's still in its stuff sack. I figured he must have slept on his boat." She rose to her tippy-toes and peered over the edge into the dory.

"He didn't do that," said Olaf. "I was on the middle raft all night, and he would have had to climb over me to get to the dory. He'd have woken me up."

"Son of a bitch is probably passed out in the willows," said Mungo.

Fritz let out a long sigh. "Okay, let's have a look around and see if we can find where he's hiding."

When a cursory check of the tents and the paths that led through the willows did not yield the desired result, Fritz organized us into teams for a more thorough search. When that bore no fruit, he sent people to each end of the ledges to look for footprints or tumbled rocks in case Wink had managed to climb the cliff face like a mountain goat. Finally, he laid out a search grid that took us back over the same ground.

As we marched along poking under the small trees and shrubs, I heard Brendan ask, "Is this what you call the 'missing man formation,' Dad?"

Fritz said gently, "No, son. That's when you fly aircraft over a pilot's funeral. We plan to find this man alive."

When it was clear that Wink Oberley was no longer present at the Ledges Campsite, we pried open both hatches of his dory and even probed an oar into the water all along the river below the lowest ledge.

"This is serious," said Fritz. "When we were digging through his dory, I checked to see if both primary and spare PFDs were present. They were. Is anyone missing a Paco Pad or any other kind of air mattress?"

All shook their heads. Glenda called from the kitchen, "Wink's Paco is still up in my tent. You don't think . . ."

"We should call the Park Service," said Mungo. "There must be a protocol."

Fritz strode quickly toward his raft, jumped from the ledge to the oarsman's seat, and opened the ammo can that held the rented satellite telephone. Scrambling quickly back up onto the ledge with the phone and a three-by-five card that listed emergency numbers, he began the struggle to connect to a satellite. While we waited, the rest of us paced up and down the rock, fiddled with equipment, or stared obsessively into our coffee mugs.

Fritz grumbled, "The battery on the telephone is really low. Has someone been using this phone without telling us?"

No one answered. I gritted my teeth, worrying that I might have left the thing switched on when I phoned Faye from the confluence of the Little Colorado. But I had switched it off; I could remember doing it. Who had run down the one good battery?

As Fritz struggled with the telephone a discussion arose regarding who had seen Wink last, what state he had been in at that time, and what might have become of him.

Mungo said, "Dell and I turned in at about ten thirty, and except for Wink, we were the last ones up. I told him to put the fire out before he turned in, and he said yeah, sure, and just waved us on, but you can see that it was left to burn itself out. He'd put away a couple more beers by then on top of that single malt he swiped, and each time he went down to the river to piss he looked a little more wobbly. He got to the point where he was spilling his beer. You don't think . . ."

"I don't want to think," said Dell. "I don't want to think at all that I might have gone to bed and left him to fall into the river drunk."

It was out, the obvious answer, and we all stared at it just as if it were a dead animal we had found lying in the ashes of the campfire.

"Did he actually drink all that whiskey and beer?" I asked.

Jerry said, "He swiped half of Don's granola bars, but I'll bet they're still floating in his bilge."

"He was crumpling the empty beer cans," said Dell.

We all fell silent as Fritz continued to watch for a sat-phone connection.

When Fritz was finally able to get a call through to park headquarters, he shifted automatically to his pilot's radio communications voice, employing the calm I had come to expect of him as he made his calls from the aircraft he and Faye flew as a charter airline. When he lost the connection in the middle of the conversation, he stared up at the canyon walls as if he could see the satellite that had just winked out of sight beyond the rim. Then he began to pace. "They're sending someone. At least, I think they are. The connection quit, right in the middle of that part. I'll call again in a minute. I need to think."

In the end no amount of thinking changed our circumstances. Fritz made another call to the park and was assured that a search party was coming, though it would take a few hours to arrive. A helicopter would respond to our distress, and we should all just sit tight.

"Tiny and I had planned a second layover day," said Fritz. "Unfortunately it's going to have to be here."

We all did our best to put a pleasant face on the day, some taking out a book to read, others starting a quiet game of cards. Nancy Skinner pulled some knitting out of the bottom of a dry bag, and organized a tutorial, teaching several of the men how to knit. No one said anything more about what had happened, lest our fear that Wink had drowned become real.

Fritz used the time to reorganize our raft, cinching everything absurdly tight, and after a while he pulled out the satellite telephone one more time and began the tedious task of getting a connection through to

Tiny, then Faye. That connection lasted long enough that I could say hello. "This sucks," I told her.

"Big-time," she replied, just as the connection died.

Fritz switched the phone off and put it away in its box. "I am appalled by these batteries," he said. "For what we're paying to rent this thing, you'd think they'd give us something that could hold a charge."

I said, "We came down here to get away from it all, so to hell with the sat phone and the whole technological revolution. Look at this camp; we're living in the Stone Age. Let's just relax as best we can."

"Iron Age," said Brendan.

I lifted an eyebrow at him.

"My teacher at school says Stone Age means all you have is rocks. We're at least in the Iron Age. You have your rock hammer, and I have my pocketknife, and the oarlocks are metal, too. And then there's the rafts. Was there a Rubber Age?"

Fritz ruffled Brendan's hair and kissed him on the top of his head. "My clever son," he said.

It was getting on for the later part of the afternoon when a Park Service helicopter came low overhead on its way toward a landing upriver, and a short while later, Ranger Seth Farnsworth pulled up to our moorage in a motor-powered Zodiac raft that had been deployed from the chopper. He climbed out in his Park Service green pants, tan T-shirt, and green cap and set to work assessing our situation. He was polite and efficient and kept his questions respectful while maintaining a sense of remove.

Finally, Mungo Park broke the formality by saying, "I take it this isn't your first drowning."

Ranger Farnsworth shook his head. "No, it is not." He looked up along the cliff face. "I can't see him climbing out of here."

"We already checked for climbing routes," said Fritz. "Though I can't see him making it up this cliff alive. He'd had several ounces of Scotch, remember, and a number of beers. And the moon wasn't up."

Farnsworth nodded. "But Oberley is well known in the canyon. He was an experienced river runner and a little unpredictable, so I'll just have a look." He started his engine and churned upriver a short distance. The helicopter reappeared, providing air support, searching the cliffs and heading downriver when the Zodiac had to stop before the next rapids.

The Zodiac came back into view, searching the eddies for any signs of the remains of an unlucky man. When he returned to the campsite Farnsworth said, "I found no sign of him, and I expect we won't find him for quite some time. Bodies tend to sink in this cold water and not come up for days or even weeks."

Nobody said anything.

Farnsworth said, "I'm sorry for your loss. I suppose you're here for another night, then?"

Fritz gazed up at the patch of sky that still blazed over the lengthening shadows and said, "Where do we go from here? I mean, aside from the obvious." He made a gesture that said, *We go down the river.*

The ranger gazed at the half-sunken dory. "You'll need to get his gear to the take-out at Diamond Creek. It looks like that may be something of a chore, but the rule is that you pack out what you bring in."

Behind me Nancy Skinner mumbled, "Garbage in, garbage out."

"Are we going to find him floating in an eddy?" asked Dell.

The ranger shook his head. "Typically a body sinks and stays down for about two weeks. You'll be long past it before that happens."

After the ranger had gotten back into his raft and taken his leave, and the helicopter had clattered away toward the South Rim, we all stood around the cold fire pit for a while staring into the ashes of the fire Wink had allowed to burn out. Glenda Fittle held her arms folded tightly around her chest, staring at her feet. She seemed to have shrunk to a smaller size over the hours of the day. "Maybe we should hold some kind of memorial service for him," she said.

People shifted nervously. "I suppose you're right," said Jerry.

Fritz stepped swiftly into the leadership void. "I agree. One of our number has apparently . . . died, and it would help the rest of us . . . put this behind us. Does anyone know if Wink was religious?"

Nancy said, "He was hanging out with those über-Christians."

Glenda pulled back in shock. "What are you talking about? Wink always laughed at the idea of religion. He recognized the value of spiritual traditions, but organized religion . . . well, that was anathema to him! He said so! Many times!"

Nancy stepped up and put an arm around her. "That's okay, dear. You've had a nasty shock. We all have."

"We don't even know for certain that he's dead," said Mungo.

Glenda burst into tears.

Fritz once again stepped into the breach. "Okay then, we'll each put some thought into this and come back together in an hour and have an observance that shows respect. If anyone else has any ideas, then great. Meanwhile this evening's dinner crew can get started."

Nancy steered Glenda over toward the camp chairs and sat her down. The three kayakers headed for the kitchen area. Gary lit a burner under a pot while Lloyd and Olaf headed out onto the rafts to fetch ingredients. The rest began to wander this way and that, leaving Fritz, Brendan, and me standing at water's edge staring up into the sky.

Brendan summarized our situation with an economy of words. He said, "Missing man, Dad. Missing man."

APRIL 17–18: THALWEG

WE LAUNCHED FROM LEDGES EARLY THE NEXT MORNING. FRITZ HAD Brendan help row as he tested the drag caused by the dory, which followed us with reluctance.

"How's it coming?" Don called from his raft. Jerry was rowing, and even as petite as she was, she was easily pulling ahead.

"Not so good," said Fritz. He didn't elaborate.

I was sitting in the bow. "Shall I recite 'The Rime of the Ancient Mariner'?" I asked.

"Please don't."

Don said, "Perhaps we should have someone row it for a while. One of the kayakers could tow his boat behind it, or lash the kayak on top of one of the rafts. You're going to exhaust yourself."

Between clenched teeth, Fritz said, "I don't want anyone having to mess with this thing."

I stopped trying to make light of the problem. Fritz was doing penance, plain and simple. Being a reasonable man, he felt blame for what had happened. I could hear his voice in my head, saying, *I'm the trip leader. I should have prevented this. All of this.*

We stopped three miles downriver at the mouth of Havasu Canyon, a lovely narrows where Havasu Creek carved a meandering slot through ribs of Muav Limestone. Several of our party climbed out and hiked up that side canyon while Jerry and Nancy and I huddled in the shade of the canyon walls, lounging back in our rafts and chatting.

Jerry said, "I hiked up Havasu to the travertine pools on another trip. They were really pretty, but a flash flood tore them out, so I'm just as happy to save my energies this time."

I asked, "What's up there farther? The river guide has a whole page for this creek, which is kind of unusual."

"It's the Havasupai Indian Reservation," she said. "They have a town—Supai—and you can eventually rim out, though it's a long way up there. This is where Eddie McKee described the Supai Group. He named the formations he split out after several of the 'temples' that cap the cliffs up there. Wescogame . . . Manakacha . . . what are the others?"

"Bottom to top it's Watahomigi, Manakacha, Wescogame, Esplanade," I said.

Nancy snickered. "You science nerds are a riot."

"We exist to entertain," I said, opening up the river guide. "So it looks like a long way out to Supai and the rest of the world."

Jerry said, "Oh, I'd say it's about fifteen miles to the nearest thing like a highway, and that's probably a gravel road. I hear it's kind of a mule trail at best, like you wouldn't get a car in there. It connects out to Kingman or some place like that. Oh, look, here are our returning heroes. Shall we get some snacks ready?"

Nancy said, "I'm always ready for snacks. I vote for adult candy bars." She opened up a rocket box and pulled out a handful of granola bars. "These include the most important food group: chocolate."

We passed around munchies and got back on the river. Stuck for a place to stow the wrapper of my granola bar, I folded it up and put it in the mesh pocket on the front of my life vest. It was nice to be in a place that had almost no trash, and I intended to keep it that way.

Fritz was pulling hard at the oars.

"I'll plot the thalweg," I told him.

"The who?" asked Brendan.

"Thalweg. It's a two-bit term for the line along the river where the current is fastest."

"You're making that up."

"It's a loan word from German. Actually a compound word, from *thal,* meaning valley, and *weg,* meaning way. So if we want the water to do as much work for us as possible, we follow the valley way. It's the most efficient route, as the river turns and wanders through the canyon." I didn't add that staying in the thalweg would also keep us out of the eddies, which might be unpleasantly decorated with the corpse of our recently departed doryman.

"I have a much better idea to add efficiency," said Brendan. "Let's just burn the thing."

Fritz's eyebrows shot up. "There's an idea."

I slapped Brendan a high five, but staring into the eddies got me thinking: Now that the immediate issue of whether or not Wink could be found at Ledges was past, questions still remained. How exactly had he left the campsite? And where would he be found? There was something about the whole scenario that did not quite stack up for me. I had been accused once or twice by FBI colleagues of having a spider's sense for the slightest twitch in the web of evidence, which was apt: For me, evidence was, much like a web, a pattern, and sometimes the pattern matched something I'd seen before, while other times the pattern was new. Either way, if the pattern did not hang together then something was wrong, and it bugged me, and I picked at it, searching for another bit of the design, until the overall picture made sense.

Nothing about George "Wink" Oberley made sense to me. Why would he work so hard at lying, making things incredibly difficult for himself, when he was bright and able enough to make his way through honest means? Why, for instance, had he come on our trip? What had he gained through that? Perhaps if he loved anything he loved this canyon, but why then would he make such a point out of provoking everyone around him into wishing he were anywhere else?

Yet Wink had been kind to Holly Ann, the girl from the Christian fundamentalist trip. Why be nice to her when he was such a shit to everyone else? I couldn't match up Wink's obvious attempts to look nice and play nicely with the rest of Holly Ann's group, which had been a lie, with his kindness to Holly Ann, which had seemed genuine. It was all just terribly confounding. I rolled onto my back on the floor of the raft and watched the sky and the rims of the canyon walls make their slow minuet, pondering our line of flow.

"Hey, Dad," I heard Brendan say. "I like this thalweg idea. I see how things drag over here and start turning around the wrong way, making an eddy, and then over there on the other side of the river, there's another eddy turning the opposite way. But if you stay in between them, the water runs fast and straight. That's the place to be, Dad, running straight, staying out of the confusion. That's the difference between you and Wink, Dad. You're smart. You let the water help you and don't get caught up in places that are going backwards."

I smiled for the first time that day. With every turn in the river, Brendan was growing up, growing wiser, sorting things out for himself and beginning to make his own discernments in life. Momentarily at peace and flowing within my own thalweg, I closed my eyes and took a much-needed snooze.

We camped that evening at the mouth of National Canyon. Camp life was subdued but much calmer, and Mungo exhorted us all to put together some skits and acted them out for each other. I felt badly that someone had to disappear to make a happier campfire life possible, but I reasoned that Wink had brought his woes on himself.

The morning of April 18, we launched and headed on down the river like a well-oiled machine. The rapids were all fairly small, and we made reasonable time, even though we had to stop periodically to bail out the dory, which had grown increasingly waterlogged. We stopped

at Fern Glen Canyon to enjoy a nice stroll up through its cool depths and made it to Cove Canyon to camp.

All was going well with camp setup when I heard Mungo shout, "Em! Your life vest is going down the river without you!"

It was floating away into the gathering current, starting to bob its way into the heavy riffle that fed around the small jumble of rocks from the side canyon.

I jumped up and charged down to the raft to get the spare life vest so I could chance swimming out to grab the runaway, but as I dug underneath our tarp to the place where Fritz had stowed our spare, I realized that it wasn't there. While I dithered around trying to figure out what had become of our spare, Gary McClanahan clipped on his own vest, pulled on his spray skirt, hopped into his kayak, and set forth to retrieve my errant vest, which hadn't gotten all that far.

"You're my hero," I said, as he returned.

"Pleased to assist," Gary said. "You maybe got a beer for your hero?"

A small peanut gallery had now gathered on the beach. "What was it doing loose?" asked Nancy, as usual cutting to the pith of the matter.

"I laid it on the beach while I was carrying gear up to our tent site," I said. "And yeah, I know better. But there isn't any wind, so I figured I didn't have to secure it right away."

Brendan said, "I saw a raven pecking at it."

"Why would a raven be interested in my life vest?"

Gary said, "Looks like it was after that granola bar wrapper in your vest pocket."

"But the wrapper's empty."

"Doesn't matter, it's shiny. Those birds will peck at anything that's shiny."

Brendan said, "He fussed that thing clear into the water."

Sure enough, there was a little tear in the nylon mesh of the pocket, and a matching hole in what was left of the wrapper.

"Cheeky little bastards," said Mungo.

Just like Wink, I thought. *Picking at shiny things with nothing in them.*

Brendan took the dripping-wet life vest out of my hands, said, "I'll tie it up with ours by the tent," and headed up the slope.

I followed him, looking for Fritz, whom I found lying on his camp mat inside the tent. I said, "Our spare life vest is missing."

He opened one eye. "That's all we need. I suppose we'll lose our deposit on the rental."

I crawled into the tent, lay down next to him, and ran a hand through his hair. "I have a theory about this," I said.

Fritz squeezed his eyes shut. "Em, I do not wish to hear it. I just want to get that piece of shit dory down this river and get everyone remaining in my care out of here alive, do you understand?"

I reeled back. It wasn't like Fritz to curse. I blurted, "But I think Wink is still alive."

Fritz rolled up onto his side, putting his back to me. After a while, he said, "I'm not sure which I'd like less, losing a trip member or having one out there someplace playing games. Either way, I'm stuck towing that damned dory down Lava Falls."

"Tomorrow."

"Yes."

This was a new Fritz. I knew him as a man of courage, the man who had flown fast jets by night over hostile territory, but now, for the first time in our acquaintance, he seemed truly scared.

APRIL 19: LAVA FALLS

W E WERE LATE LAUNCHING ON THE MORNING OF APRIL 19 BECAUSE
Fritz had the dory up on the beach at Cove Canyon trying to patch the
leaks. "Why are you doing this?" I asked him. "I like Brendan's idea of
making a bonfire. We could use it to send smoke signals to the gods of
bad juju, and maybe they'd get off our back."

"I told the Park Service I'd get this thing to Diamond Creek and
I will," he muttered and shot more caulking into a gash big enough to
run his hand through.

When we did at last get onto the river, the dory did seem to ride a bit
higher for a mile or so, and Fritz didn't have to row quite as hard, but
still his mood did not lift. I wanted to spit. Even though he was no longer with us, Wink Oberley was managing to screw with our enjoyment
of the river.

Two miles out from Cove Canyon a motorized Park Service raft
with two women on board appeared from upriver, sped up to us, and
slowed as it came alongside. I recognized botanist Susanne McCoy in
the bow and, standing at the controls, Maryann Eliasson, the ranger
who had checked us in at Lees Ferry. She called, "Are you the Calder
party?"

"Yes," said Fritz. "I'm Fritz Calder. How can I help you?"

"Oh. Uh, well, I'm just checking on you, actually. I hear you've had some trouble."

Fritz nodded grimly.

"Well, sorry to hear it," said Maryann. She nodded toward the dory. "It looks like it's taken on some water."

Fritz again nodded. "We're managing okay. Thanks for checking."

Maryann was a little thing, not much over five foot two, and her chubby little life vest added a cuteness to her muscular, authoritative stance. She seemed to tarry a bit, staring at Fritz a moment longer than was quite necessary.

Yes, he is gorgeous, I wanted to tell her. *Feast with your eyes, dear, but don't sit down at the table, because that chair is taken.*

"See you at the falls, then," she said and opened up her throttle.

Another mile and a half downriver we came upon a plug of dark rock that stuck up out of the river about fifty feet, taller than it was wide. "Brendan, look," I said. "It's Vulcan's Anvil. It's what we call a volcanic neck, the rock that cooled slowly inside the throat of a dying volcano. For the next eighty-five miles, we'll be seeing volcanic features. They're extremely young, geologically speaking, all under a million years. Recent argon-argon dating studies say that this neck is about six hundred thousand years old, but that's three times older than the earliest fossils of what we consider modern humans."

Brendan lifted his sunglasses and stared at me.

I smiled back at him. "I've made a decision, Brendan. You're a smart kid, so you'll make your own mind up about things one way or another. I know your mother's Bible says that God created everything in six days a little over six thousand years ago, and in my own way I do respect her decision to believe whatever makes the best sense to her, but we are in the United States of America. Half of my ancestors came here because an almighty being back in England was dictating to them who and what and how they should worship and threatening them with all manner of persecution if they presumed for a moment to question what the king believed. Almost four hundred years have passed since those ancestors climbed into leaky ships and sailed across an ocean to a place they'd never been just so they could think their own thoughts, and when we declared our independence and rights over two hundred years ago we wrote it down in ink that we meant to keep things clean by separating church and state. Now I find myself in a nation that's starting to have the same kind of squabbles all over again, and what does that tell me? That humans are always going to disagree on things that matter deeply to them. So I've decided that the best I can do for you is answer your questions as honestly and completely as I can and trust that as you grow up and prosper and outlive all of us disagreeing adults, you will make your own personal peace with these ambiguities."

Brendan thought about that for a moment. "End of speech?" he asked.

"End of speech."

"Cool," said Brendan.

All too quickly, we arrived at the top of Lava Falls. Everyone pulled off to the right bank, tying up next to Ranger Eliasson's motorized raft, and we got out to scout it and listen to its thunder. A jumble of broken-up hunks of basalt formed a talus slope, but decades of boatmen had beaten a pathway through it leading up to an aerie from which we could assess the coming challenge. A hundred yards farther along the trail I could see the ranger and the botanist, taking a good, long look.

We joined them, and I stared out across the crash of water that was rushing past us. Here was the last truly big rapid and, by most accounts, the meanest of the bunch, the size 10 that set the top of the scale for all other rapids on this river.

Mungo folded his arms across his life vest. "There's the Cheese Grater," he said, scowling at an immense rock that stood up right in the middle of the biggest waves. "I wrapped a raft around that monster the first time I came through here, and I can tell you it was one unholy mess getting that boat out of there."

I felt slightly sick. I turned to Fritz. "How 'bout I hike down to the bottom of the trail and photograph everyone as they come through?" I said. "It looks like there's plenty of room down there below Cheese Grater to pull over and pick me up."

Fritz seemed to melt with relief. "Are you sure? I'd hate to have you miss anything . . ."

"I'll see you at the bottom, I said."

Ranger Eliasson turned to Fritz. "I am truly sorry that you're having to clean up after that . . . person," she said.

"Thank you for the sympathy, Ranger Eliasson."

"Please call me Maryann. So how are you going to get it down there?"

"To be honest, I'm more than a little bit concerned. I really have no idea how it's going to handle. It took on so much water in Dubendorff that Wink couldn't control it, and he hit a rock. Hell, the thing seems to go looking for rocks now. None of us know how to row it with any authority, so we're not going to try to row it through the suds, but it's like the wrong kind of sea anchor. I'm really concerned that if we try to tow it through, or let it precede our raft on a line, we're going to have a serious problem."

Maryann said, "Why don't you let me sneak it around to the left there? I've got more control with a motor. I'll tie it with a quick-release knot and let it run out ahead of me, and if it goes out of control I'll have Susanne here release the line. Then if it stacks up on Cheese Grater or winds up in an eddy below too bashed up to float, it's not your problem."

Susanne added, "It can become one of the famous wrecks that dot this canyon, and maybe make a little compost for a nice growth of poison ivy."

Fritz smiled for the first time in days. "This all sounds great, but really, I couldn't ask you to—"

"You're not asking, we're offering. Come on, Susanne," said Maryann and trotted down the path toward the boats, where she produced a massive auxiliary pump and got to work on the dory.

Fritz followed after her and wrested the pump from her hands. In a blink the two were bent to the task together in very tight quarters, and I felt a twinge of jealousy, mixed in with gratefulness that this tiny woman was bringing a much-needed solution to Fritz's dilemma.

Turning my back on the scene, I headed on downriver toward the eddies below, searching for a good vantage point from which to watch *Wave Slut* crash its way into eternity.

The Cheese Grater was beautiful, in a dark and sinister way. Uncounted tons of rushing water had carved flutes that gave the rock a nasty serrated edge that faced into the current, and the steep drop and massive hydraulics of the rapid seemed bent on hurling all comers straight into it. I could see no elegant V pointing toward the safe route through chaos, only a narrow chute and a long, steep spill-off.

Suddenly Gary, Olaf, and Lloyd shot down through the gigantic waves in their kayaks, disappearing and reappearing through the dancing jets of spume, their paddles flying with the effort to stay upright. Only Gary stayed right side up the entire time; Olaf flipped but recovered quickly, and Lloyd rolled over twice. All three eddied out across the river from me to await the rafts.

Mungo was the next to line up on the rapid, with Molly and Glenda in the bow. There was a major drop just below the pour-off. They had to sneak around to river right and then pull hard to make it to the left of the Cheese Grater. They pitched and bucked with the rapid drops and wallowed over the waves.

Hakatai appeared next, pulling at the oars of Don and Jerry's raft while the couple crouched in the bow grinning like schoolchildren.

Dell and Nancy came next. After almost spinning a circle between the first drop-off and the Cheese Grater, Dell managed to pull left and sneak around the hungry rock.

Fritz and Brendan came last of our group. Here was a man in his element, charging into the fray with his beloved son cheering and pumping an arm in delight. The raft bucked and settled, spun, and bolted forward as Fritz suddenly threw back his head and howled at the fun he was having, and Ranger Eliasson had made it possible. I decided that she was my new best friend.

All eyes swung upriver again to watch the ranger's descent. She brought her raft broadside toward the lip and stood with hands on hips, assessing the lay of the water. The botanist was in the bow, left hand on a safety strap, right hand gripping the release line that ran to the dory. As the sticken craft slid sickeningly down into the first waves it wallowed and shuddered and filled to its gunwales in no time flat. Maryann was seated at the helm now, the controls to the engine in her right hand, holding on with her left. The dory lurched forward, spun, and hit Cheese Grater hard. The water had it in its fist now and ground it miserably along the side of the massive rock.

Maryann shot her raft around the combined hazard of the dory and the rock then deftly dodged below, yanking the imperiled boat out of the rut of water that held it. Her face fierce with concentration, she towed the boat down out of the rapid and into the eddy below, where Fritz waited with Brendan.

"You were amazing!" I yelled, as I came along the edge of the river toward the ranger's raft. "That was some incredible rope work! I grew up herding cattle, and it was just like you were working a bull!"

Maryann offered me a demure smile. "Another way to do it would have been to tow the dory behind me and charge through the rapid as fast as my engine would take me," she said, "but I prefer finesse. And I've been told to put safety first." She beached her raft, climbed out, and examined the damage to the side of the dory. In a low voice, she added, "And this was for all the women you've abused, you sorry son of a bitch!"

I wanted to hug her. I said, "I enjoyed watching it hit that rock myself. Having that man on this trip has been a very long walk in exceedingly tight shoes."

She nodded curtly to cover her embarrassment and swiftly got about pumping water out of the dory. To Fritz, she said, "I hope this doesn't make it even tougher to get this hulk down to Diamond Creek."

As he took the tow line from her hands. Fritz awarded her a serene smile.

Deciding to ignore this exchange among warriors, I climbed quietly on board our raft. Fritz rowed us back out into the stream, and we immediately shot down through the final riffles of Lava Falls and out into the thalweg.

Maryann idled her raft alongside ours. "How far are you headed tonight?" she called over the water.

"Whitmore Wash," he replied. "It's another eight miles, but we've got to make up for lost time."

Maryann said, "Then I'll continue to tow the dory. I'm going that way myself, and I'll put it on the beach for you."

"I won't try to talk you out of that," Fritz said.

I was glad that several yards of water separated our rafts. Otherwise, he might just have hugged her.

Diary of Holly Ann St. Denis
April 19

Dear God,

   Things haven't been right in the five days since we came off the
river. At first Mom was all happy because she could have a real shower
and get all prettied up. We came home here to our house in Las Vegas
and had a real party with pedicures and everything. She even let me put
some color on my toenails, not just the clear stuff, though I didn't tell
her that I was sorry to see my river feet change to town feet. She seemed
all happy, running around the house singing, even some of the rowdy
songs she sang in the days before she accepted Your Son as her personal
savior and married into the church.

   Then things began to change. She was awake a lot in the night and
said she had to go to the church office and the bank and get some things
straightened out, and one morning she was out somewhere when I woke
up. She talked about taking a trip and how I should pack some favorite
clothes, but then all of a sudden her mood turned very strange, sort of
a mixture of worried and angry. I wonder if it's because she has to deal

so much with "Uncle" Terry, who likes to tell her he knows better than she does what to do with church donations because he was "Daddy" Amos's right-hand man. They had a big fight, really yelling, and I hid in my room and put my hands over my ears so I couldn't hear.

Then "Uncle" came over yesterday and said a ranger from the Grand Canyon was trying to get hold of her but she shouldn't call him back because the church didn't need that kind of publicity. He said he'd told the ranger that she was unavailable for comment, but if the ranger found his way to her door she should refuse to answer any of his questions and that went for me, too. He was downright mean to Mom, looking at her all nasty. He grabbed her arm in a way that scared me and hauled her off into the kitchen to talk where I couldn't hear them. After that Mom got worse and worse.

Today Mom has gotten so bad she's like she was before she found Your Son Jesus. She won't get out of bed and won't open the curtains. Dear Heavenly Father, I miss the Colorado River. I really liked living out of doors, and the river guides made nice food and I got to play my guitar for You under Your Heavens. Mom seemed happy enough on the river, at least when her feet didn't hurt, and I felt so close to You there, and now things are all going wrong. I wish we could be back there now.

APRIL 19: WHITMORE

THE CANYON OPENS OUT WIDER TOWARD THE WEST, AND THE CLIFFS that hug the river channel are lower and festooned with dark basalt flows. Basalts form oddly brittle rock, cooling into hexagonal pillars that can be knocked over like matchsticks by flowing water. As we rowed along, I told Brendan about the evidence that eruptions of these basalts had at times overwhelmed the river, creating short-lived dams that backed the waters up into temporary lakes.

After many hours' travel through a red and gray landscape of deepening desert, with cacti appearing more and more frequently along the widening slopes, we came around a bend to Whitmore Wash, a side canyon that opened to a wide delta at river level. Its gravels were decked heavily with tamarisks, forming a grove that obscured the campsites from us until we were right on the beach. As we pulled up, a strange thing happened: A great big man lumbered out of the thicket and started yelling at us. He wore an orange plastic rain poncho and had a knitted ski mask pulled down over his face, and great sprigs of tamarisk spouted from the top of it. "You can't camp here!" he roared, in a booming low voice. "No camping! This space is reserved!" He waved his arms, shaking additional stalks of brush over his head in threat, and stumbled even closer, limping heavily.

Ours was the last raft to arrive at this scene, and Fritz stood up at the oars to face the challenge. "Is there a problem?" he asked loudly, in his calm pilot-commander voice.

"This site is reserved!" the man roared again. "It's reserved for the Calder party!" Suddenly he lurched toward our raft. "Are *you* Fritz Calder?"

"Who wants to know?" Fritz asked, keeping his voice steady.

The great galoot shook his branches at us one more time, then dropped them on the gravel and yanked off his ski mask. "Tiny wants to know!" he shouted in a higher, much more familiar voice. "How ya doin', chump?"

Fritz sprang from our raft and charged up the beach to embrace his friend. "How'd you get here? This is wonderful! Tiny, you old sot, you don't know how glad I am to see you!"

As the two big men slapped and hugged at each other, another tall person walked out from behind the cover of the tamarisk: Faye Carter, my friend and Fritz's business partner, grinning to beat the band. Now I ran from the raft, so glad to see her I couldn't help shrieking with delight. "How did you get here?" I demanded to know. The others were up on the shore now, securing their craft to the thickest stands of tamarisk and greeting the visitors.

Faye gave me a bone-crushing hug. "When we heard what had happened up the river, we figured it was time to saddle up and get down here." She pointed up the wash toward the north. "There's a dude ranch up there—the Bar 10—and they have a nice little airstrip. Tiny got out of the hospital last week, and he's feeling pretty good now, so I flew him down here. The ranch arranged to bring us down by helicopter. There's a helo pad just a half mile up the river, and we caught a ride down here with a park ranger who was towing a dory with some ugly holes in its sides."

"Then you've met Maryann Eliasson."

"Her and Susanne McCoy. They're just down the way there doing some studies on the tamarisk. Nice folks."

"Very nice. The ranger is a bit too admiring of Fritz for my comfort, but aside from that . . ."

"You can't argue with her taste. And don't worry, I told her that the man is taken, and Fritz didn't seem to matter much once she spotted Tiny! It seems she has a taste for enormous men. Besides, she wouldn't want to mess with you."

"Not one bit. So where's your gear?"

Just then a helicopter came thundering in overhead, flew along the river, up over the cliff to river left, and descended out of sight.

Faye said, "They come out of Las Vegas to meet up with rafts so people can take on the canyon à la carte, floating down only as far as Diamond Creek. The folks at Bar 10 make arrangements like that, too. Or if you're sick of camping by this point, you can rim out and the Bar 10 will feed you up and fly you from their strip out to Las Vegas. It's a neat outfit they have up there. You can stay in covered wagons, and they have trail rides and such."

"Wonders never cease." I stared after the helicopter, a bit put out to have my sanctuary invaded by machinery. After almost three weeks camping on the river, life had become blessedly simple. "Do you have gear with you? Are you staying the night?"

"Yes, ma'am." She led me up along a little creek to the place where they had stashed their belongings. "I've made arrangements to hike up the trail in the morning and get met by the four-wheel brigade. Tiny would like to stay and run the rest of the trip with you. He's made an amazing recovery, but he's not up to much hiking."

"The man's insane. He left hunks of himself all over I-80."

"Both facts have been amply established."

I didn't care how crazy Tiny was; Fritz had visibly relaxed the moment the man joined us. He was smiling again, laughing, his old happy self. Leading the trip had weighed heavily on his shoulders. Things had not gone to plan from the moment Wink joined the group, and when he left it as he had, the load on Fritz had become unbearable. He needed his friend.

We had our tents set up and a mess of tamale pie cooking in the Dutch ovens when Maryann and Susanne appeared at the campsite. "We hate to ask," Maryann began, "but another group has just arrived at the lower campsite, and it's late. They'd have to head a couple of miles farther down the river to find a site large enough for them, and it's possible that it's already taken. Would it be all right if we joined your group?"

Tiny answered for all of us by offering her a beer. "The more the merrier, little lady."

She waved off the beer. "I'm on duty, and that's Ranger Eliasson to you," she said saucily, but then she rolled her weight onto one hip and added, "Rain check?"

"I'll check you with a whole thunderstorm," he purred.

As another helicopter clattered overhead, Maryann jumped into action, shouting for everyone to stay at the camp. Backing off a hundred yards to open ground up the delta, she created an exclusion zone for the aircraft to land. I noticed then that she had already mounted a length of flagging that had been tied to a tree, a telltale for wind direction. She was expecting this helicopter: Why?

Faye peered at the descending craft. "That's not a commercial helo," she said. "What the hell?"

"It's Park Service," I said.

The noise of the helicopter magnified as it bounced off the near walls of the canyon, and now we felt the downwash of the rotors. It turned and I could see the pilot surveying the ground through the Plexiglas floor of the cockpit, looking for a clear spot to settle.

Maryann stood between the camp and the helicopter, waving her hands to guide it in, one hand, both hands, now crossing them in an X to indicate that it was down. Her hair blew back from the blast, but she stood still, waiting for the pilot to shut down the engine. The blades began to slow then, and the whine of their slices through the air descended and stopped.

The passenger's side door opened. A booted foot came out, then a leg, and then the rest of the man, decked out in a flight suit. He had some age to him, but he was fit and trim if a bit stiff along his spine. He moved down from the cockpit of the aircraft in one long step and settled a Park Service green cap on his head using both hands, straightened his flight suit with a tug, faced the campsite, squared his shoulders, and began to stride toward us. Maryann had to trot to keep up with him. She was saying something to him, her hands moving in a pleading gesture, but the grim expression on his face did not change. She led him straight to Fritz.

The man spoke. "Are you Fritz Calder?"

"The same. May I offer you a beer?"

"No, thank you. I mean to place into evidence your mineral hammer."

Fritz narrowed his eyes in confusion. "My what?"

"I believe you call it a rock hammer. Or perhaps it belongs to your wife, Emily Bradstreet Hansen." He began to scan the faces in our group, limning which one might be me.

I shot a look at Maryann, who now stared at the ground, curling up even tinier. "This is Ranger Weber," she announced. "He is chief ranger for the park. As such, he holds a Class One Federal Law Enforcement Commission, and . . ."

I stepped toward Weber. "You can have my rock hammer if you wish, sir, but would you please first explain why you want it?"

He swung his face my direction. "I am investigating a homicide."

"The rock hammer's right over there, sir," Maryann said miserably, pointing toward our tent.

Ranger Weber strode briskly to where she pointed, produced a plastic bag, turned it inside out over his right hand, and used it like a glove to requisition my hammer, flipping the bag right side out again and sealing it shut. Shifting the bag to his opposite hand, he then produced a felt-tipped pen and wrote the date and his name across the seal. Pulling out additional bags, he said, "Now I need your pocketknife, Mr. Calder. In a separate bag, please."

My stomach sank. I knew this behavior in a cop, and his reason for being here was all coming together in a flash: Wink's body had been found, and judging by the beeline Weber was making toward that hammer, he'd been killed with an object of that size and weight. But where? And when? And if Maryann Eliasson knew all of this, why hadn't she told us?

On the next mental click, all of that came clear to me as well: She had been sent that morning to locate us and keep an eye on us. For all I knew, there was no other group camping at Whitmore that night; she had wangled her way into our camp under orders from her superior, and she had done a damned fine job of sneaking her job in plain sight.

"But—"

Fritz fumbled his pocketknife out of his pocket. He seemed lost in inner space, his gaze staring inward, his face drawn. He hadn't moved.

Ranger Weber strolled back toward him with the slow deliberation of a bull. Five feet short of Fritz he stopped and held out a second bag.

Fritz dropped his knife into the bag.

After repeating the performance of sealing the evidence, Weber stared up into Fritz's face as if measuring his height. He spoke again, this time addressing him more formally. "Lieutenant Commander Frederick Calder?"

I had never heard Fritz addressed by his military rank, but the term had a decided effect on him. He seemed to snap awake. He stiffened up into a military brace and nodded.

"Will you come with me, please?"

Fritz did not move. "If you will kindly tell me where are we going," he said firmly.

"To the South Rim. I am placing you under arrest for the murder of

George Oberley." He began the familiar drone: "You have the right to remain silent . . ."

As the words of the Miranda rights tumbled past him, Fritz turned to Tiny, handed him his beer, said, "You're in charge," and then turned to me. His expression was blank, unreadable. "Take care of Brendan," he said, then marched toward the helicopter with the selfless cooperation he had learned while in uniform.

Weber marched after him, and I had to run to catch up. "But what's the deal here? Are you going to be gone overnight? Won't you need a change of clothes, or your toilet kit, or—"

"A jacket would be nice," Frtiz said levelly. "It might be cold at altitude."

We had reached the helicopter. I spun on Ranger Weber. "You wait a minute, okay? I've got to get the man his gear!"

Weber nodded permission but kept his attention on loading Fritz into the helicopter.

I ran and dove at the tent, thinking, *This is ridiculous! Fritz didn't kill anyone! If my rock hammer were still here I would use it to bash the engine on that machine so he could not leave!* I tore into Fritz's dry bag and pulled out his day pack, stuffed it with his jacket, hiking boots, the pouch that held his toothbrush, razor, and comb. I found a clean pair of socks and a T-shirt that wasn't too bad. My hands were shaking. I was swimming in adrenaline.

Outside, I ran to my husband to hand him the pack, but Ranger Weber snagged it out of my hands. I threw myself at Fritz then, leaning into the helicopter, and wrapped my arms around him.

Ever so gently, he patted me on the back. "It's better this way," he said. "We'll get it over with, and there will be less fuss."

"What are you talking about?"

"Just take care of Brendan," he whispered into my hair. "Trust me, sweetheart."

I let go and stepped back. I could see Brendan standing by the kitchen stoves, holding on to the table like it was the only thing keeping him from sinking through the ground.

Fritz said, "He loves you, and so do I." Then he checked his harness, put on the headphones that Weber handed to him, and nodded to the pilot just as if he were in charge. Ranger Weber climbed into his command post in the front of the aircraft, gave the pilot his own nod, took off his hat, smoothed his thinning hair, and put on his headphones.

Maryann drew me away, outside the exclusion zone. The engine started then, first the rising whine of the engine and then the great rotors beginning to move, spinning up into a blur, a disk that now tipped forward as the bird lifted, nose toward the river, rising higher and higher as it reached toward the east, dwindling finally into a dot and a distant thunder that faded into the darkening sky.

APRIL 19: PARTY ENDED

"You!" I shouted at Maryann Eliasson. "You tell us *now* what happened to that son of a bitch Oberley! I want to know why my husband and that boy's father is being taken away like a criminal!"

The rest of the group moved toward her, too, and Susanne McCoy moved in to take a protective place behind her. Susanne said, "Now, everybody, please calm down. Maryann did not like following the orders given to her, and she is as shocked as the rest of you that Major Calder has been removed from this beach."

Maryann found her voice then. "That's true. I was told to keep him here for questioning. That's the whole story, I swear it! But yeah, Wink Oberley's body has been found. And he was murdered."

Chaos broke out then, everyone asking questions and demanding answers at once. Maryann had to raise a hand to ask for quiet. "This is serious business," she said, "and I'm sure you all want to help get Fritz back here as quickly as possible. From my take on the man he is not a killer—or at least not a murderer."

"What in hell do you mean by that?" I demanded. My brain was running a million miles an hour.

She turned scarlet. "I mean that he was in the military, and he dropped bombs, right? So in a manner of speaking—"

"Stuff it right there!" I told her. I wasn't going to tolerate that kind of thinking. "This whole mess makes no sense, so let's all calm down and figure out how to deal with it."

Brendan broke his own stasis of shock. "My dad didn't kill anyone!" he said. "If anyone killed Wink it should have been me!" He made a fist and pounded his chest for emphasis.

My brain filled with words: *Look after Brendan, you said . . . but what does that look like, Fritz? What exactly do you do for a thirteen-year-old boy on the brink of manhood whose dad has just been arrested for the murder of a monster who'd been terrorizing him?*

A weird thing happened: I got an answer. Inside my head, I heard Fritz say calmly, *Call the bluff.*

The bluff. Things began to snap together in my mind. I said, "Wait, our life vest went missing, remember? What if Wink swiped it, swam to Havasu, and hiked out? The man walked around in shorts, a T-shirt, and flip-flops when the rest of us were up to our chins in fleece, and he knew this river like a second skin, so he could have survived that swim, and he knew that sharp turn in the current he'd have had to make to get into the side canyon. And there's no way he was as drunk as he was trying to make us think." Turning to Mungo, I said, "He took your Scotch to the latrine and probably dumped it in the bushes, and he was spilling as much beer as he was drinking later on, maybe all of it. His behavior was over-the-top awful for days before he disappeared, like he was consciously trying to provoke Fritz. And he hardly seemed to be trying to keep that dory afloat anymore. It was like he was planning to disappear and wanted to make it look like Fritz killed him."

Brendan let go of the table. "He kept going over to that church group that was camping near us," he said. "And the night at Nevills I saw him hiding in the tamarisk. When that woman with the wrong sandals came by, he whistled to her like a little bird. They thought no one was watching them. When he tried to touch her she pushed his hand away, but she smiled at him."

The kid has the makings of a spy, I thought. I said, "There has to be a connection there, Maryann. When did that group come off the river?"

She knit her brow, thinking. "I think it was the fourteenth. I'd have to check."

I said, "The fourteenth. The next night Wink disappears. Don't you see it? He was staging his own death, and maybe someone in that group was in on it."

Brendan said, "This book I was reading says a lot of the people who die here are never found, so this is the perfect place to look like you've died."

Maryann shook her head ruefully. "It would be just like him. Always starting things rolling and never taking an ounce of responsibility for anyone he hurts in the process."

Faye said, "And he'd been run out of Princeton. And his wife wanted him to get a damned job and feed his kids."

Maryann said, "But wait, he *is* dead. It's not just an act!"

I said, "Then something went wrong with his plan. Come on, tell us what you know. Where was he found?"

She closed her eyes. "Right here," she said, "or more precisely, just beyond those tammies at the upriver edge of the gravel bar. Seth Farnsworth saw him. Saw *it*. Said it was pretty gross."

"Right here?" said Jerry. "Seriously? That man messes up the evening even when he's dead! So okay, he disappears from Ledges on the fifteenth and is found here *when*?"

"Yesterday." Maryann shook her head. "The whole park's been humming with it. You're right, Brendan, people die here, but we never get used to it, and this time it was someone a lot of us knew, and even if we weren't all exactly happy with him . . . well, it's got everyone upset."

Jerry said, "Can you call Seth Farnsworth on your radio?"

"The radio won't work here." Maryann threw her hands wide in exasperation. "Listen, you've got to understand also that this is an official situation. Weber takes his position really seriously, and if he thought I was making investigations without his say-so, well . . ."

Brendan said, "That's my dad who just got arrested!"

Jerry said, "Maryann, you probably don't know that Em here is a detective. You've got one of the finest forensic minds on the planet right here at your disposal. She's famous for the work she's done."

Maryann looked at me like I'd just grown a second nose.

I said, "I'm a geologist, but yes, I do a lot of forensic work with the local police."

"And the FBI," said Faye. "Where do you keep your sat phone, Em? I think it's time we called in a few of our brethren."

"Whoa!" said Maryann. "Wait just a damned minute! We're on national park ground here, so it's national park jurisdiction!"

Susanne said, "He may have been found here, but if the murder took place on the opposite bank, then it would be Hualapai land, because the obvious way to get a body here is by helicopter. It doesn't make a whole lot of sense that a body could get all the way here from Ledges without getting caught in an eddy."

Maryann said, "You have a point." She pursed her lips, thinking. "That part's been bothering me. And if you want to kill someone, you don't put the corpse in a life preserver before you toss it into the river, because then it's more certain to be found."

I said, "Then someone wanted him found, and wanted him found here. Who?"

Maryann said, "You're right, the helo pad is on the other side, river left, and thus is under tribal jurisdiction."

"Or would that be Bureau of Indian Affairs?" said Susanne.

"Or again FBI," said Faye.

I said, "I'm still liking the idea that he hiked out through Havasu Canyon."

Maryann said, "The top of that canyon's a long way from anywhere."

"Then someone could have picked him up," said Jerry. "Maybe Julianne."

"What?" said Mungo. "Didn't you see the hole she beat in his dory?"

"With my rock hammer!" I said.

"Sure," said Nancy. "But she was just as crazy as he was. And maybe they had a plan that he was going to disappear and join her somewhere and they didn't want anyone going looking for him at her place." Jerry said, "But what kind of a monster would leave his kids?"

A stifled sob brought our attention to Glenda. She had contracted, head down and arms brought up tight against her breast, hands balled into fists.

Nancy said, "Sorry about all that, Glenda, but didn't you know he was boffing someone else on the upper half of the trip?"

"It's just so embarrassing," she sniffed. "And Jesus Christ, everyone, the man is dead!"

I said, "He damned near drowned Brendan on Sockdolager! He untied the raft the kid was sitting in, and the only thing that saved him was that he had his life vest on!"

Brendan grabbed my arm. "Don't tell them that!"

"Why not?" asked Mungo. "You did famously, kid! You came all the way down that rapid underneath that raft!"

Brendan leaned into Mungo's face. "Don't you see? Dad was mad as blazes, and that's why the rangers think he killed Wink!"

Maryann said, "I don't think for a minute that your father committed murder, Brendan. Wink Oberley has been pulling stunts like that for years, and far less honorable men than your father have managed to restrain themselves."

Silence settled across the camp. Only then did I notice that the sun had completely set and that it was getting cold.

Tiny said, "Okay then, let's get out of here early tomorrow and get on down the river so we can help our friend. We've still got thirty-seven miles of river to navigate, and our shuttle drivers won't be there with our vehicles until the day after tomorrow anyway. By the time we get to Diamond Creek, we need to have a plan."

Faye said, "I'm flying out of the airstrip up at Bar 10 tomorrow morning. I'll get our company's lawyer on task and see about bailing Fritz out."

"They'll have him in the holding cell at South Rim," said Maryann.

I said, "As long as the batteries hold out, I'll be on the sat phone making inquiries. Maryann and Susanne, you did not hear a word of this. I'm sure your Ranger Weber takes his job seriously, but if, when we get to Diamond Creek, Deputy Dawg still likes Fritz for this murder, so help me I shall pull out all the stops and show him how it's really done!"

Maryann pondered this for a moment, then said, "I believe that I am officially off duty now. Tiny, where do you keep your beer? And speaking of words you did not hear, I have a sat phone call or two to make so I can catch up with my old friend Seth."

We ate dinner and discussed plans further and then, as the embers in the fire pan winked out, we each wandered off to our own sleeping bag. I gave Fritz's to Tiny and shared mine with Faye. It was a long time before Brendan found sleep that night; I know, because we all pulled our camp mats out onto the sand and lay in the warmth of our sleeping bags staring up into the night sky, sending messages to Fritz by way of the stars.

"We're coming, Dad," Brendan said, just before he drifted off.

APRIL 20: NO JOY

PILOTS HAVE A JARGON ALL THEIR OWN WHEN THEY COMMUNICATE OVER radios. One of the strangest phrases is "no joy," which means anything from "I am unable to establish radio contact" to "I can't spot the enemy aircraft you just said is bearing down on me." These words ran like a squirrel in a cage inside my dreams all night, and in the morning, when Maryann still had not been able to establish radio contact with Seth Farnsworth and Faye had to leave to hike up the Whitmore trail to meet with the four-wheelers from Bar 10 Ranch, it began to sound like a klaxon.

"I am so sorry I can't stay with you," Faye said, as I stuffed granola bars into her day pack. "I left my daughter with—"

"You already explained all that, and I need you up there in the world making phone calls," I assured her. "You've got to get that lawyer online, get Fritz bailed out, you've got my list of questions that need answers, and you know who to ask. Now, just get going before I lose my mind!"

"You'd think that ranger guy would have figured out by now that Fritz isn't the one. I keep watching the sky for that damned Park Service helicopter, bringing him back."

"Trust me, so do I. Now be careful going up that trail. It looks like there are a lot of tight switchbacks."

"Okay, okay."

I walked her to the head of the trail, near a place where ancestral Indians had painted a series of images in red iron oxide pigment on white stone. I was lonely coming back toward the campsite but came across Susanne McCoy, who was studying a patch of cacti covered with waxy, lipstick red blooms. "There seem to be more cacti at this end of the river," I said, trying to make pleasant conversation. I was having a hard time thinking of anyone with the Park Service as a friend just then.

Susanne stood up and turned to face me. As if reading my mind, she said, "You should know that Maryann will do whatever's in her power to make things right."

"You don't mince words."

"No, I don't, and that's because like you, I'm a scientist, and we both know that scientists are just another sort of detective." She turned and swept her arms out in a gesture that took in all the plants in the land-scape. "This is where I do my forensics. I look for the bit that doesn't fit, that thing that has changed. Right now I'm watching for changes from global warming trends, the evidence of crimes we didn't know we were committing, but also from stupid human tricks like putting that dam in. Yeah, I know, we use the energy, but look at what's left of the plants that used to flourish along the high-water line over there on the opposite bank. See it? The spring runoff used to come way up the bank. You can see exactly how high because that's where the last of the leafy green forbs and shrubs like hackberry, catclaw acacia, and mesquite grow. These plants needed the high water stages to get started. What's left survives because it has roots that go deep, and what you see is at least as old as the dam. Then down at river level we have the nonnative tama-risk. So like you, I'm watching for things that should be there but aren't or things that are there that shouldn't be. I liked your summation of what might really have happened with Wink."

"Right, the opportunist who wasn't truly flourishing. He shouldn't have been on this river trip. He shouldn't have been at Princeton. He shouldn't have been in the Army Airborne Rangers. He shouldn't have had his head up his ass."

"Or his dick up any number of women," she said simply. "But given that he was all those places, where did he go from here?"

"And how did he get back? I thought about that one all night, and each time I see a commercial helicopter come in here I want to ask the pilot if he carried anyone in two days ago who answers to Wink's description. The only problem is that even if we can establish that he went out via Havasu, he didn't come back as a corpse."

"Because the pilots wouldn't allow that."

"Exactly. Pilots take their jobs very seriously, which includes the safety of those on board. They do not carry people who can't get on and off under their own steam. So I'm looking for another vector, such as this trail behind me. Perhaps he came back in past Bar 10, and his corpse was carried down that trail on a mule. I've asked Faye to check with the ranch to see if there's any way anyone could slip past their notice."

"Why kill someone somewhere else and then go to the trouble of bringing the body back to the river?"

"Simple: Wink went to the trouble of making it look like he'd died in the canyon, then whoever killed him would take advantage of that subterfuge by bringing him back here, in order to obscure the evidence. It's the old game of misdirection. Obviously Ranger Weber doesn't see the sleight of hand."

"Then how would you prove that he left the canyon and returned?"

I shrugged my shoulders. "There's where the forensics come in. You look for that telltale indicator that not only says that things have changed, but that something has been brought in from somewhere else. There will be particulates on the body, perhaps up underneath the fingernails, and his stomach will contain a meal that wouldn't have come from here."

Susanne smiled. "Oh, I like that! Something exotic from a buffet in Vegas! And the botany would be all wrong. There would be pollen from even farther out into the Mojave or the Sonoran Desert, or from places overseas that ship things to Vegas."

"If he was in Las Vegas."

"Everything weird shows up in Las Vegas sooner or later. So what do you need in order to make your investigation?"

"Access to the corpse would help," I said. "But I'll bet I'd be the last person Ranger Weber wants to have sniffing at that body. Conflict of interest and all that."

"Well then, there's the difference between scientists and cops: We're looking to eliminate what's not true, while they're assuming everyone is lying."

"Do you have any idea where the body would be taken?" I asked.

Susanne considered my question. "This is Mohave County. The coroner's office would be in Kingman."

We walked back toward the campsite, where we found all hands busy reloading the rafts. Tiny had Brendan busy hefting and hauling, and the lad hustled past me carrying an oversized load from our tent. "Excuse me," he said with grave importance. "Coming through."

When he was out of earshot I turned to Tiny. "Thank you," I said. "He barely slept last night."

"Keeping busy is not the cure, but it soothes," he said. He tipped his head toward Maryann. "She got a call through to HQ, and the Man won't be bringing our man back today."

"Shit."

"I agree wholeheartedly. Meanwhile, let's get this show on the road."

"Can you row?"

"Not really. They had me in traction for a while. My neck is pretty screwed up."

"Understatement."

"Yeah."

"Thanks for coming, Tiny. It would be an even bigger mess if you weren't here."

"I'll accept that praise however faint or left-handed." He lifted one of his huge hands and used it to pat me on the head, then shambled down the beach toward the rafts.

We shoved off at around ten with Brendan at the oars and Tiny riding on top of the load in a reclining camp chair that we had rigged for him. Maryann had the dory under tow again, breezily stating that it was evidence in an ongoing investigation, and I didn't argue. She asked where we planned to camp that night, waved good-bye to all of us while gazing longingly on Tiny, and opened up her throttle. As I watched the binary rig disappear down the river, I wanted to kick myself, because she was right, the dory was evidence. I vowed to examine every inch of it if I got another opportunity.

The river was wide and lovely but lonely without Fritz. Minutes and hours slid past in a mental storm that clashed with the clear skies and serene landscape. We stopped for lunch somewhere and continued on, clocking down the miles toward the end of what was supposed to have been a joyous journey through river, rock, and time. I had trouble holding in my mind the reality that Wink was dead; I had felt so certain that he had simply slithered away like the snake he was, and yet his body had been found, and it had displayed evidence that another human had killed him. He had died by another man's hand, not just the ragged run-out of his own miserable luck. My brain flew crazed loops around the idea that Ranger Weber thought that Fritz was that man. How could he? Fritz was such a kind and gentle person. He could not have killed anyone. Could he?

APRIL 21: PULLOUT

THE MORNING OF OUR LAST DAY ON THE RIVER DAWNED COOL AND CRISP in the desert air. We were camped near Granite Park, a place where the river split around a central island of gravel and cobbles. The sandy ground along the river's edge was dimpled with the burrows of doodlebug larvae, and beyond the braces of willows and ferocious lines of cacti the ground rose and rolled back to a desert scrub of ocotillo and barrel cacti.

I sat in our raft and one last time took the satellite telephone out of its protective box, switched it on, and called Faye Carter.

"Em! How are you doing?"

"Lousy," I said.

"I'd offer comfort, but let's conserve connect time. The lawyer has been working on getting someone lined up in Arizona. I've got child care coverage lined up, so I'm standing by to fly wherever you need me to go. And I've got a message from your workplace that sounds urgent: Some girl who says she knows you from the river has been trying to reach you. Write down this number."

"Who?"

"Her name is Holly Ann St. Denis. She said it was about Wink Oberley and that she met you on the river."

"The girl who played the guitar! This is good!" I said.

"Who is she?"

"She was with that religious group."

"Whatever." Faye dictated the number.

I read it back. "Did she say what it was about?"

"She said she'd speak to you only. Now here's the bit from Bar 10: The place is wide open and they'd have seen anyone who came or went. There was unusually little air traffic over the ranch in that time period, i.e., none. And it's like forty miles across open desert to get to the nearest highway. He did not leave nor return through that quarter."

"Do they track other aircraft?"

"No, but I'm working on getting the records for any aircraft that made short trips from surrounding airports during the time of interest. And like you asked, I've got the names of the people who found the body, but I'm having trouble getting phone numbers. The only person from that group who was available to talk to me said the corpse was unrecognizable but—"

The connection ended. When the next satellite rose above the horizon I dialed the number Faye had given me for Holly Ann. I got a recording: "Praise God! Leave a message!"

I told the telephone, "Hi, Holly Ann, this is Em Hansen. I'm coming off the river today. In about five or six hours you'll be able to call me on my cell phone. Please do. Here's the number—" The connection went dead. I dialed again and left my number. On my next satellite connection I talked to Faye again, but she said she'd already given me what she had, and I switched off to spare the batteries. I put the phone away and took a last walk along the river's edge, trying to focus on the sprays of yellow flowers that bloomed in profusion there.

Tiny held court at breakfast. "I hardly got to spend any time with you all, and I wish the circumstances could have been better, but it's been great anyway," he said. "Maybe we can all get together later in the year and float the Green River through Desolation Canyon, or some other stretch of God's watery heaven. Anyway, in the meantime we've got a mate to get out of hock. I'm to blame that he's there. Fritz is being held for killing a guy I should never have invited on this trip; no offense, Glenda. Well, we got us one of the best detectives in creation here, our own Em Hansen, but the law's gonna look on her as something of a hostile 'cause they're holding her man. So we all gotta help, right?"

A general hubbub of consent followed, and Jenny reached out and gave me a hug. I had to squeeze my eyes shut so I didn't burst into tears. I had never had so many friends pull together on my account, and their love almost knocked me over.

Jerry said, "I organize things for a living, so I'm running your nerve center."

"That would be great," I said, "and can you and Don head to the South Rim? Fritz should have someone there with him as soon as possible." I fought back a wave of fatigue laced with more jangled emotions. "Sorry, everybody, my brain has been sliding in and out of a strange fog. Okay, so, I really need to see that body. Anybody who can come with me into Kingman, I'd really appreciate it."

"I'm with you," said Mungo.

"Sure," said Molly. "What's in Kingman?"

I said, "I'm going to have to get into the county morgue."

"How jolly," said Nancy.

I felt oddly swoony and put my hand on my stomach.

"Are you all right?" asked Jerry.

"It's probably that I haven't eaten yet."

She turned to the kitchen table and produced a bowl of oatmeal and a mug of herbal tea.

I lifted the tea to my nose. For some reason it smelled awful, and I couldn't help wincing. "Sorry," I said and handed it back to her. Not being able to eat scared me, and I thought, *I've been through plenty of murder cases, so why's this one getting to me?*

It's probably that your husband is the prime suspect this time, said another part of my brain.

"Sit down," Jerry said, shoving a chair up behind my legs. "Eat the oatmeal."

I did as she ordered. I took small spoonfuls and, between mouthfuls, did my best to outline how I hoped to open up the truth once we came off the river. We would return to paved roads, cell phone towers, and high-speed Internet via Peach Springs, a town on the Hualapai Reservation. An hour and a half down a two-lane highway lay Kingman, where, if there was to be any justice, the coroner would let me get a squint at Wink's remains.

My self-appointed village discussed the vectors each carload would follow upon leaving. Some would eventually go north into Utah, some would drive west toward California, and some would head east toward interstate highways that would lead them home to Colorado. But first, all agreed, we must spring Fritz.

We launched soon after and made a beeline for Diamond Creek, not even stopping at Pumpkin Springs to look at its colorful travertine deposits. We were a village with a mission, and the sooner we got after it the better. Our shuttle arrangements were for early afternoon, and we meant to be there, de-rigged and ready to load up and get on up the gravel road toward some answers.

Diamond Creek was an unintentionally ugly place, an abattoir for raft trips. Hualapai Indians checked our permits and pointed toward the route out. At the appointed hour, our shuttle drivers jounced down the road driving several of our vehicles and pulling a flatbed trailer that carried two more. I was never so glad to see Fritz's SUV, which Brendan and I packed in a flaming hurry, hurling gear into the back. The rental company appeared next, and we had our rafts deflated and rolled up and loaded in no time. As I handed them the box containing the satellite phone, I said, "I'll need to know all calls that have been made from this thing."

The agent from the rental company said, "Don't you know who's used it?"

I wasn't sure how much to tell him, so I said, "One of our party left before paying his tab, and I want to know if he made any calls first."

Maryann stepped forward and took the phone out of the man's hands. "Sorry, but you're right, Em; this is evidence." She gave me an embarrassed wince. "Weber's orders. Anything that might be evidence is evidence."

I gritted my teeth. "So Wink is still costing us even from the far side of the morgue."

Maryann said, "With my own eyes I saw you return this item. I am seizing it from the rental company, not you." She stared up at the man. "I am a federally commissioned officer of the law. I hereby seize this for a federal case."

The man's eyes widened. "Wow, bummer," he said. "Someone died?"

"Yeah, Wink Oberley," said Maryann.

"Oh. Shit. Oberley." The man shrugged as if his skin had suddenly grown a layer of slime and he was trying to knock it loose. Having thus shaken himself into action, he began to walk around his load to cinch down his cam straps before leaving.

That left only the dory, which Maryann had towed all the way to the pull-out. I asked her, "Does Weber want this thing, too? Fritz didn't have time to tell me what we were supposed to do with it."

"The Man didn't say anything about that bucket," she said drily.

"Either way, I'm going to give it a good going-over."

Don and Maryann helped me pull open hatches and shine a flashlight into far nooks and crannies.

"I was wondering where these got to," said Don, lifting a sodden granola bar from the hold. "But there's not much else in here except his basic gear."

The tally of equipment was surprisingly short: Aside from a short Paco Pad and a much-battered sleeping bag, we found only his life vest and a cheap spare, his hat, a pair of flip-flop sandals, and a small dry bag containing three T-shirts, a pair of cargo shorts, a fleece jacket, a pair of athletic shoes, a minimal collection of toiletries, and a tattered paperback. "Well, I don't know what I expected," I said. "This is what Seth Farnsworth found when he came to Ledges, and nothing's changed. Wink was carrying some of our fresh produce, but we ate all that. I wonder what he had in the forward hatch that he didn't want me to see."

Maryann said, "He tried to keep you out of here?"

I bent and stuck my head back inside that space. There was nothing there. I straightened up and faced the ranger. "Yeah, and he got pretty hotheaded about it when I got nosy, like there was something special in there he didn't want me to see."

The Hualapai in charge ambled over to the dory. "What about this boat?" he asked. "I don't see a trailer for it. You are taking it, eh?"

Maryann explained what had happened to its owner.

The Hualapai shook his head. "Bad," he said. "But it still goes."

It began to occur to me that getting that hulk to Diamond Creek and off the river was only part of our requirement: We must now get it up a rutted, stony road to . . . where? I turned to Tiny. "Did Wink have a plan for getting this thing out of here?"

Tiny looked worried. "He said he had a pal who'd show up with a trailer."

I said, "I wonder if he meant that, or if that was just some vague plan he had, or if he planned all the while to leave it to the rest of us to drag it out of here."

The man from the rental company shook his head. "Don't look at me. We don't have a place for it on our load. Maybe if you wanted we could pick it up another time?"

"When indeed?" I muttered.

"Damn it!" said Brendan. "When is Wink going to quit messing with us?"

The head Hualapai adjusted his sunglasses. "We could make arrangements to keep it for a while as long as you can get it out of our way. There'd be an additional fee, of course."

So now we had to pass the hat to pay for the keep and removal of a dead dory? I wanted to kill the man all over again.

"It's evidence," said Maryann. "I'll haul it."

As I thought this thought a truck appeared at the top of the road with a trailer bouncing along behind it. It was Hank, Wink Oberley's beleaguered friend. He bounced his rig down the road, kicking up dust, and, with the deliberation necessary when driving a rutted road, eventually pulled up next to the dory. The near truck window slid open, knocking loose a shroud of silt, and one skinny elbow appeared over the windowsill. "Where's Wink?" he asked.

"Gone," said Mungo.

"He left before I even got here? Gone where? Did he run off again? That sumbitch, he stole my new shirt! A nice plaid with buttons and a collar, even. I'd just got it in the mail from Cabela's, on sale for $16.95. So where's he hiding himself?"

"In the morgue," said Mungo.

Hank threw open the door and jumped down to the ground. "He what?"

"Gone. Dead. Not here. In the morgue. Sorry, lad."

Hank turned and leaned his face against the metal frame of the window of his truck and began to mumble to himself in little words I could not quite make out.

I said, "Come to think of it, where is that plaid shirt? It's not in his gear here. Did he have it on the night he disappeared?" A bit late for decent manners, I added, "Sorry, Hank, but as you can see we've got a mess on our hands, so we're a bit distracted. Sorry for your loss."

Jerry Rasmussen opened Wink's dry bag and peered inside. "Nope, no plaid shirt, and I could swear he was wearing something else that last evening by the fire. Glenda, do you remember?"

"I went to bed, you'll recall."

Jerry persisted. "He didn't slip anything into your gear, perchance?"

"God, no," said Glenda. "Uh-unh. I repacked everything last night and I would have noticed."

I said, "All the more reason that we've got to get a look at that corpse. If he wasn't wearing that shirt, then he had to have taken it somewhere else, and that proves that he left the Ledges alive."

"What the hell are you all talking about?" cried Hank.

Mungo said, "Wink was murdered."

Hank began to shriek. "No! No, no, no! What am I going to tell Eleanor?"

"Who's Eleanor?" I asked. "Was that his wife?"

"She's *my* wife," sobbed Hank. "Oh Jesus, she's going to be so upset!"

"Why? Did she know him?"

"Know him? She's his half sister! Oh hell, she's going to be beside herself! She hated the asshole, but he was all the blood kin she had left." He began to talk rapidly, blathering personal information out of shock. "They had the same daddy, and they were both in and out of homes when they were kids, but she kept finding him again and he'd run off and get into one kind of a fix or another, and then—" He broke off into a strange keening. "Oh, how am I going to tell her?"

Maryann said, "So wait, then she's a next of kin? Because we need someone to identify the body." She caught my eye and nodded toward Hank, as if to say, *Here's your route into the coroner's office.*

"Right!" I said. "Let's get this thing loaded up and get on up that hill and give your wife a call!" I felt bad asking a grieving sibling to crack into a morgue, but I had my priorities: Get Fritz out of custody first and make amends later. "Besides," I said, "she'll want to know who really killed him so she can spit straight."

Glenda kindly put an arm around the brother-in-law.

Everyone grabbed hold of the dory and on Tiny's one-two-three-lift got it up onto the Park Service trailer and cinched down before Hank quite knew what was happening. We strapped the oars across the top and the personal gear down through the forward hatch.

I hurried over to Maryann, who was just climbing into the cab of a Park Service truck. "Okay if I make a couple more calls?" I asked.

She shrugged her shoulders.

I took confiscated satellite phone and asked Hank to call his wife to tell her she was about to make a trip across the state in a private plane. "It's a Piper Cheyenne, a big turboprop," I said. "I'm having a commercial pilot fly down to pick her up and get her to Kingman so she can identify her brother's remains." Next I dialed Faye and said, "I need you to fly to Page, Arizona, and pick up a woman and bring her to Kingman, arriving in about two and a half hours. I'll pick you and your passenger up at the airport and drive you into town. I'm passing the phone to a guy named Hank, and he's going to give you the woman's name and phone number in case she tries to stay home."

We thanked the Hualapais and paid our tab for using the pull-out and formed up a conga line of vehicles climbing the dusty slope. Glenda took the wheel in Hank's truck and I made a mental note to thank her afterward. We climbed through a dusty desert, easing across places where flash floods had turned the road to a wash of naked cobbles, and continued past grazing burros and ocotillo and other desert scrub.

At length we achieved Peach Springs, parked the vehicles at the first thing resembling a grocery store, and piled out under Mungo's instructions to observe one last important ritual of raft trip communal living: our first taste of ice cream in three weeks. I had an ice cream sandwich, but was so wound up that I couldn't eat more than two bites. Brendan went for one of the cones that had been rolled in nuts, and we bought two cones for Hank, who had suddenly become cavernously hungry.

Gary, Nancy, and Olaf finished their ice creams first. "We're on our way, then," said Gary. "We'll check the helicopter places in Las Vegas, and if we find anything, we'll call you. If not, we're on our way west, and we'll try to catch up with that woman who had such lousy luck birdwatching, Kathryn Davy."

"Thanks, guys. Let's all get together later in the summer."

Gary and Nancy each gave me a hug, and Olaf waved from the safety of Gary's truck.

"I'm not a mouse," I told Olaf. "I don't bite, and I sure won't crawl on you in your sleep."

He gave me a thumbs-up but maintained his distance.

So this is it, I thought. *Three weeks living in close proximity with these rascals and now off we go, scattering to our separate corners of the real world.* But I didn't have time to grieve the loss of the camaraderie of the river. I switched on my cell phone and handed it to Brendan and asked him to monitor it while I found a restroom at the filling station across the road from the market. I had an overwhelming need to vomit and wanted to do so in peace. When I returned he was talking to someone on the gadget.

"Yes," he was saying. "Uh-huh, this is Brendan, Em's stepson; you remember me! So what was it you needed to tell her? Oh, here she is now!" He turned to me, beaming. "It's Holly Ann," he told me, thrusting the phone toward me. "I think she's got something for you."

I put the phone to my ear. "Holly Ann?"

"Oh, I'm so glad I found you! Ms. Hansen, I—I don't know if this is quite correct to ask you, but there's something wrong, and I think it's got to do with Dr. Oberley."

My mind raced: How much did she know? I said, "How can I help you, dear?"

"Is he there? Can I talk to him?"

I closed my eyes. "No, he's not here, Holly Ann. I'm afraid we've got some very bad news for you."

Her voice went up an octave. "Please tell me he's not dead!"

"Where are you calling from?"

"Las Vegas. Brendan said you're in Peach Springs; that's about three hours' drive. Is Dr. Oberley all right?"

"No, he's not." I was calculating drive times, mentally running between Kingman, South Rim Village, and Las Vegas. "I'm afraid he has passed from among us," I said, sliding automatically into the kind of language I thought fundamentalist Christians might use. I preferred to use the more direct term: "dead."

Holly Ann paused awhile, then said only, "I thought so."

"Excuse me? How did you—I mean, did you have some kind of a clue that this was going to happen?"

"No. But I felt it." She sounded resigned. "I can't explain these things. It's like a knowledge. Mom says it's a gift from God, but I can't say as I like it."

"And when did this . . . knowledge descend upon you? I mean about W—Dr. Oberley?"

She began to stutter. "I don't know. Well, it was a couple of days ago, I guess. Listen, I gotta go. I'm sorry to bother you."

"Wait! I need your help! Can we meet?"

She was silent for a long while, and I wondered if she had broken the connection. I said, "Holly Ann?"

"Give me a minute. I'm praying over it." There was a silence. "Okay, yes. We can meet."

I said, "Great! Would you please keep your cell phone switched on? We just got off the river, and we're trying to make plans, and I'll need to figure out how soon I can get there, so can I call you back?"

"Certainly. And God bless you, Ms. Hansen."

"Thank you, Holly Ann. Right now I need all the blessings I can get."

Jerry appeared at my side. "Watch what you pray for, dear," she said with a smile and handed me something in a paper sack. "I picked this up for you at the drugstore over there. Don and I are off to the South Rim, and we'll report in as soon as we've seen Fritz with our own eyes. You be careful and don't overdo, you hear me?" She shook a finger at me and, still staring at me with mock sternness, climbed into her side of their SUV.

As their vehicle turned onto the highway, I opened the drugstore bag and peered inside to see what on earth Jerry had purchased for me. What I found did not compute, though of course nothing in my life made much sense just then. Why would she think I needed a home pregnancy test?

APRIL 21: KINGMAN

FAYE MADE HER FINAL APPROACH IN THE CHEYENNE, TOUCHED DOWN smooth as silk, taxied, and pulled up at Air'Zona Aircraft Services, Kingman airport's fixed base operation.

Eleanor climbed down out of the aircraft looking dazed. She was a round woman, built squarely like her brother but gone to flab, but for all her mass she drifted across the tarmac like a dry leaf caught in the wind. She scanned our faces, and when Hank stepped forward to greet her, she grasped his hand as if it were the handle on a cane and leaned on it. "Am I dreaming all this?" she asked him.

He reached out his free hand and brushed a lock of hair tenderly from her forehead. "I wish it were just some bad hallucination," he said.

I led the way with Faye and Brendan in our vehicle, keeping an eye on the rearview mirror to make sure that Glenda, Hank, and Eleanor didn't get lost. The airport was eight miles out of town, and we had a few turns to make once we breached the city limits. Kingman was typical of desert towns, simultaneously bleak and homey in its square, sun-drenched architecture and its spare attempts to look like an oasis. We pulled up along West Andy Devine Avenue in front of the county offices, strolled in, and inquired where we might find the morgue.

A man seated at a desk dialed a few numbers and talked and eventually told us to take a seat. We waited. I focused my nerves on a copy of the *Kingman Daily Miner,* which brandished the motto TRUSTED LOCAL NEWS LEADER FOR KINGMAN, ARIZONA & MOHAVE COUNTY. The day's headline was KINGMAN HOMES GET MAKEOVERS IN ROCK AND ROLL PAINTATHON. I decided that if anyone was beginning to hallucinate, it was me. I gave up on reading and got up and began to pace, and Brendan got out of his chair and paced with me.

"I wonder what Dad's day is like," he said.

"We have to just keep putting one foot in front of the other," I said.

"We're detectives," he said.

I nodded. "You're doing very well at this, Brendan. You have good instincts, and you use the right kind of logic and make excellent observations and you never forget a thing."

He smiled faintly. "That's the scientist part of me. Like you said, we make observations and come up with hypotheses and then we test them."

"Exactly."

"And we have to believe, too."

"Tell me what you mean."

"I do not believe that my father killed that stupid man."

"I don't either," I said.

At last a technician in a white lab coat presented himself to us and asked what we needed. Eleanor identified herself as next of kin. "I'm here to . . ." She began to cry.

"I can only take kin in there," said the man. He looked from face to face.

Eleanor turned to me.

I said, "Okay, Cousin Eleanor, Hank and I will come with you. The rest of you wait here."

Brendan said, "Turn your cell phone to vibrate."

I did as Brendan suggested and followed the man down a network of hallways and into a chilled room that had big drawers mounted along one wall. The place stank of chemicals. He asked Eleanor to sign a paper, then opened one of the drawers. Inside lay a gray plastic zippered bag covering a form the size and shape of Wink Oberley.

The technician grasped the zipper but then stopped and turned to Eleanor. "You know that scavenging birds got to him before he was found?"

Eleanor's eyes grew wide, and she shook her head. Tears rolled down her cheeks afresh.

The man said, "Perhaps you ladies would like to close your eyes and let the gentleman have the first squint."

Eleanor snapped her eyes shut, but I stepped forward to make sure I had as good a look as possible. I told the technician, "This isn't my first time at this sort of thing. Open it up, please."

"Okay then." He drew the zipper down along the bag, letting the plastic sag open around the corpse's head and shoulders.

For a moment I thought the man had opened the wrong drawer. The face was mangled, but there was more to my unrecognition than that. Something was different, very different. Then it hit me what had changed. "He's had his hair cut!" I said.

Hank said, "You're right, he was all shaggy when we last saw him, and look, he's clean shaven, too!"

I heard Eleanor gasp, which meant that she had opened her eyes. In a tiny, squished-up voice, she asked, "Is that Georgie? Really?"

Using her question as an excuse, I gestured for the technician to open the bag farther. "Did he have any birthmarks?" I asked.

He opened the bag to below the navel.

I could see deep scrape marks running alongside the coroner's incisions. "What made those scrapes?" I asked. "He was always scratching his belly, so he had his shirt up a lot, but I don't remember all that." I caught the technician's eye to make sure that he could swear on a witness stand that I had not touched the body and said, "Would you do me a favor? Do you have a magnifying glass of some sort handy?"

The man fetched a large magnifier attached to a light source and switched it on. "What did you want to look at?" he asked.

"Down there in those scratches," I said. "Do I see a fine gravel, or is that my imagination?"

The technician leaned down toward the magnifier and had a closer look. "Yeah, that's bits of gravel. Why?"

"Well, I was wondering exactly what kind of gravel it is, you see. This man was murdered, so any particulate matter that's gotten stuck to the wounds as the blood coagulated might have significance in the investigation, don't you think?"

The technician nodded. "The coroner would have made a note of that."

"Can we see his notes?"

The man shook his head. "It's a murder case, after all. It's evidence, like you say."

"Well then, here's my point: I'm a geologist, a forensic geologist, and that looks very much like asphalt in those scrapes. I'd like to know if I'm right about that. In fact, I demand to know if I'm right about that, because at this moment my husband is being held for this murder, and I can guarantee that he was not anywhere near any asphalt for over two weeks before this cat went missing from our group. Do you get my drift?"

Eleanor turned to Hank. "What's she saying, Hankie?"

To the technician I said, "The Park Service might like to know that they're holding the wrong man for this murder."

Eleanor suddenly reached out and grabbed me by the hair, pulling my head around to where she could stuff her nose up against mine. Her tears had instantaneously been replaced by rage. "Just who the fuck are you?" she demanded.

Hank said, "Let go of her, honey! That ain't gonna help!"

I struggled to free myself, but Eleanor's grip was formidable. I heard the drawer roll shut. Pain shot through my neck and scalp, and my stomach was about to blow from the stink of death, but the emergency was over. I had found the evidence I needed. Fritz would be freed.

I heard a door opening and footsteps approaching. Out of the corner of my eye I saw two men coming from around a divider at the end of the room: One was an older man in another white lab coat, and I thought, *Coroner?* and the other wore Park Service green and a flat-brimmed straw hat. *God help me, it's Chief Ranger Gerald Weber!*

"Do you want to explain yourself?" Weber demanded.

"Yeah. Just help me get this woman off of me, okay?"

"I don't know," said Weber, "maybe you'll feel more talkative in that position."

"I can clear my husband," I said. "The evidence is right there in that drawer."

Weber raised his eyebrows at Eleanor. She let go of my hair.

I said, "I take it you've been listening?"

Weber nodded.

"Well then, what's your problem? He disappears from Ledges looking like a shaggy dog and shows up at Whitmore with a haircut and shaven and all shot full of asphalt. You want to tell me how any of that happened if my husband killed him?"

The coroner's tone was pleasant and collegial. He said, "She's got a point, Gerry," and to me added, "So that's asphalt? How do you know? I hear you have quite a name as a forensic geologist."

Now it was my turn to get angry. "You guys were *waiting* for me to show up?"

Weber nodded. "Yes, I told Maryann to report your movements, so I flew over here to protect my evidence. You may have noticed something we didn't, but even if that proves to be asphalt, you still haven't given me an alternate perp. If your man didn't kill him, I need to know who did, and you have to agree that all the other the evidence points to your man."

"What evidence?" I asked. "All I know is that you took him away and took my rock hammer with him. If you want me to help crack this case, you're going to have to share everything with me."

The coroner turned to Eleanor. "Thank you for coming, madam. Do you identify these remains as your brother?"

She nodded, her head wobbling like it might come off her neck. "He had a scar there on his right hand, and this one on his tummy," she said. "That's from a bicycle accident when we were kids."

"Thank you. My technician will show you back out to the waiting room." He waited for them to go, then said to Weber, "Shall I show her?"

Weber nodded his assent.

The coroner re-opened the drawer, rolled the body onto its side and pointed to a stab wound just to the right of the spine at heart level, then lifted a flap of skin at the back of the scalp, exposing the skull. "This one on the head would have knocked him out, and the bleeding would eventually have killed him, but this stab wound here finished him off. From the angles here you can see that the assailant was quite tall, like your husband."

I turned back to the coroner. "Time of death?"

"Difficult to assess, given the temperature of air and water, but I'd say he died the evening before he was found, plus or minus."

"What was he wearing?" I asked.

The coroner described the life vest and the clothing.

I nodded. "Hank's shirt. Wait," I said, feeling my cell phone vibrating in my pocket. I flipped it open, read Brendan's text, and said, "They're in the lobby."

"Who's in the lobby?" asked Weber.

"Holly Ann St. Denis and her mom, Lisette Carl. They—"

Weber turned and headed quickly out the door. "I've been looking all over hell for that woman!"

To the coroner I said, "Please join us in the lobby and I'll explain how to run tests on fine particulates," and headed out the door, close on Weber's heels.

APRIL 21: WHAT HAPPENS IN LAS VEGAS

LISETTE ST. DENIS CARL STOOD IN THE LOBBY OF MOHAVE COUNTY'S Offices wearing a new pair of high-heeled sandals, a lovely spring frock and even more makeup. It looked ghastly, and her hairdo sat askew.

Brendan met me halfway down the hall and walked with me to the lobby. "Pretty good, huh?"

"Yeah, pretty good! How did they know where to find us?"

"You told me to stay on it with the cell phone. Well, we talked again, and I told her where we were going and why."

"And she just sort of decided to join us?"

"Not exactly. She asked if you were going to do some detective work like on those TV shows. So I said if she wanted to see the real item she'd better get here as quick as a bunny, and get her mom to drive her. I have a feeling they know something."

"Nice work."

"It's how we roll."

Ranger Weber strolled up to the mother and daughter. "Ms. Carl? I've been trying to reach you," he said. "It's been reported that you overheard a person threatening George Oberley's life."

Lisette's eyes grew wide. "I don't know anything," she said.

Holly Ann said, "Tell him the truth, Mom. Tell him what you told me in the car. Tell him the whole story."

Lisette seemed to drink in the strength of the girl's conviction. "Okay." She closed her eyes, opened them again, faced Ranger Weber, and spoke. "I don't know how you know all this, but it's true that I overheard a very heated argument at Cremation Campsite, but that's not important."

"Why not?" Weber demanded.

"Because George left the Grand Canyon alive."

"How do you know that?"

"Because he asked me to pick him up on the road that leads into Supai," she said. "And I did." She put a slender hand across her heart. "I'm sorry. I truly did not know that there was anything I should be reporting to the law."

"*When* did you pick him up? And where did you take him?"

"I picked him up just after dawn on the sixteenth. I took him into Las Vegas and—" Her voice caught, and she closed her eyes, shutting out the world.

Weber took a step closer to her. "When did you last see him? And where?"

"In the driveway outside our church," she said. She opened her eyes and turned to Holly Ann. "I'm sorry for what you're about to hear, dear." To Weber, she said, "I took him to the church vestry, where my deceased husband used to dress for his sermons, and I let him use the shower there to clean up." With a dramatic flourish, she added, "And I cut his hair so he could be civilized in the presence of God."

I asked, "Did he tell you how he got to your meeting place from the river?"

Weber shot me an *I'll ask the questions* look.

Lisette said, "He told me he had a wet suit hidden under one of his hatches." Her voice began to wander and become childlike, as if she were telling a fairy tale. "That and an extra pair of those heavy sandals you people wear, and a little backpack with extra gear and some food and water. When we last spoke at Nevills, he told me that he would call me on a special telephone he could use so I'd know when to pick him up. He said there was a place called Ledges and he'd get your group to camp there, and he could swim to that canyon that leads to where the Supai Indians live."

I said, "Ranger Weber, you will therefore find his fingerprints on that satellite phone. But Lisette, why did he take our spare life vest?"

She seemed to be losing her focus, distracted by cars moving about in the parking lot outside the windows. "He said he could swim that distance just fine, but I told him I was worried about him, because he said it would be difficult to swim out of the current at just the right instant and get into the mouth of Havasu Canyon. So he said he'd borrow a life vest. Once he was up and on the trail he put the wet suit into his pack and began to hike very quickly. In places he even ran. The moon was very bright and pretty that night. He had a head lamp, but he didn't use it because he wanted to make sure no one at Supai Village saw him. He's so strong, you see; a real man! So he was able to get all the way up there before daylight, and there I was waiting for him."

"Tell them why, Mom."

Lisette raised her shoulders in a coquettish little gesture. "He was going to take me away!" She arched her neck like a cat being stroked. "We met in such romantic circumstances . . . He was in Las Vegas for a geology conference, he said, and our eyes just met across a crowded room . . . We were going to go away together, get away from all the pressures . . ." She glanced at her daughter. "And take Holly Ann, of course."

Holly Ann stared at her hands, her lips set in a straight line. I had the feeling this wasn't the first time she had heard this sort of story from her mother.

Lisette's voice took on a wheedling tone. "Really, sweetie, this time it would have been perfect! I swear it!"

Faye's cell phone rang, interrupting the story. She put it to her ear, listened, said, "Great," and handed the phone to Weber. "It's for you," she said.

For once, Weber couldn't find an intimidating stare. "Me?"

"Yeah. It's a friend of mine with the FBI. He's got some information for you about a stray helicopter flight that disappeared off the radar near Whitmore Wash the evening of the seventeenth."

Weber put the phone to his ear, nodded, nodded again. When the caller was finished speaking, he said, "Let me get your number," and wrote it down on a small pad of paper he produced from his shirt pocket. When he had handed the phone back to Faye, he said to Lisette, "It would seem that your brother-in-law Terry Carl made an extra trip back to the canyon. Tell me about him, why don't you?"

Lisette turned white.

Holly Ann told her mother, "You tell him or I will!"

Brendan moved to Holly Ann's side and gently took her hand.

Lisette squeezed her eyes shut. "I can't and I won't!"

Holly Ann's lips began moving, praying in silence to the Heavenly Father who supported her in all things, including and especially the trials of growing up as parent to her own mother. Out loud she said, "'Uncle' Terry took over the church's books after 'Daddy' Amos died, and he found out about the account that had been set up for Mom."

Lisette shrugged her shoulders, a last-ditch effort to look innocent. "A girl has to look after business," she said.

I put two and two together. "He caught you embezzling?"

"I wouldn't call it *that*," said Lisette. "More like getting paid for my hard work. Amos encouraged it, called it a tax loophole. And those people wouldn't have sent in all that money if I hadn't cried on camera all those times!"

You and Wink deserved each other, I thought, but said, "So for the record, is Terry the tall guy with the Adam's apple who was leading prayers at your camp?"

Lisette's attempts at playing the gamine suddenly vanished. She stared into space, watching memories play back in her mind's eye, scenes that drained the blood from her face. "He's six foot four," she said. "He—"

Brendan said, "And he knows how to fly a helicopter. He flew Super-Cobras for the marines."

"That's right," said Holly Ann.

Faye said, "And he flew an AStar out of McCarran Airport in Las Vegas the evening of the seventeenth."

Weber shook his head. "I thought I'd checked all of that, but—"

Faye popped him on the shoulder. "It helps to know how to talk to pilots. We're a mangy bunch, but we stick together." She turned to me. "The guy who owns that bird is one of their parishioners. He said that Terry told him it was important church business, and God wanted things quiet."

"But wait, he was killed with your rock hammer," said Weber. "Explain your way out of that one, Ms. Hansen."

"Wink was a geologist, too," I said. "And you have more to tell us, don't you, Lisette?"

Brendan said, "I'll bet it was his own hammer that was used."

Genuine tears began to roll down Lisette's face. "Georgie asked me to buy it for Holly Ann," she said. "He was going to give it to her to let her know she could go to college and study whatever she wanted. And we would have had the money if Terry hadn't gotten in the way!"

"Tell the rest," I said.

"Terry caught Wink hiding in the vestry, and he was so angry! He—he took the hammer, and . . ."

Weber said, "What happened then, ma'am?"

Lisette's eyes were wild. "I can't tell you that! He said if I told on him he would tell everyone on television what I did with their money. He'd found our passports and took them. And he was going to take Holly Ann, and . . ."

Weber said, "Did you see Terry Carl strike George Oberley with a square-headed hammer?"

Lisette sobbed. "Yes! Georgie fell down, and I—I was scared, so I ran away! I thought he would follow me, but—but he didn't!" Tears were streaming down her face now. "I thought he loved me, but he didn't call ever again!" She turned to her daughter. "I just wanted a nice life for you. You understand, don't you?"

Holly Ann put her arms around her mother. "It's okay now, Mother. These people will find Terry and make him go away where he can't hurt us anymore."

Brendan patted Holly Ann on the shoulder. "And there's something else you need to tell us, isn't there, Holly Ann."

The girl looked to the boy. "What do you mean?"

"Tell them about how he touched you."

Now Holly Ann turned pale. Her lips moved again, but no words came out. I wanted to take her in my arms. She was the real deal, a woman who asked for guidance from that grace that binds us all and got real answers. And she was a child, an innocent stuck carrying the burdens of the so-called adults around her.

Brendan said, "What he does isn't healing, Holly Ann. It's called molestation. You're under age and you didn't want it. I saw what he did and I will testify under oath and he'll go to jail for that, too. He's going away for a long, long time to a place where he can't hurt you ever again."

River trips can teach many things, especially if one is ready and willing to learn. Brendan was only thirteen years old, but already he was a man.

APRIL 21: THE VIEW ACROSS FOREVER

FRITZ WAS STANDING ON THE WALKWAY AT THE SOUTH RIM OF THE Grand Canyon near the El Tovar Hotel when we reached him that evening. He was staring into the vastness of open space and time and stone, hands in pockets, taking in the view. He seemed so relaxed and at peace that passersby might have taken him for any other tourist, not a man who had just been released from false imprisonment. The great vault of the heavens was sprinkled with stars. The occasional tiny dot of moving light traced the presence of a satellite, man's voyagers across the heavens.

"Dad!" shouted Brendan, running toward him.

Fritz grinned and caught his son in his great, strong arms. He mussed up his hair and spoke closely into his ear. "Thank you, son. I hear you put essential pieces of the puzzle together and got me out of that cell."

"You're welcome, Dad."

Fritz loosened one arm and gathered me in as well, and the three of us formed up in a group hug. Fritz didn't say anything to me, but he didn't have to; the way he nuzzled his lips up against my neck told me everything I needed to know.

Jerry and Don Rasmussen had followed us from the parking lot where we had left our cars. I waved them over.

"Thanks," said Fritz.

"Our pleasure," said Jerry.

Don nodded his agreement. "I don't know if they're still serving dinner in the dining room, but I know for certain that you can get something in the lounge until eleven."

"Sounds good," said Fritz. "I'm starved after what I've been fed over the past forty-eight hours."

I said, "Brendan, why don't you head on in with Jerry and Don. I want a moment longer out here, okay?"

Brendan said, "I'm okay to wait with you."

Jerry caught my eye and grinned. "Oh, come on with us, Brendan," she said. "I'll bet they have cake!"

For the moment Brendan became just a boy agan and left cheerfully with the Rasmussens.

"Something on your mind?" asked Fritz, pulling me in for another hug.

"I have something to tell you," I said. "I promised you once that I wouldn't take chances with my work as a detective, and I've kept that promise, even today, when it was your neck that was on the line. I called in the big boys to do the work that would have put me at risk."

"Thank you," he said, kissing me along one side of my face and into that ear. "I knew I could count on you."

"Well, I want you to know that I hereby double that promise."

He straightened his neck and looked into my eyes. "What's up with you?" he asked. "It's not like you to . . . What's going on?"

"It's just that I'm going to be very busy for quite a while to come, with new responsibilities."

"What are you talking about?"

"Remember that first evening at Nankoweap?"

"I sure do."

I pulled out the little test stick Jerry had bought for me and handed it to him.

"What kind of busy is this?" he asked. "I can't see."

"Don't you have that little flashlight in your pocket?"

"Yes, I do," he said, producing it. "I'm the Eagle Scout, remember? Always prepared."

"Always."

In the soft glow cast by the tiny light, I saw his smile widen into a grin. "Always," he whispered, as he gazed on his first knowledge of the child who was growing in my womb. "Always and forever."